THE SISTER CODE

A Suspense Thriller

Eliza McCullen

Published by Laurie Cameron

Copyright © June 4, 2021 Laurie Cameron

All rights reserved

The characters and events portrayed in this book are fictitious. Any similarity to real persons, living or dead, is coincidental and not intended by the author.

No part of this book may be reproduced, or stored in a retrieval system, or transmitted in any form or by any means, electronic, mechanical, photocopying, recording, or otherwise, without express written permission of the publisher.

ISBN-13: 979-8515803735

Cover design by: Laurie Cameron
Printed in the United States of America

FOREWORD

As I read the final draft of this book, finished in January of 2021, I was absolutely amazed that my imaginary world was becoming a reality . . .

I began writing this book in 2018, stalled out for a while, then resumed writing at the beginning of 2020. Suddenly a deadly virus began to spread throughout the world and the whole world was shutting down. People were asked not to go to work but to shelter in place. All non-essential businesses were closed. Flights were cancelled. Thus faced with endless hours at home, it seemed a perfect time to finish that book. And yet, every time I sat in front of the computer, I couldn't help but think how irrelevant the story was considering what was happening in the world.

I finally decided that I could only write this book in a post pandemic world. So, I imagined that a vaccine would be developed, and life would go back to normal. In my imaginary world, this normalcy would occur in 2021. Since my original story began in May 2020, I simply fast forwarded it to May 2021. I finished the first rough draft in January of 2021 when hospitals were being overwhelmed by the illness while at the same time vaccines were being developed.

Then I put the manuscript on the back burner and, fortuitously, didn't pick it up again until May 2021. As I read my draft, I was absolutely amazed that my imaginary world was becoming a reality. Several vaccines have been developed, the economy is recovering in fits and starts. Infections and hospitalizations here in the US are declining rapidly. Of course, in many parts of the rest of the world, the virus is raging out of control. As I write this, I don't know where it's all going to end.

In this story, the pandemic is in the past, but the devastation is not ignored. There are no masks, no social distancing, no vaccine hesitancy. Las Vegas looks like it did when we visited this city in 2019. The scene at the Basque restaurant is crowded and strangers share tables. Since it was written long before the first scene took place in May 2021, there are inevitably inaccuracies in this post pandemic world. That said, the story will be around long after the last remnants of the pandemic are behind us and such inaccuracies will be forgotten.

PROLOGUE

Winnemucca, Nevada

Hugh Nicolas got up early in the morning and, like always, took his coffee out to the porch to greet the day. He sat in his rocking chair and propped his feet up on the porch railing to watch the sun come up. Just to the side of the porch was a pinion pine that had been there when he and his wife had built the cabin.

He had heard somewhere that pinion pines could live as long as three or four hundred years. He figured this one was at least a hundred years old. Some of the branches were devoid of needles, thrusting out of the canopy like gnarled old arms.

This morning, an owl perched on one of those old branches. He was heavily built, with a barrel-shaped body, and striped underbelly. His long, earlike tufts stood at full attention. His huge yellow eyes stared directly at Hugh.

Hugh stared right back at it. "What are you looking at?" he groused. "I know what day it is. You don't need to remind me."

According to local Indian legend, the great horned owl was the most uncanny and most dangerous of owls. Being active mainly at night, these owls were believed to be a protector of the underworld, associated with prophecy and divination. If Hugh hadn't been a believer of this lore in his youth, he certainly was now.

As he watched, the owl turned his head to one side, then the other. Then he turned his head all the way around before spreading his wings and taking off, soaring silently up into the blue dawn.

Hugh swore to himself, feeling that familiar black depression that came over him on this one day of the year. He finished his coffee and went inside to get ready for work.

As he left the house, he glanced at the old pinion pine. The owl had returned and was settled back on his roost. Hugh stopped and stared. "What are you doing here? Can't you leave a fellow alone?" The yellow eyes stared intently at Hugh and Hugh felt a tingle of foreboding run up his spine. Then he shook his head and clomped over to his pickup.

He took the winding road from the foothills of the Winnemucca mountain where he and his late wife had purchased their plot of land and descended into the valley. From there the road ran straight through a terrain of sagebrush and grassland before reaching town. It had been a particularly dry winter and now in the early spring, the vegetation, which normally burst into life for a brief period before the dry summer, looked sad and bedraggled.

When he arrived at the sheriff's department an hour later, he was uncharacteristically short with his receptionist as he strode past her on the way to his office. "Hold any calls, Marsha," he said and entered his office, closing the door behind him.

He threw his jacket over the back of his chair, sat down, and rummaged through his desk drawers until he found what he was looking for: a manila folder so old that it had turned a dark yellow, its edges frayed from much handling. He placed it on his desk in front of him and stared at it for a moment before opening it.

Carefully, he pulled out the stack of photographs, being careful to handle them only at the edges. Even now, he felt the same horror he had felt so long ago when he had found the collection at the scene of the crime.

Twenty-three snapshots of youths, ranging in age from three to eleven years old wearing nothing but underwear and a tag attached to a string around each child's neck with a number on it, stared up at him. Nothing but skinny arms and legs and protruding rib cages, pathetically vulnerable in their near naked state. The worst were the eyes. They were blank, drug-induced, hopelessly staring into the void that was their future.

Twenty-nine years ago, he and a task force of law enforcement officers had busted up a pedophile ring. The children in the photos were being auctioned off to the highest bidder, a group of wealthy businessmen, men in turbans, and politicians. Hugh recognized a few of them. As the arrests were made, the children were gathered up and taken by child services into foster care. And then they were never seen again.

Hugh longed more than anything to shove the folder back into his desk drawer and forget it ever existed. But he felt honor bound to pay his annual respects to the children in that folder, children who were supposedly rescued, only to disappear once again. He would like to know what happened to them, but he had been "advised", literally on pain of death, not to pursue it.

CHAPTER 1

Prescott, Arizona

Cate turned her heater to its maximum level and pressed her hand to the vent hoping to feel just a smidgen more warm air, all the while cursing her useless brothers. What was the point of having so many of them if they couldn't at least fix her car? She barely got any heat out of the old girl these days, the brakes were starting to make strange noises, and you could move the steering wheel approximately three inches in either direction before any apparent steering actually took place.

In all fairness, it wasn't really her brothers' fault that they were reluctant to put their heads under the hood. On many occasions, they had urged her to junk it and get something more reliable. The last thing she needed, they told her, was to break down at some god-awful hour of the morning in the middle of nowhere. There were just too many deserted roads in the county where a body could get lost for days. Or worse yet, break down in some dodgy neighborhood in town where meth users and dealers hung out.

But the truth of the matter was that she couldn't afford to buy anything new. At least not until very recently. For the past six months, every penny she made went straight back into the business. Now though, she was starting to see some light at the end of the tunnel; business was returning to normal.

By the time she crossed town, the sun had risen high enough in the sky to banish the cold night temperatures of the high desert, offering far more warmth than the car's heater. She pulled into the reserved parking space at the back of the pub and switched off the ignition, listening to it shudder as the engine shut down. She patted it on the dashboard affectionately, then locked up and headed to the pub.

When she pulled the door open, she found Patrick, their chief cook, already hard at work. The aroma of slow cooked corned beef, lamb stew bubbling on the stove, and brown bread baking in the oven hit her full force. As she reached for a pasty that was cooling on a baking tray, Patrick smacked her on her hand.

"Those are for our customers, brat." He had been telling her the same thing since she was a kid coming in after school. "Besides, you got a visitor."

Cate glanced at her watch. "A visitor? But the place doesn't open for another hour."

"I would say that this particular visitor isn't your run-of-the-mill customer. I put her in your office." Cate grabbed a cup of coffee and made her way past all the tantalizing goodies to her office.

She pushed open the door and peeked inside. A woman sat primly in one of the visitor's chairs, hands folded on her lap, knees crossed demurely. She stood when Cate entered the room, smiled, and offered her hand.

"Oh, hello. You must be Caitlin Connelly?" She wore an elegant blue suit with a white silk blouse unbuttoned at the collar to reveal a creamy neckline and a hint of cleavage. Her skirt reached the top of her knees, exposing shapely legs, and feet shod in blue, low-heeled pumps. Blond hair was neatly coifed in a chignon.

"That's right. I'm Cate. How can I help you?" She offered a professional smile, taking the soft, manicured hand in her own.

"I am ever so glad to meet you," the woman said. She spoke with a distinctly southern accent. Soft and cultured, it was quite a contrast to the local western accent Cate was accustomed to. "My name is Victoria Saunders. You don't know me, but I've come here on a somewhat unusual quest."

"I see. Well why don't we both take a seat and you can tell me about it." Cate pulled her chair around the desk and scooted it next to Victoria's, then settled in, clutching her coffee cup. Victoria reached into a smart leather briefcase resting next to her chair and pulled out a manila envelope.

"You see, this document shows that you are my sister."

Cate, who had just taken a sip of coffee, nearly choked, spewing coffee unceremoniously onto her lap.

"Oh, my goodness. Oh dear. I am so sorry," Victoria stood and, pulling a tissue from her Vuitton purse that exactly matched her shoes, blotted gently at the spill. "Well, you're lucky that those jeans are a nice dark color. It hardly shows . . ."

"Victoria?" Cate glared at her. "It's okay. Really."

"I-I guess I should have tried to ease you into the idea, but, well, there's no easy way to do that, is there?"

"Not really. No." She regarded Victoria suspiciously and reached for the envelope. Extracting the report, she held it with a shaky hand. It contained both her name and Victoria's, a couple of bar charts, and a table with a lot of numbers.

Victoria scooted her chair closer and bent her head over the report. "See, it's all about your genetic code, the total number of centimorgans that you and a relative share. I don't really get it completely, but they measure the amount of matching DNA segments between two people. Now there are a total of 6800 centimorgans in all your chromosomes. You get about half from your mother and half from your father. Full siblings don't get the same chromosomes from their parents unless they are identical twins. But because they share DNA from their parents, they will generally share less than 3380 of these centimorgans but no less than 2500 centimorgans. You follow?"

"Not really."

"Yeah, I get you. I swear I have read these sites on the internet at least fifty times and I still don't really get it. What I do get is that with all this new DNA testing and online searches you can find a match with your relatives. Well, that is if you are both in the system. Which it seems you are. You did get your DNA tested, right?"

Cate gazed at the earnest face of this beautiful stranger. Was she for real? Or was she trying to pull something over on her? Then she remembered that she had, in fact, done a DNA test. She had been with an old college friend tossing back a few beers, when the friend pulled out two test kits. Her friend had been studying her family's genealogy for years, which naturally led her to look into DNA testing. When she had ordered a test kit, by some mix up, she got two kits. So she talked Cate into doing the test with her. That was over a year ago and Cate never gave it another thought.

Now Cate said, "Yes, but that was a long time ago. I forgot all about it."

"Did you ever check the results?"

Cate shook her head.

"Well, guess what? You have a sister."

"No way. I come from a big family, four brothers. No one ever mentioned a sister. My family is very close. If there had ever been another girl, surely they would have told me. In fact, if you were my sister, you would be part of my family."

Victoria's blue eyes darkened with concern. "I know this is really difficult to accept. Believe me, this DNA test came as a real shock to me as well. But these tests are ninety-nine percent accurate."

"Then how . . . ?"

"I honestly don't know. But I can tell you how I came to find this out. My mother had breast cancer—"

At that moment Patrick rapped softly on the door and stuck his head. "I'm ever so sorry to interrupt you fine ladies, but there's a supplier here that Cate needs to see."

"I'll be right there," Cate said. In fact, she was glad of the interruption. This woman and the bombshell she had just dropped, it was all a bit too much to take in just now. She needed time to think. She turned to her visitor. "Listen, we do need to talk, but right now, I have to attend to business. Maybe we could meet later?"

"Oh, of course. I completely understand. Business first." Victoria reached for the envelope, but Cate held onto it.

"How about this afternoon?" Cate suggested. "Things usually slow down around two o'clock. Could you come back at, say, three?"

"Absolutely. I'll come back then."

* * *

Cate scowled as she watched the woman, Victoria, hasten out the back door. Patrick, who had taken in the interplay between the two women, laid a comforting arm across Cate's shoulders. "Are you all right, my child? You're white as a sheet. What did that woman say to you?"

She turned into Patrick's embrace for a moment, soaking in the comfort that he offered. Then she stood back and regarded him solemnly. "She told me she was my sister."

"Jesus, Joseph, and Mary. No wonder you're all shook up. Did she give you any reason for this wild tale?"

Cate showed him the report that she clutched in her hand. "DNA. She said we came up as a match in DNA tests."

"Well, now, surely the tests are wrong."

"I don't know, Patrick. I mean, they say these tests are pretty reliable. But if it's true, I just can't work out how." She glanced at his face, so familiar to her since she was a child, now so full of sympathy and concern. "I need to think about this."

"Sure, I understand. I'll tell the vendor to come back another time."

"No, Patrick, don't do that. We really need to get new equipment ordered."

Indeed, some of the stuff Patrick used to produce his stews and breads were so old that she wondered how he managed. He never complained about it. Like every business on the planet, it wasn't certain if they would be there by the next day. Now that life was finally getting back to normal, business had picked up to the point where he couldn't afford to have something break down and still keep up with daily orders.

"Why don't you just meet with him?" Cate said. "We've talked everything over and you know the budget as well as I do. I trust your judgement."

"Right, sure and I can do that. Now you just have a seat there and I'll bring you a nice cuppa." He closed the door to her office gently, returning a few minutes later with a steaming cup of tea laced with plenty of milk and sugar.

Cate sipped at the overly sweet brew and let its comforting effects flow over her. Slowly her mind began to settle down some. She looked at the report Victoria had given her. The name of the company and the website were provided in the header. On impulse, she logged onto her laptop and entered the website address. It took some digging, but before long, she was able to find her own DNA test results. And sure enough, the report indicated that they found a match to a close relative. The data mirrored what she was seeing in Victoria's report.

She stared at it for a long while until the din around her, the everyday noise of a restaurant starting to open, reached into her conscious. Right, she thought squaring her shoulders, she would get to the bottom of this. If any of it was true, her family had a lot to answer for. And that included her "sister." But just now, she would attend to business. There were a hundred little details she needed to take care of in order to get the pub ready to open at eleven.

Luckily, most of the tasks were routine, because questions kept bubbling to the surface. She was the baby of the family, the only girl. Her four brothers teased her unmercifully, all the while trying to shelter her from the rest of the world. She wondered sometimes if that was why she could never find a suitable boyfriend. Was it because any decent guy was intimidated by her brothers? Or maybe because in her own mind none of the guys she met could ever measure up to even one of her brothers.

And now, after all this time, it turned out she had a sister.

How was that possible? Didn't they have to have the same parents to have matching DNA? Cate's parents would never give up a child of their own. Which meant Victoria was not their child. But if Victoria wasn't their child, then neither was she. She thought about her mother and father, how warm and loving they were, how they folded everyone to their bosoms. It would be just like them to take someone in. Which was the only conclusion Cate could come to.

She was adopted. No, that just couldn't be.

But the more she thought about it, the more convinced she became of the truth of this. It wasn't just that she was the only blond in the family. She had this vague memory of landing in her parents' home as a very young child. Of course, people don't remember those first few years of life, but this memory seemed to have been seared into her brain. It sort of sat there in the back of her mind, until today's conversation triggered it.

As she worked the pub floor during the noon hour rush, taking orders, bussing tables, tending to the register, the memories pushed their way forward. She remembered bouncing around a bit amidst a lot of boys. She remembered seeking comfort in her dad's arms. He was so big and strong, and his arms wrapped protectively around her. But no matter who she snuggled up to, the image stayed in the back of her mind of another boy with big blue eyes peering out of an excruciatingly thin face who had held her tenderly before kissing her goodbye.

Then another thought struck her. Her father always called her his wee foundling. But what did that mean? If she wasn't mistaken, it meant an infant that had been abandoned by its parents and was discovered and cared for by others. Was that what her father meant? And her brothers used to talk about how the stork had brought her to them.

So when her oldest brother Ethan showed up for a late lunch at the pub, Cate pulled a beer from the tap for both of them and sat next to him at the bar. He was the dark one of the bunch with deep brown, wavy hair that curled around his collar. He kept it tucked under a newsboy cap. His complexion was fair which only served to accentuate dark gypsy eyes. She looked straight into those eyes as she took a sip of beer.

"Ethan, was I adopted?"

Ethan grabbed up his glass and took a large gulp. "What? Why are you suddenly asking me this, Cate?"

"So it's true, isn't it?"

"Well, kind of."

"Kind of? What the hell does that mean?"

"You just showed up one day. We didn't think anything of it because there was always a stray kid or two in the house. Someone whose parents were out of town or in hospital or whatever. They'd stay for a few days and then off they'd go again, back to their own homes. But you just never left. It must have been about six months after you showed up that Dad announced that you would be staying for a while longer."

As Cate listened to her brother talk, she became more and more agitated. "Ethan, you're saying I just 'dropped' into the family? Why hasn't anyone in the family ever talked about this? And if I am adopted, then who are my real parents?"

"Now calm down, Cate. I didn't mean to upset you."

"But," Cate sputtered, "of course I'm upset. All my life I've known who I am: the youngest child and only girl in the Connelly family. At least that's what I thought. Until today."

"Look, I'm sorry. I figured Mom and Dad had told you. The truth is, I don't know the whole story. But why are you asking these questions now?"

"I had a visitor today. She claims to be a blood relative, and believe me, she is not a Connelly. I didn't have time to get the whole story this morning, but she's coming back this afternoon." Cate glanced at her watch. "In fact, I better finish my work before she gets here."

"Now, hang on, Cate. You're telling me that some stranger came to see you this morning who claims to be related to you?"

"Mm-hm."

"A complete stranger?"

Cate nodded. "She showed me a DNA test." When Cate saw

Ethan shake his head in disbelief, she grew impatient. "Well, you did say that I was adopted. So why should it surprise you that I have a sister out there somewhere?"

Ethan regarded her solemnly as she hopped off her stool. "Okay, Cate. But just . . . be careful, will you?"

She saw the look of concern darken his countenance. Just like all her brothers, they were ever protective of their little sister. "Don't worry big brother, I can take care of myself. And right at this moment I trust my sister a whole lot more than I trust any of you."

CHAPTER 2

Prescott, Arizona

Victoria hustled down the street to her car after her meeting with Cate, her mind in a whirl, her emotions in a jumble. Mostly she felt relief that Cate hadn't outright laughed at her or told her to go jump in a lake when she told her what she was about.

Victoria might have done just that if someone showed up on her doorstep with such a story. She was an only child. She didn't have any brothers or sisters. She was shocked when she got an email from DNA Family Tree notifying her of a match, a sister.

She thought about contacting Cate by writing or telephoning, but that kind of news just had to be done in person. She had to go there and try to meet Cate face-to-face. So, she got in her car and drove—for three days. When she finally arrived late last night, she was exhausted, and her nerves were so frazzled that she decided it was best to check into a motel. The next morning, she got up, put on her best business suit so as to be taken more seriously, and headed over to the pub.

But she didn't reckon on it being closed at that time of the morning. She should have. It was a pub after all, but there you have it. She wandered around to the back of the building. No one was home. She returned to her car to wait for someone to show up. That someone was a man in his sixties with a balding head and a bright red beard. When he pulled into the parking spot at the back and made his way to the door, she intercepted him.

"Excuse me, sir, I was wondering . . ."

The man jumped about a foot, he was so startled at the appearance of another human being just a few feet behind him.

"Oh, my Lord," Victoria said. "I scared you, didn't I? I am so sorry."

The man looked her over from head to foot, taking in her business attire and her concerned expression. "Well, now, that you did," he said with a soft Irish burr, "but no harm, no foul. Now what can I do for you, Miss?"

"I . . . I was hoping to speak to Caitlin Connelly. She does work here, doesn't she?"

"Yes, yes she does. Runs the place is what she does. But she won't be in for another hour."

"Oh." Victoria hung her head in disappointment.

"Well now, see here. Maybe you'd like to come inside and wait in her office."

"I don't want to be any trouble."

"No trouble. Besides, it's a bit nippy out here. So come on in. I'll fix you up with a nice cup of tea. Or is it coffee you'll be wanting?"

"That's very kind of you, sir. I wouldn't mind a cup of coffee. My name is Victoria, by the way," she said, offering her hand.

"Nice to meet you, Victoria. My name's Patrick." He grasped her hand in a warm dry handshake.

She entered through the kitchen and gazed around her with interest. She was by no means an expert on such places, but there was no doubt that this place had seen a lot of miles. A huge old butcher-block table with its scarred surface and edges worn smooth from years of use took center stage. Large industrial ovens stacked three high, once the color of stainless steel, had blackened over the years. Along one wall was a shelf heaving with pots and pans and baking trays. Opposite, a large stove stood with a huge pot bubbling on it.

Patrick escorted Victoria to Cate's office, where she settled in with some reading material that she had brought with her and waited nervously for Cate to arrive. He lived up to his promise and brought her a large mug of coffee. As he puttered in the kitchen, the aroma of meats, breads, and herbs wafted into the office, setting her stomach to grumbling.

Patrick must have read her mind or heard the rumblings of her stomach, for he soon brought her something he called a pasty warm from the oven. It consisted of pastry dough wrapped around beef, potatoes, and onion and baked until crisp and golden. As she slowly savored the treat she thought, now this is comfort food.

She plucked at the last crumb and waited another half an hour before she finally heard the back door open and a woman wish Patrick a good morning. It had to be Cate. This is it, she thought, closing the magazine and standing to greet her sister for the first time.

Cate was a petite woman, standing just over five feet tall with a trim figure. She wore jeans and a chambray shirt over a white tank. Her thick blond hair was tied back in a ponytail where wisps tugged loose to frame a face with delicate features. Wide blue eyes looked at Victoria with interest.

It could have gone badly, the way Victoria had just jumped right in. But the fates or the faeries or someone must have been smiling on her because she managed to get Cate to hear her out. At least until Patrick interrupted them and Cate had to attend to pressing matters of business.

Now as she returned to her car, she sent up a prayer to those faeries. She had placed a lot of hopes in this meeting with her sister. It wasn't just that the DNA test results showed that she had a sister. It also showed that her parents weren't her parents. Her father had had no choice but to acknowledge the fact that she was adopted, but he wouldn't tell her anything more. And her mother was dead.

Victoria was still mourning the loss of her mother when she made this momentous discovery. Why hadn't her mother ever told her about the adoption? Victoria had loved her mother, a sweet, genteel woman, so dearly. She even moved home to take care of her as she fought an aggressive cancer that eventually killed her. Victoria felt cheated that even as her mother was dying, she chose to keep this secret from her.

Things had only gone from bad to worse as she struggled to make a life for herself after her mother passed. Savannah, that charming coastal town known for its southern hospitality and grace, no longer felt like home. She felt increasingly estranged from her father and was unable to relate to her childhood friends. Perhaps it was a coward's way out, to flee from the family home. Except that it was no longer home. Somehow, somewhere, she needed to start over again. She needed to start from a firm base, a knowledge of who she was. She was hoping Cate had some answers.

* * *

Cate spotted Victoria the moment she entered the pub late in the afternoon. She had changed into skinny jeans that hugged her curves and had let her hair loose so that it swirled in thick blond waves to the small of her back. Cate stood and waved her to a small booth in the far back corner. As Victoria strolled towards her, she thought what a striking contrast she was to the masculine ambiance of the pub.

And a striking contrast to me, her own sister, she thought with a twinge of irony. She glanced down at her attire—worn jeans frayed at the hems, a functional button-down chambray shirt, sneakers that had seen better days. The one similarity, her blond hair, hadn't seen a hairdresser in months. She tied it back to keep it out of the way, but she couldn't keep wisps from escaping from the front and from around her neck.

Tucking a loose lock of hair behind her ear, she stood next to the booth awkwardly. How did one greet a long-lost sister? As she held her hand out, Victoria took it in both of hers and smiled warmly. "Hello Cate. It's so good to see you again." She looked around the pub. "What a lovely place."

Cate flashed her a crooked grin, then gestured for them to sit.

"What?" Victoria drew her perfectly plucked eyebrows together. "You don't think this place is lovely?"

Cate glanced around at the old place with affection. A heavy oak bar ran along one wall, behind which a huge variety of libations were on display from whisky to wooden kegs of beer. At the bar itself were five beer-tap handles including ones for Guinness and Murphy's Irish Stout.

The bar was separated from the dining area by a wooden railing. Cozy booths with padded seating lined one side while the main floor contained a mix of bar-height tables and those more suitable for families. The ceiling was pressed tin and the walls were covered in a collage of vintage photos and typical Irish pub signs—*May the road rise up to meet you*; *May you be in heaven before the devil knows you're dead*, etc.

"Not lovely exactly," Cate mused. "Homey comes to mind."

A waiter came over to the table with two coffees.

"I hope you don't mind that I took the liberty of ordering these," Cate said.

"Oh, my heavens no. I love coffee." She looked up at the waiter, blinked her eyes with their long lashes. "Could you be a doll and bring me some cream and sugar please?"

The waiter grinned and said, "Right away, miss."

Cate leaned across the table. "If you're not careful, you'll have him eating out of the palm of your hand."

Victoria grinned. "Mm, sounds delightful."

Cate burst out laughing and for the first time felt the day's tension start to ease. "Are you really my sister?"

Victoria's expression turned serious. "Indeed I am. Can't you see the resemblance?" Cate took in Victoria's perfectly groomed hair and pushed a stray lock of her own behind her ear. She glanced down at her rough hands with short blunt nails, then at Victoria's, which were soft and perfectly manicured. Before she could reply, the waiter returned with the requisite cream and sugar.

"Thanks, Ken," Cate smiled up at him. "Can you please see that we are not disturbed?"

"Of course, Cate." The waiter nodded, then looked Victoria over with curiosity before he left them to their privacy.

"Now then," Cate said, "let's hear your story."

"Right," Victoria plunged right in. "See, my mother died of breast cancer."

"I'm sorry to hear that."

"Thank you." Victoria blinked back tears. "It was a very difficult time, as I am sure you can imagine. Anyway, she had some genetic testing done to help the doctors decide on the best treatment. Not that it did her much good. The type of cancer she had was very aggressive and the doctors couldn't save her.

"Then about six months after she died, I decided to have some of my own genetic testing done to determine if I had those same mutated genes she had. That's when I learned that my mother was not my mother, genetically speaking."

"How terrible."

"Yes. I was shocked. I mean, I was beside myself. I went straight to my father and demanded answers. He admitted that I was adopted, but when I asked about my birth parents, he clammed right up." She paused for a moment. "The more I thought about it, the more I reckoned there was something, I don't know, underhanded about the adoption."

"Oh, surely not," said Cate.

Victoria smiled sadly. "You don't know my father." She took a sip from her coffee, then continued. "Then I got an email telling me I had a match, a sister, in the database. I was overjoyed. All my life I longed for a sister and now, it turns out I have one.

"The report said you lived in Prescott, Arizona, so I started searching the net until I found your family pub. There you were in a photo with your parents and four brothers. For weeks, every morning when I got to work, I sat at my laptop with my first cup of coffee and stared at the photo on that website.

"I dreamed about having a sister. And all those gorgeous brothers. My oh my. But staring at a photograph just wasn't enough. So, I came here, hoping to meet you and your family."

Cate felt a surge of sympathy. "I guess sometimes I didn't

really appreciate all those brothers growing up. They were just there. And good company, mostly. For sure I was never lonely. In fact, sometimes, I longed for a little solitude. And of course, they could be a real pain. Especially when they started getting all protective of me, being the only girl and the youngest."

Victoria smiled. "Sounds like they really love you."

Cate nodded.

"So tell me. I'm just dying to know all about them." Victoria face showed avid interest.

"Well, let's see. Ethan is the oldest. He's always been really . . . driven, I guess you could say. All he ever wanted was to follow in his father's footsteps. So he joined the police force as soon as he could. My dad was a cop. He's retired now. Anyway, Ethan moved up the ranks really quickly and now he's a supervisor of a multi-agency statewide task force in Phoenix."

"Impressive. Is he married?"

"Yes, with two young kids. A boy and a girl. Needless to say, they are the apple of their daddy's eye."

"Of course," Victoria smiled encouragingly. "And the others?"

"Next would be Michael. He's an FBI agent also working out of Phoenix. Not married, but has been engaged, like, forever."

"Oh, that's sweet. And interesting that he is also in law enforcement."

Cate quirked an eyebrow at Victoria. "So is Liam, my third oldest brother. He's a cop here in Prescott, a patrol officer. You know, working the streets, keeping the community safe, that kind of thing. He's had some opportunities to move up in rank but, so far he hasn't made any moves. I think he likes being able to meet people, providing service to the entire community. It suits him."

"Lordy," Victoria beamed. "So your family is like the *Blue Bloods* of the west."

Cate grinned. "You could say that. I was a cop too, until I left the force to manage this pub."

"Really?"

Cate nodded. "I've been at it about six months now. Trying to get it back on its feet after the economic crash."

"Yes, it's been quite something hasn't it? There were times when I despaired that things would ever get better."

They sipped their coffees in a moment of reflection.

"And the fourth brother?" Victoria asked. "I suppose he's a police officer, too?"

"Ryan. No, he was the only one that wasn't interested in the 'family business'." Cate waved quote marks in the air. "He was very artistic. He moved to New York City to make a name for himself in the art world. He worked in restaurants to pay his rent and was just beginning to be discovered. Then the pandemic hit. He caught the virus early on. It took him really fast."

Victoria reached for Cate's hand, held it gently. "What a shame. I am so sorry."

"It devastated all of us. It's like there's this hole in the family where Ryan used to be." Cate looked around the pub for a moment, then back at Victoria. "And you know what's ironic? All my brothers chose careers where they often have to put their lives on the line. Except for Ryan. Being an artist. Who would have ever imagined?"

She brushed impatiently at her eyes. "Anyway, those are my brothers. I guess they are my adopted brothers. I checked out your report online. It all seems legitimate. Then I got a chance to talk to my oldest brother Ethan at lunch. He confirmed that I was adopted, but he didn't know much more than that. He said I needed to talk to my parents."

Victoria wrinkled her brow, concerned. "Is that going to be a problem?"

"Well, yes and no. To be honest, I'm a bit hurt by this whole thing. I mean how come they never mentioned the fact that I was adopted?" She took a sip of her coffee and sighed. "And now it will be much more difficult. See, my dad had a stroke over a year ago and he has trouble talking." Cate smiled. "Only my mother can understand what he is saying. But I'll see them tomorrow and find out what I can. How long are you in town?"

"Oh, I don't have any definite plans . . ."

CHAPTER 3

Prescott, Arizona

Early the next morning before she was due at the pub, Cate drove over to her parents' house, a great rambling affair on the outskirts of town with a large fenced-in yard. Memories of her childhood came to her unbidden. She and her brothers had spent endless hours romping there, climbing on the monkey bars and swing set, playing catch and tag football, and just generally messing around.

There was still the old tree where her older brothers had built a tree fort. The fort was gone, but the steps made from small scraps of wood nailed into the trunk were still there. They tried to keep her and Ryan out, saying they were too young, that only those initiated into their club could join. But that only made her and Ryan more determined to claim their space. Whenever the other boys were elsewhere, they would sneak up and hang out. From that height they could see well beyond their family property, to neighbors' houses down the road, and beyond to the rolling hills where the high desert scruff gave way to distant mountains covered in ponderosa pines.

Cate would often catch Ryan gazing into the distance, his smoky, dark brown eyes turning pensive, even at such a young age. He wasn't like the others. There was a dreaminess to him. He saw the world in colors and textures. As he grew older, he spent much of his time indoors drawing, first with crayons, then with colored pencils that their parents bought for him, then watercolors and oils. Ryan had chosen a different path. Moved to New York to become an artist.

Until the pandemic. So unimaginable, like something out of a sci-fi novel. The whole country taking shelter to try to stop its spread. The pub, like every other business, was shut down for awhile. At the same time, Cate's parents were forced to furlough their staff, many of whom had worked there for years. The shock of losing Ryan along with the stress the pandemic took on their livelihood caused their father to have a stroke.

As she pulled into the driveway and she saw her mother through the kitchen window, her thoughts returned to the present. Her father, she knew, would be sitting in his recliner in the living room watching the news. When she entered through the kitchen door, her mother put down the spoon she was using to stir some oatmeal on the stove.

"Caitlin, love, how good to see you." Neila smiled, embracing Cate warmly.

"Hi, Ma." She peeked into the pot on the stove. "What are you cooking?"

"Oh, just some porridge. We were just about to sit down for breakfast. There's plenty of it. Have you eaten yet?"

Cate's stomach growled. She'd been too anxious to talk to her parents to eat anything that morning. "No, I haven't. Gee, it's been ages since I had some of your porridge."

"Good, I'll just dish you up a bowl as well." Neila smiled. Then she looked at Cate more closely. "Cate? Is everything fine?"

"Yes, Ma. Why do you ask?"

"No problems at the pub?"

"No, no problems at the pub."

"Well something is up. I can see it in your eyes."

Cate smiled. "I never could hide anything from you, could I?"

"Nope. I'm your ma," she said succinctly.

"Actually, Ma, that's what I came to talk to you about."

"Oh? Now this sounds serious." Her mother dished out three

bowls of porridge and put them on the table that was already set with milk, cinnamon, and brown sugar. "What is it?"

"Was I adopted?" Cate asked baldly.

Neila looked up sharply at her daughter. "Yes. But you are every bit as much a Connelly as your brothers."

"How come you never told me?"

"I don't know, Cate. It just never came up."

"But how did I come to be adopted?"

"It's kind of a funny story, that. Your father came home one night with you in his arms. And you," Neila smiled softly at the memory, "you had your arms wrapped tight around his neck like you were holding on for dear life. Until I put a bowl of soup in front of you. Then you practically lunged at that bowl, grabbing it with both hands and slurping it down. Poor thing. You were half starved."

"So . . . where did I come from?"

"Your father kind of rescued you from a real bad place. He was working on some sort of task force back then. He wouldn't tell me much. Whenever I asked him about it, he would just shake his head. 'Neila,' he'd say, 'you're better off not knowing.' Then he'd go all silent on me.

"Well, it got to where I never really wanted to pester him any more about it. So, you stayed with us. We saw to it that you got enough to eat so that your ribs were no longer sticking out, cleaned you up, bought you some new clothes.

"The boys were just tickled about you, being a girl, and with your fine blond hair and eyes as round as saucers. Once you got over your initial shyness, you were a regular spitfire. I reckon they'd have done just about anything for you."

Cate smiled. She remembered well enough. Whether it was learning how to ride a bike or doing homework, all she had to do was ask and one of her brothers was at her side. "But I still don't get it. How could Dad just come home with me in his arms? Was I legally adopted? What happened to my birth parents?"

As Cate quizzed her mother, her father entered the room. He took a seat next to Neila. Neila patted his leg affectionately. "You got something to say, Joe?"

"'os 'eggus," he uttered.

Neila regarded him steadily. "What are you trying to say?"

"'os 'eggus," he repeated.

"Oh, for heaven's sake," Neila said. "Let me get you your letters." She stood and left the room, in search of the box of letters that Joe used when he had something important to say. While she was out of the room, Joe reached across the table and grasped Cate's hand in his big paw. He nodded at her and said, "'uv 'oo."

"I love you too, Dad," Cate said.

Then Neila returned with the letters. Joe rummaged in the box until he found what he wanted. He laid the letters out on the table: Las Vegas.

"Oh, yes. Now I remember," Neila said. "You were working on some joint task force with law enforcement in Nevada."

Cate frowned. "And then, somehow, you found me?"

Joe nodded.

Cate stared at her father as possibilities began to float around in her head. And none of those possibilities was pretty. Las Vegas was most known for its gambling and prostitution. She had studied criminal justice in college and now she recalled a case study about child prostitution. "How old was I when I came to you?"

"You were three," Neila said.

"Was I...abused?"

"No. Oh good heavens no. You were undernourished and dirty, but I never saw any bruising, nothing like that." Cate looked at her father. He was shaking his head vigorously.

"What about my parents?" Cate persisted. "Do you know who they are?"

Joe shook his head, no.

"Did you try to find them?"

Joe nodded vigorously, yes.

"But you couldn't find them," Cate supplied.

Joe nodded again.

Neila regarded her daughter. "Cate, why all these questions? Why now?"

"Because yesterday I met my sister."

Neila clasped her hands to her mouth as tears spilled down her cheeks. "Oh, my heavens."

CHAPTER 4

Prescott, Arizona

When Cate got to the pub later that morning, she closed the door to her office and called her brother Michael at the FBI office in Phoenix.

"Hi Cate. What's up? Are Mom and Dad okay?" She could hear the anxiety in his voice. She rarely called him at work unless it was something urgent, which in this case, she thought it was.

"Mom and Dad are fine, Michael. I'm calling you about something else."

"Okay, shoot."

"I need a favor from you. I'm looking for any reports on a joint law enforcement operation in Las Vegas around the time that I was three years old. That would be around 1993."

"That's a pretty strange request. Do you mind if I ask you why?"

"It's kind of a long story..."

"How about a five-sentence summary?"

"Okay. I met my sister yesterday and—"

"Whoa, wait a minute. Last I checked you were an only girl."

"Yeah, that's what I thought too. But this woman, her name is Victoria, she brought me a DNA report that shows that we are sisters. You know I was adopted, right?"

"Yeah, now that you mention it..."

"So, she's trying to track down her birth parents and was hoping I would know something. I went and saw Mom and Dad this morning and Mom said I came home with Dad after some kind of joint law enforcement operation in Las Vegas. Dad, of course, couldn't give me any of the details and Mom didn't know a lot about what happened. So, I thought maybe you could find out more."

There was a long pause at the other end. "Michael?"

"I'm here. I'm just trying to process all of this."

"I would really appreciate it if you would help me out here."

"You know that you're a Connelly, right? Nothing's going to change that."

"Of course. You're my family. You and my other brothers and Mom and Dad. I wouldn't have it any other way. But now I want to know the rest. How I ended up here, who my birth parents are, how I got separated from my sister. Just everything."

"I suppose I could look into it a bit. Those records are old. I would have to get access to the archives."

"Great. Thank you, Michael. Thank you so very much."

"I . . . well . . . you're welcome, I guess."

* * *

Cate got an email from Michael just as the lunch rush hour was winding down. She waited until Victoria showed up, then they went to her office and closed the door. She opened the email and read it aloud. The bust involved a child trafficking ring in May of 1993.

"It says that the FBI rescued twenty-three children in Las Vegas from the grips of a multistate human trafficking ring and arrested thirty-six traffickers. The bust was part of a joint operation encompassing multiple stings over four days. Three FBI field offices were involved, along with twelve other law enforcement agencies across the states of Arizona and Nevada."

"Oh, my goodness, Cate. What were they planning to do with those children?"

"I don't know, child pornography, prostitution, and worse."

Victoria's face lost most of its color. "That's . . . so sick. Oh, those poor children."

Cate sighed. "Sadly, it happens. There are a lot of sick people in the world."

"What about the traffickers? Did they say anything about them?"

"Let's see. It refers to another section of the report for persons arrested. But that part of the report isn't included."

"What about the names of the children?"

"It seems that part isn't included either."

Victoria slumped in the visitor's chair. "Well, that helps a whole heck of a lot."

"Not very useful, is it?" Cate scrolled through the short report. "There is one bit of useful information: the name of the Special Agent in Charge of the case. I wonder if he's still around."

Victoria brightened. "If he is, maybe he could tell us more."

"Exactly. Meanwhile, I'll talk to my brother again, see what else he can tell me."

Just then the waiter popped his head into her office. "Cate, I have bad news for you. Kerry is down with the flu and Josh has a family emergency."

Cate frowned. That meant they were two wait staff short for the dinner rush. "Don't tell me this. We're expecting a busy night."

Victoria said, "Let me help. I know my way around a restaurant."

"Oh, no. I couldn't ask you to do that."

Victoria rummaged in her purse for a moment. She pulled out a hair clip and started to tie her hair into a neat ponytail. "Nonsense. Just tell me what to do. I am yours to command."

Victoria was good, Cate had to admit. When a family of six came in, she helped push two tables together and took their drink requests in short order. A couple of guys came in and sat at one of the tall tables. They ordered dinner and a couple of large beers. She watched as Victoria deftly parried their flirtatious overtures.

Then her brother walked in with his partner.

* * *

Victoria did a double take when two men entered the pub and, spotting the only vacant table, made a beeline for it. She recognized the younger one. He was Cate's brother. She had stared so many times at the picture on the website that she would have known any of them on sight. But what she hadn't reckoned on was how very attractive he was in person.

He stood about six-feet-four and had broad shoulders tapering to a narrow waist. As she watched him saunter towards the table, she took in a tight butt and long, long legs clad in police blues. Chestnut colored hair, badly in need of a haircut, curled around his collar and framed a wind-burned face. It was a face with nicely chiseled masculine features. Except for the lips. They were full and sensuous.

When Victoria brought them menus, his green eyes fixed on her.

"You're new here," he said. He leaned casually on the table and she could make out well-formed muscles on his biceps and forearms under his uniform shirt.

"Oh gosh, no," Victoria said. "I'm just helping out. They're short-staffed tonight, so I told Cate I'd be happy to pitch in."

"Is that a fact?"

"It is. And you must be one of Cate's brothers. I recognize you from your website."

"Well now, that's interesting. I must confess I have never looked at it."

"Oh but you should, It's really quite nice." Then she offered her hand. "By the way, my name is Victoria."

His hand was large, dwarfing hers in its powerful grip and he held on just a little longer than necessary. "I'm Liam. This is my partner, Matt."

Victoria nodded and smiled at Matt. "Well, now, what can I get you two?"

As Liam and Matt drank their beers and ate their dinner,

Victoria glanced over from time to time. Liam's steady gaze never seemed to leave her as she worked the floor, hustling orders to customers, and bussing tables as needed.

Cate's brother wasn't the only one to catch Victoria's attention. About a half hour before the pub was due to close, a couple of men walked in and sat at the bar. Victoria didn't know a soul in the town where she found herself, but there was just something off about these two guys, like they didn't belong.

One had dark hair and a beard, the other looked like he hadn't shaved in some time. Under the whiskers, Victoria could see a scar running through his cheek. When she brought them menus, she glanced at black beard's face and caught him staring at her. His eyes were dark and flat, soulless. As she walked away, she could feel those eyes boring into her back.

They declined the menu and ordered beer with whisky backs. Making short work of the first shot, they ordered a second, then sat back and drank their beers more slowly. Their eyes travelled around the place and Victoria got the impression they were scoping it out.

They tried to order another round, but bartender refused to serve them, pointing at the clock. Victoria's shoulders sagged in relief when they sauntered insolently to the door.

At about the same time, Cate chased the last customers—two regulars who were enjoying their third Guinness—out of the bar. They were reluctant to go, but Cate was adamant.

As she ushered them to the door, she asked, "Who's driving?"

"Don't worry, Cate. We got a ride all arranged."

"Good, then." She pushed them out the door and watched them amble down the street, turning into a bar in the next block.

She locked the door and turned and slumped against it. She spotted Victoria cleaning up the last table. "Victoria, stop working and come have a drink."

Victoria took a last swipe at the table, then grinned. "Well now, I don't mind if I do."

Cate took a seat next to Victoria. The bartender was just polishing up the last of the glasses. "What'll you two ladies have?"

"How about a bourbon neat?" Victoria said.

"I'll have a beer, thanks, Ben."

"Coming right up."

As they took their drinks, Cate said, "Victoria, you are such a lifesaver. How can I ever thank you for pitching in, besides paying you, of course?"

Victoria pulled the clip from her hair and shook her hair loose. "It was my pleasure. And, of course, the money will come in handy."

"Where did you learn to wait tables?"

"College. My father paid for my tuition and room and board, but I had to earn my own pocket money. So, I waited tables. When I got to be twenty-one, I started tending bar. Let me tell you, I can make a mean Bloody Mary." She took a sip of bourbon. "By the way, did you see those two guys who came in right around closing?"

"Yes. One had dark hair and a beard. The other had one of those permanent five-o'clock shadows," Cate said.

"Yeah, they were creepy." She turned to the bartender. "You saw them, right, Ben?"

"I did. And I agree with you, Victoria. I didn't like the look of them. They reminded me of some of the guys I served when I worked back east. One of the bars I worked was in a rough neighborhood, a lot of mob stuff going on, you know? It got so I could tell a wise guy the minute he walked in the door."

"And those two guys. They reminded you of them?"

"A little bit, yeah. It was the look in their eyes. Cold. You know?"

"Yes." Victoria nodded her head emphatically. "Exactly. I wonder what they were doing in here."

CHAPTER 5

Prescott, Arizona

When Cate called her brother the next morning to ask for more information on the report, he had sent her, he promised to get back to her by the end of the day. Meanwhile, Cate was still short-handed at the pub. Thankfully, Victoria helped out by taking on another shift. As Cate put in another twelve-hour day, she wondered what she would have done without her.

By the time she locked up, she was dogged tired and her feet were killing her. Weekends were always chaotic, but now that spring was giving way to summer, business was picking up. Somewhere back in time, residents of Phoenix, population in the millions, got the notion into their heads that Prescott made a great playground. They liked nothing better than to head into the high country to hit the town's whiskey row and toss back a few drinks with the cowboys.

As summer arrived and Phoenix turned into a convection oven, they arrived in droves to enjoy the cooler temperatures. The bars in the old part of Prescott were always overflowing. Cate couldn't complain too much as it was this steady flow from Phoenix that kept the pub afloat when she first took over.

She was grateful that they had survived during the massive economic shutdown. She discovered that even more than the need for food and shelter, was the need for companionship, comfort food, and a spot of libation. Many of the employees returned, as did the regular customers. They were all like family.

But then as business picked up, she'd had to put the brakes on things. She wanted the pub to be a place for friends and family, not a place for brawling drunks. She started closing down at ten for the sake of her sanity.

Tonight, she pulled into her driveway, thinking about whether she could afford an assistant manager. As she entered her apartment through the back door, she picked up a distinctive smell: body odor. She glanced around quickly, looking for signs of an intruder. The kitchen was divided from the living area by a high counter. From her vantage point, she could see that a couple of kitchen drawers were partially open, drawers filled with phone books and odds and ends that she rarely used.

Feeling the hair on the back of her neck rise, she stepped cautiously into the living room area. All seemed to be in order. Then she heard a rustling sound. It seemed to be coming from the spare bedroom that she used for an office. Hugging the wall, she edged toward the door and peeked around the door jamb.

Two guys dressed in black turtlenecks and dark trousers filled the space. One was standing at her desk rummaging through her drawers. The other was thumbing through her filing cabinet.

Seeing two strangers going through her things made her feel incredibly violated. Anger surged through her, blocking out all sense of caution. "What the fuck do you think you're doing?"

Both men started, heads jerking around at the sound of her voice. She recognized them. Dark hair, shadowy faces. They were the guys who were at the pub the night before. Ben, the bartender, said they looked like thugs working for the mafia. But there was no mob in Prescott.

The man who had been rummaging through her desk turned abruptly. He slammed into her midriff and ran out of the room. She fell to the floor and gasped in pain. The other man scrambled around the desk and headed for the door. As he ran past her, she reached for him, grabbing his foot. He crashed to the floor. As Cate tried to pull him in, he used his other foot to kick her in the head. The room turned black for a moment and she lost her grip on his foot.

As they ran out the back door, she willed herself to get up and follow them, but her body refused to cooperate. She curled up into a fetal position and held her head in her arms. The pain in her gut was sharp; her vision was blurred, and the walls of the room were gray. She focused on her breathing: in and out, in and out.

Gradually, the room stopped spinning and the ache in her head subsided to a steady throbbing. She sat up and leaned against the wall. With a trembling hand, she pulled her cell phone from her back pocket and dialed 911. The dispatcher was sending someone over.

Just as she was ending the call, her phone chirped at her. Caller ID told her it was her brother Michael.

"Michael?" she said in a shaky voice.

"Cate? You sound funny. Are you okay?"

"No, I'm not. Someone broke into my place."

"What?"

"They broke into my place, Michael. I caught them in the act."

"Jesus. Did they hurt you?"

"I'm okay. But they got away."

"Have you called the police?"

"Yes, just now."

"Good girl." She felt her hackles rise. None of her brothers seemed to realize that she was a grown woman, much less a trained police officer. "Listen," he said, "I'm going to call Liam. I want him to be there when the police on call arrive."

Now her defenses ratcheted up another level. "Don't you dare. Liam just got off duty. Besides, he has a lot more important things to worry about than a little vandalism."

"Cate, just humor me. I'll feel better knowing he's there."

"No, Michael. Promise me you won't do that. You know how Liam is. Super protective. Worse than you and Ethan put together. Anyway, it was probably some meth head looking for cash," she fibbed. They really didn't look like meth heads. But whoever they were, she didn't need any big brother taking care of things. She could take care of herself.

"Okay, okay. I'll leave it in your capable hands."

"Thank you. By the way, why did you call? Did you find out anything more about that bust?"

He hesitated. "No. In fact, you know that report I emailed you? Maybe you should just delete it."

Cate felt the hairs on the back of her neck rise. "Why?" She glanced at her desk in the corner, then remembered with relief that she had left her laptop in her office at the pub.

"I don't know. I've just been thinking, maybe it's better to leave sleeping dogs lie."

"But you didn't have a problem sending it to me, so what happened?"

"Nothing. Nothing happened. I'm just having second thoughts, is all."

"Come on, Michael. I don't buy it. Why the cold feet?"

"I'm not sure what you mean."

"Well, there wasn't much in the report. Most of it was missing anyway."

"That's right. The details have been redacted." She knew that the FBI often redacted certain sensitive information, usually if it concerned national security.

"But you have access, right? I mean, you are a federal agent."

"That's what's strange about it. When I tried to get more information, the system locked me out. And anyway, I can't see how anything that happened nearly thirty years ago should matter to anyone now."

"Right, so why does the report have restricted access?"

"I don't know."

"Michael, why do I get the feeling there's something you're not telling me?"

"Listen, Cate, you need to leave this alone, okay?"

"I don't know. I need to think about it. And anyway, right

now I have bigger issues."

When she ended the call, she rose slowly from the floor and did a mental check of her injuries. Her head hurt and her ribs were sore, but there didn't seem to be anything major to worry about. Then she stepped into the kitchen and poured herself a healthy dram of Irish whiskey.

What the hell was going on? What were those thugs looking for? It couldn't possibly have anything to do with that FBI report, could it? Is that why Michael tried to get her to back off? Did someone get to him?

There was something more to this story. She was sure of it. She'd be damned if she'd let some goons prevent her from finding out what. Her policing skills may be rusty, but she could take care of herself. First thing tomorrow, she had plans to meet up with Victoria. She was looking forward to discussing things with someone other than her brothers.

CHAPTER 6

Prescott, Arizona

The two sisters met over coffee at a café near Victoria's motel. Victoria listened wide-eyed as Cate told her what had transpired the night before.

"I think I agree with your brother," Victoria said. "We should drop the whole thing. I mean, it would be nice to know who my birth parents are, but heck, Cate. Someone broke into your place last night. If it's related to that FBI report that's serious stuff."

"Exactly. I want to know why."

"But your brother has asked you to back off."

"Right. All I can figure is that someone got to my brother. There had to have been some kind of alert in the system if anyone tried to access that report."

"But Cate, that's all the more reason we should leave this alone."

Cate's chin went up. "No. I am not going to let some thugs threaten me. Whoever they are, they know where I live. Besides, the report says that there was at least one child who was three years old. That could be me."

"Yes, it could be. And what about me? There weren't any infants."

"Look, if we're sisters, then we were probably taken at the same time."

"So?"

"I don't know. Maybe you were, like, sold in a separate deal."

Victoria frowned. "Like to my father."

Cate gave Victoria a sympathetic glance. "How you ended up adopted by your parents is anyone's guess. Your fate could have been a lot worse."

Victoria shivered. "The whole thing gives me the creeps just thinking about it."

"Which is why I can't just let this thing go."

"Then what are you going to do?"

Cate thought for a moment. "Our only lead is the SAC for the case."

"SAC?"

"Special agent in charge. I need to find a way to track him down and see what he has to say."

"But how do you know he is going to tell you anything?"

"I don't. But I won't know until I try."

Victoria regarded Cate for a long moment. "Okay, then. I can't let you do this alone."

"You don't have to do anything. I can do a little snooping on my own."

"No. No. If my father was involved in this in any way, I want to know. So, what's the plan?"

**

It took Cate a while to track the special agent in charge down. Since he was retired and she didn't know where, she couldn't do a simple google search. Even if she could, she probably wouldn't find him. Retired FBI agents were often fairly secretive about their whereabouts.

Her brother could probably locate him, but he wasn't going to help her. She needed to find a source that wouldn't alert any of her brothers what she was up to. Finally, she remembered a colleague in Colorado. She had helped her track down a suspect that managed to escape custody and found his way into Arizona. She dialed the number. A rusty voice answered.

"Paula, this is Cate Connelly. Do you remember me?"

"Hell yeah, I remember you." Cate could see her on the other end of the line. Mid-forties, built like a brick house, a weathered face. She was the salt-of-the-earth type of officer. "You helped me big time catch that arsonist suspect. You saved my butt on that one. So, what can I do for you?"

"I need a favor that requires a little bit of discretion."

A hoarse chuckle came from the other end of the line. "Discretion is my middle name. Tell me what you need. If I can help you, I'm all yours."

"I'm trying to locate a retired FBI agent by the name of James Peterson. And I don't want any of my brothers to know about it."

"That shouldn't be too hard to do. I'll just talk to my colleagues here at our FBI field office."

"That would be awesome," Cate said.

"I don't suppose you want to tell me why you are looking for him."

"It involves an old case. Almost thirty years old. It seems the old records are pretty spotty, so I was hoping he could fill me in."

"Right, sounds interesting. I'll see what I can do. Meanwhile, how are those rascally brothers of yours? Still keeping the peace in the state of Arizona?"

"You got it."

"And you? Are you still kicking butt on the force?"

"Well, actually, I left the force. I'm running my family's pub now."

A long pause followed. "Well, I don't quite know what to say. You were a hell of a policewoman."

Cate smiled into the phone. "Thanks, Paula. It's nice to be appreciated."

"You bet. Listen, if you ever decide you want to get back into it, there's always room for you here in Denver."

"I'll keep that in mind." When she ended the call, she stared at her phone for a moment.

Return to the police force? Now there was something she hadn't given a lot of thought to recently. Her parents had invested their entire life savings into the pub. It was to be their nest egg, supporting them through their retirement. So when the first shutdown due to the pandemic ended, Cate took leave from her position as a cop to help her parents manage the pub. They barely weathered the storm and then, just when it looked like the economy was turning a corner, wham. The virus began to spread . . . exponentially. Arizona soon became one of the world's hotspots, the virus spreading out of control. The pub was closed indefinitely, and Cate returned to her job on the force.

Looking back on that dark, uncertain period, Cate was forever grateful that she had family, her brothers, to lean on. When the vaccines were developed and life slowly returned to "normal," Cate decided to resign her position on the force and try to bring the pub back to life.

At the time she resigned, she'd been having doubts about remaining a cop. Or at least, being a foot soldier, like her brother Liam. As a patrol officer, she dealt mostly with petty criminals, mostly doing incredibly stupid things.

Part of her had her eye on bigger things. There was a wide world outside of Prescott where real crimes took place: domestic terrorism, bank robberies, child pornography, federal hate crimes, etc. If she was going to put her life on the line, she wanted to be tackling those kinds of issues. What stopped her were her brothers. They were already apprehensive about her being a cop. God forbid that she should do something like join the FBI.

So when her parents needed her, she decided to make a clean break and sort out her feelings. That had been several months ago. And she was still running the pub. She had never broached the topic of the future with her parents; it was easier to just keep on going on and not think too much about it.

*　*　*

That afternoon, Paula called her back with a telephone number and an address—in a small community on the west side of Las Vegas. Cate stared at her notes, composing her thoughts, then dialed the number. A deep, strong voice answered the call.

"Hello, is this Mr. James Peterson?"

"Yes, this is Jim."

"Hello, Jim. My name is Cate Connelly. My father is Joe Connelly. I don't know if you remember him."

"Joe Connelly. Of course I remember him. How is he?"

"Well, that's just it. He's okay, but he had a stroke recently and so he isn't able to communicate, you see. And that's why I'm calling. I understand that you headed up an FBI operation about thirty years ago in Las Vegas. My father was part of that joint task force—"

"I know the one," he said sharply.

"Oh. Well, the thing is the old report doesn't contain much information and so I was hoping you could fill me in."

She listened to a long pause. "You say you're Joe Connelly's daughter?"

"Yes."

"I might be able to help you out, but not over the phone."

"How about email?"

"I trust email even less than I trust the phone."

"What if I came to see you?"

"I guess that might work. Where are you calling from?"

"Prescott, Arizona. It's about a four-hour drive to Las Vegas. I could come tomorrow. I'd probably get there around noon."

"Right. See you then."

* * *

When Cate told her staff at the pub that she was taking a couple of days off, they were at once surprised and happy. She hadn't taken any time off to speak of since she took over the management from her parents. The staff told her not to worry, they would take care of everything.

She packed a few clothes in anticipation of the warmer climate of Las Vegas, a good three thousand feet lower in altitude, shaking her head as she placed the pitifully limp items in an overnight suitcase. One day, she would have to loosen her purse strings and do something about her wardrobe. She was tired of looking drab and washed out.

The last thing she packed was her gun. As she tucked it into the suitcase, the weight felt heavy in her hand. She hoped she wouldn't have a need for it.

She threw her suitcase in the car and waited for Victoria. They had debated which car to take. Victoria's was a sleek BMW and Cate longed to sink into the plush leather seats for the drive to Vegas. But in the end, they decided Cate's would be more practical if they needed to drive anywhere off the beaten track. So the plan was that Victoria would drive over and leave her car at Cate's place.

At the agreed-upon time, she locked up the apartment and sat on the stoop to wait.

CHAPTER 7

Prescott, Arizona

Victoria was just gathering the last of her things and carefully packing them for the trip when a knock sounded at the door. She had taken lodging in one of those old-fashioned motels that opened to the outside into the parking lot. She sure wasn't expecting anyone, especially at this time of the day. She stepped over to the door and peered through the peephole.

When she saw who it was, she about fell over: her ex-fiancé. She pulled the door open and stepped out, blocking his entry into the room.

"Noel, what in the Sam Hill are you doing here?"

"I could ask you the same thing."

She glared up at him. He was a tall, well-proportioned man dressed, as usual, in a finely tailored suit. A dark scowl marred his handsome features. A lock of black hair had strayed from his perfectly groomed head and fell across his forehead. Her thoughts flashed briefly on another, taller man at the pub in police uniform, a man whose biceps bulged as they rested on the table, a man with sensual lips. Then she reigned her thoughts in.

"That is none of your business," she said, crossing her arms over her chest.

"The hell it isn't. Do you know what I went through to track you down? It's time you stopped chasing around the country and came home."

"Home? And where would that be? Oh, you mean Savannah." Victoria's soft southern accent was laced with sarcasm.

"Of course I mean Savannah. Where else?"

"As far as I'm concerned, Savannah is no longer home. I'll be going back there when hell freezes over."

"Just what do you plan to do?"

"Just now, I'm going to Las Vegas."

"Well now, that sounds great. Just great. What are you planning to do there? Gamble away your trust fund?"

"I will do nothing of the kind. For your information, I am going there to find my birth parents. With my sister."

"That whole business again? What possible difference can it make if you find them? Besides, it's a wild goose chase if I ever heard one."

"If it is, it's my wild goose chase. Besides, we have come across some interesting old police reports out of Las Vegas."

Noel scowled and shook his head in obvious disbelief. "Police reports? Are you serious? Come on, Vicky. This is nonsense. You belong in Savannah as my wife. Now pack your bags and let's go home."

"No. You and I are finished. I told you that before. So why don't you just get yourself on outta here and go back to the hole you crawled out from."

"Why you little witch!" He grabbed her arm and tried to pull her to the car.

"Unhand me, sir, or I will scream."

"You wouldn't dare."

"Try me." In her heels, Victoria was almost as tall as he was and she glared into his face.

Noel must have sensed that she meant it. He dropped her arm and stepped back. "Vicky, this DNA thing is the most foolish nonsense I ever heard. And digging up old police reports could be downright dangerous. When you come back to your senses, you come on home. You have a wedding to plan."

Victoria sneered. "We're done, Noel. And don't call me Vicky."

The man straightened his already perfectly fitted jacket. "We're done when I say we're done." With a last, pointed look at Victoria, he strode over to his car, slid in, and roared out of the parking lot.

Victoria took a couple of deep breaths to try to calm her nerves. By all that was holy she would not to let the man shake her. She turned and grabbed the door handle to her room and swore. She had locked herself out.

"Ma'am," she heard a voice behind her and glanced back. A police car had pulled into the parking lot and a man was addressing her through the window. "Are you all right?"

"'Course I'm all right. Just locked myself out of my room is all."

She turned towards him and saw him get out of the car. It was Liam. Cate's brother.

He leaned against the car and folded his arms casually across his chest. "I saw you going head-to-head with some guy."

"So, you saw that did you? And did you also see that I chased him off?"

"I did."

"Well, for your information, that was my ex-fiancé."

"I see."

"Just what exactly do you see?"

Liam chuckled. "I see a woman who knows her own mind and a man who hasn't quite figured out that he's been dumped well and good."

Victoria smiled. "You got that right. Now if you'll excuse me, I have to go get another room pass." She turned and made her way smartly to the hotel's reception without looking back.

When she reached the front desk, she gave herself a moment. It wouldn't do for Liam to know what she and Cate were up to. Something told her that he would try to stop them, and Cate was determined. And she also decided it was best altogether not to mention this morning's incident to Cate. So when she saw Liam leaving the parking lot, she let out a sigh of relief. Then, with another room pass in hand, she returned to the room, gathered her things, threw her suitcase in the car, and headed out.

As she pulled onto the road she took a deep breath and tried to get her hands to stop shaking. When she left Savanna, she did indeed have a destination and purpose in mind. But what she would only admit to herself in the dark of the night was that there was another reason she fled. Major family events over the past few years had left her feeling anchorless, cast adrift with no idea of what to do with her life.

It started when she came home to take care of her mother. Her father was hopeless when it came to caring for someone who was ill, much less someone who was terminal. Her mother needed her. Like a dutiful daughter, she didn't give it much more thought than to come home, abandoning a job that had real career-fulfilling potential, to help her mother through her cancer and last dying days.

Her mother's death carved a huge empty space in her heart and in her life. She was left living under her father's roof. Seeing him every day, knowing that he had utterly failed her mother when she most needed him, Victoria began to feel a growing resentment towards him and, truth be told, her mother.

What kind of relationship did they really have? She had never paid much attention, they were just her parents, they seemed to get along fine. But as she tended her mother, she began to realize that there was a very good reason why they got along so well. Her mother always let her father have his way. For his every fault, she found an excuse. She was an enabler.

After her mother died, Victoria found herself with way too much idle time. In an effort to escape her gloomy thoughts and fill her empty hours, she tried looking up old friends, immersing herself in her old Savannah life. It didn't take long to realize that she no longer fit in. Most of her high school friends had gotten married and had a child or two. Their conversations revolved around mortgages and diapers. She put a good face on it but by the end of the evening her cheeks were stiff with rictus from pasting on a phony smile. And her mind felt like mush.

When her father had offered her a position in one of his companies, it was as though he had thrown her a lifeline. She didn't see the job as permanent, but at least it gave her a place to go, some intellectual stimulation, a chance to be with other people. That's where she met Noel, a very eligible bachelor, a lawyer with a very successful practice. He literally swept her off her feet.

Then she discovered that her mother, whom she had loved as any daughter would, was not her mother. Why hadn't her mother ever told her? When she asked her father, he had no choice but to admit that she was adopted, but he refused to tell her anything more. Was there something suspicious in the adoption? What did her mother know about it? Was she somehow complicit in the deal?

She might have let things go except that, while working at her father's company, she started to suspect that there were some shady deals going on. There were many inconsistencies in accounts receivable. She found excessive, unexplained cash transactions. She struggled with unreconciled bank account statements. She came across an unusual increase in employee reimbursements. Sometimes, she discovered sudden activity in previously inactive accounts.

It all seemed pretty dodgy. She began to suspect that her father was dirty. And if he was, then was the manner in which she had been adopted also dirty? What made matters worse was when she realized that her fiancé was up to his neck in her father's affairs.

At first, she tried to deny what she knew in her heart to be true. Noel was just as corrupt and dirty as her father. That handsome face and charismatic personality was a perfect cover for a man who found legal loopholes to avoid taxes and created dummy corporations to hide ill-gotten gains in offshore accounts. To think she had been so duped, so taken in by his charm. So, she broke off the engagement.

Then she ran. Ran from her job, ran from her feelings for her father, ran from her bitter disappointment in her fiancé. She ran all the way to Arizona.

Now as she drove to Cate's place, she glanced up at the deep blue, high desert skies and thought what a fine morning it was for a drive to Las Vegas. Traffic was still light that early in the day and she made it across town to Cate's place in good time. When she spotted Cate sitting on the stoop, she smiled and waved as she pulled in next to Cate's jeep. This trip with her sister she thought, hoped, might help her to least find a few answers.

CHAPTER 8

Las Vegas, Nevada

Arthur Townsend, having spent the better part of his adult life in Vegas before becoming the governor of Nevada, preferred working in Vegas over the state capital of Reno. Thus he maintained an office in Vegas where he spent most of his time.

He was just settling in there when the phone rang. He looked at his watch. It was early, just past seven in the morning, that first hour of the day when he got the most important stuff done and out of the way. There was no secretary to interrupt him with phone calls or other business-related tasks.

Since the pandemic had passed, the gambling and entertainment industry had begun to revive itself. It was a long slow process. People still liked to gamble. They would always like to gamble. But with the economic downturn, people had less money, plain and simple. Even so, Art had been inundated with the thousands of tasks required to oversee the state's recovery. Early mornings were his quiet time, his thinking time.

So why was the phone ringing?

He picked it up and barked into it. "Hello."

"Sir, this is Henry, down at the front desk. I have a man on the phone calling from Savanna, Georgia. He insists on talking to you. I told him that you weren't receiving calls at this hour of the day, but he insisted you would want to talk to him. His name is Forrest Saunders."

Art raised an eyebrow. He hadn't heard from Forrest in quite some time. "Right. Okay. Put him through." He waited for the called to connect. "Forrest, how the hell are you?"

"I'm good, Art. Real good."

"Hey, I heard about your wife. Very sad. Let me offer my deepest condolences."

"Thanks, Art. May she rest in peace."

"And that beautiful daughter of yours? Victoria? How is she doing?"

"As a matter of fact, that's what I'm calling you about."

"Oh?"

"Well, now, you know how hard-headed some women can be. And I'd say Victoria is about as hard-headed as they come."

"Is that right?" Art said, wondering just where this conversation was going.

"It seems she has come across some information in a most round-about way. It all started when her mama died. She had breast cancer, you know. So, Victoria had a DNA test to see if she carried the same genes."

"I see." Art felt a burning sensation in his stomach.

"'Course you know that her mama wasn't her real mother, biologically speaking, that is. She found out that she was adopted. And now she's downright determined to find her birth parents. I tried to dissuade her, but that just made her dig her heels in further."

As Art waited for him to continue, he reached into his desk drawer for a bottle of antacid and shook a tablet out.

"I guess she found out she had a biological sister over there in Arizona and tracked her down. Now this sister started doing some digging. Seems she has some relatives that are in the law enforcement business. I guess this sister managed to dig up some old police reports out of Las Vegas."

"Is that right?" The burning in Art's stomach intensified. He shook out another antacid tablet.

"Well, now, she and this sister of hers are on their way to Vegas."

Art sat up straight. "Now that's interesting. Do you know what they are planning to do?"

"No, I don't. But I thought I would give you a heads-up."

"Thanks for letting me know, Forrest. I'm not sure that they are likely to find anything, but I'll keep my ear to the ground."

"That's probably a good idea. And Art, keep me informed, would you?"

"Will do."

Art ended the call and stared at the phone for several minutes. What possible reason would these women have for coming to Las Vegas? It had to be that damn report. He hadn't given it a thought in years. Then, a few days ago, he got a message from his colleague at the FBI. Art maintained connections throughout law enforcement. It always paid to keep tabs on them. Like this time. His colleague got notified that someone had got on their intranet and opened the old file, one that he hoped never to see the light of day again. He told him not to worry, because the pertinent information was limited to eyes only.

Still, Art needed to be careful. That's why he sent a couple of his guys over to Prescott, to find out what was going on. But, of course, they had botched it. Nearly got caught ransacking the woman's home.

He stood and turned to his large picture window. In the distance he could see the Strip with its neon signs and dancing fountains fronting bigger-than-life resorts. From his vantage point, he could see the golden lion perched on the pedestal in front of the MGM Grand resort, rearing his large, regal head. It glinted in the brilliant morning sun.

His quick mind sifted through all the possible avenues that these young ladies might be following, which led him to one road in particular: the lead SAC on that long-ago case. The man had always been the one vulnerability he couldn't shut down without having the whole thing blow up in his face.

He turned back to his desk and dialed a number he knew by heart.

"Talk to me," a scratchy voice said.

"Mac, it's me. We may have a spot of trouble."

CHAPTER 9

Las Vegas, Nevada

As Cate and Victoria reached the outskirts of Las Vegas just after noon, Victoria entered the address for James Peterson into her GPS on her phone. Peterson's house was on the western edge of town, near Red Rock Canyon, which meant they had to navigate clear across the city.

Cate, used to the small city of Prescott, found the drive on the fast-moving interstate just a little nerve wracking, but Victoria steadied her with her calm navigation. Even so, she was relieved when they exited the freeway and found themselves in a quiet suburb with orderly streets, tidy houses, and the occasional shopping center.

They turned into a residential neighborhood. "It's right here," Victoria pointed to a neat adobe-style home with a tidy front yard landscaped for the desert with agaves, salvia bushes, and lots of gravel. When they pulled up to the curb, they looked at each other.

"Ready?" Cate said.

"I am. Let's go."

They followed the sidewalk to the front door. The afternoon sun blazed down on them and Cate felt the sweat begin to trickle down her back. As they reached the door, they heard voices but couldn't make out the words. Someone was home. They stepped up to the door and knocked.

Suddenly a loud bang thundered into the quiet afternoon, followed by a crash and hurried footsteps.

"Stay back." Cate said as she pushed Victoria behind a tall agave. She thought about her gun tucked safely in her suitcase and debated a few seconds. There was no time. She would have to brazen it out. She pushed the door open, yelling "Police!" and took cover behind the door frame.

When no one responded, she peeked inside. There was no one in sight.

"Mr. Peterson?" she shouted. Silence. Cautiously, she stepped into the front room and looked around. It was comfortably furnished with a large couch, an easy chair, a coffee table, and a TV along one wall. There was a kitchen on one side separated by a tall counter. Straight across from the front door was a set of patio doors leading to the back. They were wide open. Had someone just run out that way?

On one side was a hallway, perhaps leading to a bedroom area, and on the other side, a large doorway. She made her way cautiously through the doorway. It led to an office.

It was in complete disarray. The doors to a filing cabinet stood open with files flung onto the floor; books pulled from couple of tall bookcases joined the files. As she slid further into the room, she saw a pair of feet just visible behind a large desk.

"Mr. Peterson?" She slid around the desk. He was lying on his back, unconscious. There was a lot of blood pooling under him. She knelt next to him and felt for a pulse.

"Is he dead?"

Cate looked across the room at Victoria, who had disregarded Cate's orders and entered the house. She stood in the doorway.

"No, he has a pulse, but it's weak. Can you call 911?"

While Victoria was giving the information to the dispatcher, Cate tried to assess the extent of his injuries. His face was bruised. One eye was swollen shut. There was a bullet wound in the upper part of his chest. She unbuttoned his shirt to administer first aid, applying pressure to the wound to slow the bleeding. Then she noticed something strange.

Tucked inside his shirt was a flash drive. With one hand still pressed to the wound, she pulled it out. Blood had seeped around the edges, but she could see the words printed neatly on a label on the outside: For Cate.

Suddenly, the sound of sirens pierced the air. Victoria went out to meet the emergency vehicles. "This way," Cate heard her say. Before Cate could think, she stuffed the flash drive into the pocket of her jeans. Then she moved aside, allowing the medics to take charge.

They loaded the man onto a stretcher and took him out. As she and Victoria stood outside and watched the ambulance disappear, they were approached by the responding officer and led to a secluded part of the yard where they were asked to wait to talk to the detectives who were on their way. Soon a whole parade of law enforcement vehicles arrived to begin collecting evidence.

* * *

Detective Cramer took down their details. He was a very pleasant looking man with guileless eyes and a kind smile. Then the older detective, Lawes, took over. He looked to be about twenty years Cramer's senior with thick graying hair and penetrating eyes under bushy eyebrows. Cate had no doubt they he had seen a lot over the years.

"Tell me what were you two ladies doing at Mr. Peterson's house?"

Cate took the lead answering questions. "He was a colleague of my father's. I wanted to talk to him about an old case they worked on together."

The detective scratched his head. "I hate to ask the obvious, but why didn't you just talk to your father?"

"He's had a stroke and can't talk."

"I see. So, what exactly was this case?"

"It was a joint law enforcement operation in Las Vegas nearly thirty years ago."

"Interesting. Tell me about it."

"They busted a child trafficking ring."

The detective raised his bushy eyebrows. "Now why would two young women be interested in such a case?"

Cate crossed her arms over her chest and lifted her chin. "We have reason to believe that we were among those children."

Those bushy eyebrows raised even further. "Say that again?" When Cate repeated herself, he peered at both of their faces in turn, then said, "Well now, that's quite a story. You mind my asking why you think that? Just what exactly happened?"

"I don't mind, except I don't remember. I was only three years old."

"And you say your father was . . . what? A member of this task force."

Cate nodded. "He adopted me."

"Is that right?" He turned to Victoria. "What about you?"

"I was a baby, so I can't tell you anything either."

"See, we are trying to find our birth parents," Cate said. "That's why we wanted to talk to Mr. Peterson. He said he might have some information that would help us."

The detective scratched his head again and Cate started to think they were being interviewed by Columbo. "Right, so you knocked on the door and disturbed a robbery in progress."

"Apparently," Cate said.

"Okay, I'm going to need you to tell us in detail exactly what transpired. If you'll come with us, we'll take you to the police station to get your statements."

As they followed the detective to the station, Cate's phone rang. She looked at caller ID. It was Liam. She was in no mood to talk to him just now so she hit the "I'll call you back" button and tucked her phone back into her pocket.

CHAPTER 10

Las Vegas, Nevada

Many hours later Cate and Victoria found themselves checking into a hotel room. It was too late to drive back to Prescott. And besides, they needed to wait until morning to see if Peterson would recover to tell them what he knew. It was Victoria's idea to stay at a Red Rock Casino resort. She had quizzed the detectives about places to stay where they could get a Las Vegas experience. Both detectives agreed that the Red Rock Casino was the best choice. Detective Lawes gave them a voucher providing a discount for two nights.

From the moment they entered the place, Cate wanted to turn around and go back to the car. Just to get from the parking lot to the lobby, they had to pass through the vast casino area with its slot machines, video poker machines, and assorted game tables, through wide hallways where enormous chandeliers reflected on spit-polished marble floors, and past a lobby bar carpeted in plush red with grand staircases on either side.

She was also acutely conscious of her state of dishevelment. Her shirt was streaked with blood and there was a large splotch of blood on the knee of her jeans, where she had knelt by Peterson, that had dried in the desert heat.

Victoria, sensing her discomfort, gestured to a seating area near the check-in counter. "Look, you stay here, and I'll get our room."

While Cate waited, her phone chirped. It was Liam. Again. This was the third time he called. She knew he would never give up so, with a sigh, she answered.

"Cate, where are you? And why haven't you been answering your phone?"

"I'm answering you now, aren't I?"

"Cate, where are you?"

"I'm in Las Vegas."

"Las Vegas?" Liam shouted.

Cate held the phone away from her ear. "Pipe down, Liam. People clear across the room can hear you."

"Cate," Liam now spoke in a low-pitched growl, "tell me what's going on."

"I'm looking for my birth parents, okay?"

"Your birth parents? Is this about your so-called sister?"

"Her name is Victoria."

"Look Cate, how do you know she's not some kind of scammer?"

Cate felt her face go red. Did he think she was that gullible? Did he think she wasn't capable of making rational decisions? She opened her mouth to say something when Victoria came strolling up with a beaming smile and a pair of room passes.

"Look, Liam, I gotta run." She pressed the end button, cutting off Liam's howl of protest.

"Who was that?" Victoria asked, seeing Cate's red face.

"My brother. They're all overprotective, but Liam is the worst. He doesn't seem to realize that I'm all grownup."

Victoria tried to hide a smile.

"What?" Cate asked. "What are you smiling about?"

"I think it's sweet how your brothers want to protect you."

"It's suffocating, is what it is."

"Okay, maybe. But did you bother to tell them what you were up to?"

"No, because they would have tried to talk me out of it. It was better this way, believe me."

Victoria held her hands up in surrender. "Okay, okay. You know them better than I do. But you might want to let them know now and then that you are okay."

* * *

When they finally reached their room, Cate was beyond relieved. She pushed open the door, and stale cool air greeted her. She made her way straight to the bathroom with her overnight case. She was desperate to wash up and change into clean clothes.

When she came out, she found Victoria splayed on her back on one of the queen-sized beds, her arms stretched out. "Holy crap. What a rotten day."

Cate stood by the window and gazed out at the view of Red Rock Canyon looming on the horizon. "You can say that again."

Victoria rolled to her side to face Cate and tucked an arm under her head. "My head is still spinning."

"Yeah, I can't quite wrap my head around it all."

"Do you think . . ."

"What?"

"Well, doesn't it strike you as a bit of a coincidence our arriving just as someone is beating the crap out of that old FBI guy?"

Cate nodded. "I've been thinking about that. They're always saying there's no such thing as coincidence, but it's hard to see a connection. I mean nobody knew we were going there. And even if they did, they wouldn't know why."

"Well . . ." Victoria said, drawing out the word into two syllables, "there is one person who knew both the where and the why."

Cate gave Victoria a puzzled look.

"My ex-fiancé. He came to my motel room this morning."

Cate gazed at Victoria, dumbfounded. "Okay, let me see if I can get this straight. You have an ex-fiancé and he showed up at your motel room door this morning?"

"Yes."

"Why didn't you tell me this?"

"I didn't see the point. He's my ex and has nothing to do with my life anymore."

"Well, what did he want?"

"He wanted me to go back to Savannah and marry him."

"And you said?"

"I told him he isn't my fiancé anymore and to get lost."

Cate thought for a moment. "But I still don't see the connection."

Victoria sighed. "I told him I was going to Vegas to search for my birth mother."

"Okay," Cate said slowly, "so he knows you're going to Vegas and why. Surely he doesn't know the name of the man we were going to see."

"Yes, but he might have told my father."

"So what?"

"See, there are some things I haven't told you. I just didn't see any relevance, but now I'm thinking otherwise."

"You mean besides the fact that you had an early morning visit with your ex."

"Yes, besides that." Victoria sighed. "Okay, so here's the deal. I think I kind of stumbled into a hornet's nest back in Savannah. It started when I came home to take care of Mama when she got the diagnosis of her cancer. Well then, after she died, I had nowhere to go to speak of."

"Hang on, a second. You came home to take care of your mother. From where?"

"See, after I graduated from college, I was working in Boston. That's where I went to school, which is neither here nor there. The point is, when Mama got sick, I quit my job there and came home. I wasn't working on account of taking care of Mama. So when she passed, there I was. No job. Nowhere to go. Then Daddy offered me a position in the accounting office at his real estate company. It was a darn sight better than hanging out at home, so I took it.

"Well, I do have a degree in business administration and I'm pretty good with numbers. Apparently, a lot better than Daddy anticipated. I started finding what you might call irregularities in the ledgers where I was working. At first, I thought it was just me, that I didn't fully understand how the numbers were kept. It took me awhile and a lot of digging, but I began to realize that there was something fishy going on."

"Like what?"

"Well, there was just a lot of money running through those accounts. Seemed like more than should have been for that kind of business."

"You don't mean money laundering, do you?"

Victoria glanced sharply at Cate. "Why, yes. That's what I was thinking, but it seemed like a pretty big accusation to go flinging around. So, I tried to get some advice from Noel, my then-fiancé. He brushed it off. Told me that some things were just over my head. Once we were married, he told me, I could quit that old job and start working on making a family."

Cate scoffed. "No wonder you broke things off."

"Yeah, no kidding." Victoria scowled. "Anyway, his words just kind of stuck in my craw, so I kept digging deeper. I started following the money at the company. Isn't that what they say, follow the money? I discovered that the money flowed through some of Daddy's other companies. That led me to working out Daddy's corporate structure.

"Come to find out that Noel represented a number of Daddy's subsidiaries, including the company I worked for. If that didn't beat all. I reckon those two are thick as thieves. Literally."

"I still don't see it. How does that connect with our situation now?"

"I figure my daddy's got to have connections to someone in Las Vegas. After all, isn't that where we think we both came from? So, if Noel told Daddy that we were coming here, Daddy might have tipped someone off." She gazed into space. "If only we could have talked to Mr. Peterson."

Suddenly, Cate leaped up from her chair. "My pants. Where are the pants I was wearing?"

"Why, it's they're there on top of your suitcase."

"Great." Cate grabbed them and pulled the flash drvie that was tucked deep inside. "I never got a chance to tell you that I found this tucked inside Jim Peterson's shirt pocket."

"No way."

"Yeah. I didn't want to say anything in front of the cops and then, with all the questioning, well, I kind of forgot it was there."

Victoria sat up. "Well, let's have a look."

Cate grabbed her laptop and inserted the drive.

CHAPTER 11

Las Vegas, Nevada

Victoria looked over Cate's shoulder as they checked out the contents of the drive. It contained of a number of reports. The first was the same report that her brother had emailed her. Only this one was un-redacted. It provided both the names of those arrested and the arresting officers. Cate felt a tingle go up her spine when she saw her father's name on the list, even though she knew it would be there.

The names of the some of the rescued children were also included along with their ages. Officers stated that they were unable to confirm the last names of several of them, as they were either too young or under the influence of narcotics. Cate perused the names of the children. Then she tried to imagine their own fates had they not been rescued. It made her heart squeeze painfully.

"Oh my God," Victoria said softy, looking over Cate's shoulder. "They were just young, helpless little children."

Then Cate said, "Look at this. In the summary section, they stated that twenty-three were rescued. But the report lists only twenty-two children. The youngest was five years old. So, where am I?"

Victoria squeezed her hand. "I don't know. But at least we have the names of the arresting officers. Maybe we can track down one or two of them."

Next was a PDF. It contained photocopies of old newspaper clippings. She scrolled through the clippings one by one. They consisted of three obituary reports: Martin Roy died in May 1995, of a hit and run. Rosa Franklin died in February 1996, during an armed robbery. Gregory Hudson passed in June 1996, in a one-car accident.

"Oh, my Lord," Victoria said. "Those were the arresting officers on the case."

"Yeah, what are the odds? I mean being a police officer is a somewhat risky business, but three of the officers involved in this case dying so close together? Why did Peterson include these?"

"Good question." Cate said. Then she opened another PDF. Like the first, it contained a set of newspaper clippings. They were dated 1989, 1991, 1992. "That's strange," she said. "These are birth certificates." She read each one with Victoria looking over her shoulder.

"Boys born to an Arthur and Janet Townsend. I don't get it."

"Me neither. But it must have been important to Peterson. Why else would he include it in the flash drive?"

Cate closed the file and moved on to a set of documents. Cate felt the hair on her arms rise. "These are intake reports by Child Protective Services, dating from 1989-1993." At Victoria's puzzled look, she explained, "When children are removed from a home, the CPS issues an intake report. I imagine the same would hold true if they were rescued from a child trafficking bust."

An hour later, Victoria sighed in exasperation. "I swear, Cate, we've looked through these reports three times. My eyes are starting to glaze over, but we haven't found a single thing for the date of the bust."

Cate closed the laptop in disgust. "I just don't understand why it's not there."

Seeing Cate slump her shoulders in defeat, Victoria said, "Well, look. I'm so hungry I could eat a horse. Let's go find a restaurant."

***

Cate sat across from Victoria in a booth at one of the many steakhouses at the resort. Victoria ordered a bourbon—a double on the rocks—and Cate settled for her usual beer. Cate couldn't decide if she was more hungry or more tired, but had settled on eating before she poured herself into that queen-sized bed waiting for her up at their room.

Victoria took a large sip from her glass and sighed. "Ah, nothing like a good old whiskey to wet a dry throat."

Cate lifted her glass. "To us."

They clinked glasses, then she sat back and took in the scene around her. The tables were arranged in an arc with a bar opposite. Despite the elegant setting, most of the patrons were dressed very casually in shorts or jeans and t-shirts.

Her gaze settled on one in particular. Unlike his fellow drinkers, he wore well-fitted black jeans and a button-down shirt with the sleeves rolled up to the elbows. He leaned casually against the bar with one booted foot propped on the foot rail. She looked up at his finely chiseled face and realized that he was looking right at her.

She glanced quickly down at her drink, took a sip. Victoria was chatting to her about items on the menu. "I think a steak will be just about right. I'm so hungry my belly thinks my throat's been cut."

"What?"

"I said I'm going to order steak. What about you?"

Cate glanced at the menu. "Yeah, that sounds good. An eight-ounce tenderloin."

"That's my girl. Now, are you going to tell me what's got you all distracted?"

Cate glanced over at the man at the bar. When he caught her gaze, he lifted his glass and emptied the last of his drink. Then he motioned to the bartender for another with a raised finger.

"There's a man at the bar. He keeps watching us. It's unnerving."

"Oh. Well, we are two attractive females," Victoria drawled. "Men do like to look."

"Yeah, maybe. And maybe I'm just a little jumpy today, but I get the feeling he's surveilling us."

"Seriously?" Victoria raised a well-plucked eyebrow. "Let me take a gander. What does he look like?"

"Tall, slender, late-thirties, shoulder-length dark hair."

"Right. I'm just going to visit the ladies room."

Cate watched as Victoria stood, flicked a lock of hair over her shoulder, and strolled between the tables and the bar. As she passed, heads turned, taking in her perfect figure and long blond hair that caressed the small of her back.

Cate smiled ruefully at her departing back and wondered if she would ever get used to Victoria's ability to draw the attention of every male in the room. Then her gaze was drawn like a magnet back to the man at the bar. She saw his eyes flicker towards Victoria, then return to her. He nodded at her and lifted his drink.

Cate felt a flush rise from her collar to the roots of her hairline. She prided herself on being able to handle men, what with all her brothers, the patrons at the pub and police training. She certainly was no blushing schoolgirl. She was a full-grown adult. But somehow, he managed to get under her skin with just one look. She was relieved when Victoria returned to the table just as the waitress arrived. After she took their order, Cate looked at Victoria.

"Well?"

"He does seem pretty intense. Like he's trying to be casual but can't quite pull it off. And I think you're right. He isn't on the make."

"So, you think he's staking us out?"

"Could be. But why?"

"All I can think is that this is about Jim Peterson."

CHAPTER 12

Las Vegas, Nevada

Across town, Art entered another restaurant, an upscale French affair that pandered to the political and social elite of Las Vegas. The hostess led him to a quiet corner where he met with a vice detective. His expression told the detective that he was not happy.

"What's the situation?"

"Peterson is in intensive care. The docs say he has a fifty-fifty chance of survival."

"And the package?"

"No sign of it."

Art's face flushed red with anger. "How could you have botched this up so badly?"

The detective shifted his heavy body in the chair. "Sir, we sent in our best. The man refused to give up anything,"

Art scowled. "And then 'your best' shot him."

"Yes, well, what could they do? They were interrupted."

"By someone knocking on his door."

"Yes, sir."

"Two women."

"Yes, sir."

"Did you get their names?"

The detective pulled a notebook from his jacket pocket.

"Caitlin Connelly and Victoria Saunders."

Art glowered at the detective. It was his worst nightmare come true. If anything happened to Victoria, Forrest would rake him over the coals. And he was suspicious of this other woman—Caitlin Connelly. That name, Connelly, rang a bell. There were some Connelly's over in Arizona. An entire family in law enforcement. If she was related to them it meant she was untouchable.

But he couldn't have those two women snooping around. Who knew what they might stumble onto? And God forbid that Peterson should die. The rascal had the goods on him hidden away in case of an untimely death.

To make matters worse, he had heard whispers of an FBI investigation into the corruption of certain departments of the police. Luckily, as governor, he was far removed from the politics of Las Vegas. He knew that he had been incredibly lucky to have skated by all the scandals unscathed when he worked for the city.

And he would continue to be safe, as long as the women kept to the present situation. If they started digging into the past, there were just too many paths leading straight to him. That could mean the end of his political career.

"Keep an eye on them. I want to know where they go, who they see."

"Yes, sir."

* * *

Sam pulled his Jaguar into the garage of his luxury apartment building at midnight, which was early for him. As soon as he walked in the door, he stripped off his snug jeans and collared shirt in favor a pair of loose sweatpants and t-shirt.

He poured himself a large glass of water and took a gulp. He was sober. Over the past couple of years, he had learned to drink his scotch very slowly. He always ordered a water back, which kept him hydrated while appearing to be imbibing.

It was all part of the image he cultivated working undercover

—the apartment, the car, the clothes, the high-end whiskey. Since he and his partner, Kyle, started their operation, they had busted a lot of criminal rings: gold smugglers out of Mexico, porno movie producers, hijackers of stolen goods and high-end cars, and some very lucrative money launderers. Hell, it was Vegas, after all.

The city was billed as "The Entertainment Capital of the World," famous for its five-star resorts, world-class restaurants and boutiques, and spectacular entertainment and nightlife. Where everything was bigger than life—cartoon architecture on a grand scale, statues of Olympian Gods, golden lions and enormous sphinxes—the city was a combination of magic and mirage.

The mirage had vanished in a puff of smoke during the pandemic. For if ever there was a place where the virus could spread its deadly illness, it was Las Vegas. Imagine the close contact at bars and theaters and restaurants where people ate together, shared drinks together, laughed together. Imagine every single poker chip, playing card, slot machine handle and button being touched by the hand of the infected coming from around the world, then shared with those who would return to their homes.

Sam had watched as the sparkling hotels and casinos had shut down, where nightlife had come to a screeching halt. A city whose entire reason for being revolved around large gatherings had turned into a ghost town. Resorts large and small were sold at rock bottom prices. Unemployment skyrocketed as people in the entertainment and tourist industries, from the maids to the performers, suddenly lost their livelihoods.

And then he watched it come back to life. As the world's scientists developed the vaccines and the virus let loose its stranglehold, people emerged from their shelters and began to rebuild. Everyone was poorer than they used to be, but that didn't stop the tourists and gamblers and families seeking a little fun in the sun from coming, if perhaps not in the same numbers.

As Las Vegas rose from the ashes, Sam saw the return of the

lowlife as well: the swindler, con artist, scammer, and cheater looking to make a quick buck. And just beyond the Strip where thousand-dollar gambits were made on the roll of the dice or turn of the card, were the homeless—those who had survived the scourge—as well as those who had joined their numbers as the economic downturn thrust them into poverty or mental illness.

When he tried to make sense of it all, it often sent him into one of those depressions that had him walking the floor at three in the morning. Sometimes he longed for the rural life in the high country he left to seek the glamour and excitement of the big city.

Life over the past fifteen months had been like riding on a roller coaster. When the town was hardest hit he found himself scrambling for basic necessities. A confirmed bachelor used to dining out every night, he'd had to learn some basic cooking skills. Somewhere along the way, as he watched with morbid fascination the news of the struggle in places like New York City, life's priorities, the things that mattered to him had shifted. He knew he would have to make a move out of Vegas, perhaps into a different line of investigations. But for now, he was hanging in there, mulling over his options.

The temperature had dropped to a cool sixty degrees and he stepped out onto his balcony and eased into his favorite lounge chair. He sipped his water slowly and thought about the two women he had been surveilling.

Even if he hadn't been on the lookout, he would have noticed them: one, an incredibly well-put-together woman, and the other, a bit of a waif, wearing a sloppy t-shirt and faded khakis. One ordered bourbon on the rocks. The other ordered a beer. Then the well-dressed one had strolled by, eyeing him with more than a passing interest. But he was more intrigued by the other one. When he lifted his glass to her, she had actually blushed. They were such an unlikely pair.

Sam stared into the night. There was no moon and the stars shone brightly despite the lights of the city. He was worried.

When he heard that Peterson had been shot and was in intensive care, alarm bells began ringing in his head.

Jim Peterson was the only cop still around that was familiar with a number of the heavies who had been arrested during a long-ago child-trafficking bust. The felons Peterson had arrested in the case were all out of prison now and as far as Sam knew, most of them were long gone, either dead or skipped the country. But there were still a couple around. From what he was able to gather, they were back to their old tricks. Most worrisome of all were rumors of a resurgence of a certain kind of child trafficking at its most heinous.

Sam and Kyle had been trying to penetrate this ring for the past three months. But they were a cagey lot and they had to work slowly to gain their trust. It would be very bad, dangerous even, if these two women got caught in the middle of their operation.

CHAPTER 13

J & R Ranch, Nevada

Not many people outside of law enforcement knew or cared that Jim Peterson had been shot and was in critical condition. Not unless they happened to read the crime section of the Las Vegas Review-Journal. But Janet knew. She had become rather an avid reader of this particular section of the paper, now posted online. That's where the real news was reported, along with the section on investigations. You didn't find it under local, business, sports, or entertainment.

The report about Peterson, though offering limited information, had triggered an unsettling memory from long ago. It took her a while to dredge it up, but eventually it came to her. She knew the man as FBI Special Agent in Charge James Peterson. He was the lead investigator on a child trafficking bust many years ago. Just to be sure, she dug up the old newspaper report that she had kept locked up in her very important secret file.

Rereading that report put her on edge. The case from nearly thirty years ago had been a turning point for her. Although she didn't know it at the time, that was when blind love for Art, her husband, had turned the corner to mistrust and eventually, loathing. She folded the old report carefully and returned it to the file.

Putting it from her mind, she settled in for an evening in front of the television. Then she saw Art on the news. He was being interviewed about water rights in the Reno Valley. She felt her anxiety rise and was tempted to reach for a Xanax. But she resisted the urge. She had been prescribed anti-anxiety meds ever since her panic attack four years earlier. The drug made her feel drowsy, weak, and uncoordinated, but had she continued to take it at the insistence of her husband. Most recently, she had started having bouts of delirium.

She hadn't realized how far-reaching the side effects were until her youngest son Carl, a nurse who had returned to school for his masters, came home for his Christmas break. He was alarmed that his mother, who tended to talk a mile a minute, was practically comatose. For her part, she remembered looking at him and wanting to say something but had trouble formulating even the simplest sentences.

That's when she decided, with Carl's help and advice, to wean herself from the drug. He also strongly urged her to see a different physician. The family doctor who had attended all of them since the boys were born pandered solely to Art's needs.

She also decided to make a permanent move back to the family ranch. It was the best move she had ever made. Her parents were getting older and welcomed her help. She took on every kind of chore, from tending the garden to riding herd with the hired hands. All those hours of hard labor in the fresh air were making her physically and emotionally stronger. She felt a renewed appreciation of the land where she was raised. So many of the ranches in Nevada were folding. Since she did not know how long theirs would survive, she started taking her camera everywhere she went.

Now, watching Art respond to news reporter's questions with poise, she was struck by how attractive a man he still was. His thick, dark hair was just beginning to silver at the temples giving him a distinguished look. His face, too, had aged gracefully. Only a few laugh lines fanned out from dark eyes. Even features that had given him that boy-next-door look in his twenties were now more chiseled, more manly.

He still had the same trim build he'd had when they first began dating. Today he was wearing a dark navy-blue suit with a crisp white shirt and a blue-on-blue striped tie. It was almost exactly the same as suit as he was wearing the day she met him, a day she remembered like it was yesterday.

CHAPTER 14

Las Vegas, Nevada 1985

She had just landed her first gig as a free-lance photojournalist documenting a fundraiser for the reelection campaign of the mayor of Las Vegas. Wearing an understated, black cocktail dress that gently hugged her slender form and armed with a high-end Nikon camera, she stepped into the opulent room with trepidation.

She gazed around to get a feel for the ambiance as well as the guests. Crystal chandeliers glittered overhead; plush red and gold pile carpeted the floors; gold guild framed ivory walls. A well-dressed crowd, men in black tuxes and women in evening attire, stood in small groupings drinking champagne and schmoozing. They were the creme de la creme of Las Vegas's movers and shakers that she would be photographing. She had studied their pictures the entire day so that she would know who was who.

She accepted a flute of champagne from one of the many black-suited waiters mingling in the crowd with their trays of beverages, reminding herself to be diligent in her drinking. It would never do to lose focus or control with this crowd. She took a small sip, then glanced up, catching her first sight of Art across the room. He was without doubt one of the most attractive men in the place. As she struggled to place him in her mental list of guests, she realized that she was staring. And he was staring right back.

She felt a spark of electricity flow between them. It was like one of those scenes in a romance novel—dashing gentleman spots young debutant, love at first sight. Yet, try though she might, she couldn't place him in her mental list. She was sure she would have remembered such a compelling face. She sensed his eyes on her. Feeling a blush rise from the modest neckline of her dress all the way up to the roots of her hair, she started to turn away. But his gaze held hers as he made his way across the room towards her. He reminded her of a predator stalking his prey.

He skirted around a clutch of socialites and then he was standing before her. "I know it's an old cliché, but I couldn't help but wonder what such a beautiful woman as yourself is doing all alone in this room full of people."

Janet smiled, feeling her face turn hot once again. "I'm working," she stated simply.

He nodded at her camera. "Let me guess. Photojournalist?"

"Yes. I was just reconnoitering, sorting out who's who. It would never do if I were to miss a shot of one of the VIPs."

"Indeed." He glanced around, took in the crowd. "I might be able to help you with that. As it is, I know most of the people here. And if I don't, well, they can't be too important."

"Oh? And you are?"

"Art Townsend, at your service. Not yet a VIP, but soon."

Janet offered her hand. "Janet Jones. Very nice to meet you." Just then the mayor and his wife entered the room, and she gave him an apologetic look. "If you'll excuse me, I believe this is my cue."

She flagged down a waiter to take her half-empty champagne flute and slipped through the crowd towards the couple. As she did so, she pulled out her press pass and looped it around her neck.

As the evening progressed, Art kept his promise to help her. Staying unobtrusively nearby, he guided her through the crowd, pointing out a photo opportunity here and there, making sure she was at the right place at the right time.

By the time the evening drew to a close, Janet was sure her feet would fall off. Finally, the speeches were finished, and the event was reaching its conclusion. She clutched her camera with its excellent collection of photos.

She turned to her companion of the evening. "I can't thank you enough for your help, Art."

"Oh but there is one way you can thank me. Have dinner with me."

* * *

He took her to a small Italian restaurant with white table clothes, low lighting, and a single candle on each table. The maître d' greeted him by first name. They selected a pricy bottle of red wine and Art gently guided her through the menu, giving her suggestions for her starter and main course.

The wine arrived and the waiter opened it with a flourish. Art lifted his glass in a toast. "To the most beautiful woman in Las Vegas," he said, taking a sip. "Now tell me about yourself, Janet. Where are you from?"

"I come from cattle country, in the northern part of the state," she told him. "My family has a ranch just north of Winnemucca. The J & R Ranch. Have you heard of it?"

"I think I have. It's a pretty big spread, isn't it?"

"Yes. My grandfather bought it in the twenties, along with a couple of other ranches."

"Impressive."

Janet blushed. "Well, I guess. If you like living miles from nowhere."

"I take it you don't?"

Janet shrugged. "I like it here. I like all the lights and the tourists and the shows and . . . just everything."

"Me, too," Art smiled at her and slipped a hand onto her thigh. She could feel it through the thin silk of her dress. It was big and warm, causing a small fire to burn low in her belly.

"What about you? Where do you work?"

"I'm an engineer. I work for the Clark County Commission. But that's only a start," he told her. "I plan to run for Commissioner."

"Is that an important position?"

Art glanced around the room and then lowered his voice. "Sweetheart, the commission governs and runs Clark County. It is *the* most powerful governmental body in the state of Nevada."

"I see," Janet said. But of course, she didn't really see. Not then.

As the evening progressed, Art's caresses became bolder. His hand beneath the tablecloth soon pushed away the silk to find her bare leg. As he gazed into her eyes and plied her with wine, his hand crept upward, ever upward until his pinkie landed on the crotch of her panties. Finding it moist with want, he leaned in and kissed her.

"I think maybe we should go somewhere a little more private."

Janet nodded, her eyes glazed with passion. She was no stranger to sex. She had had a couple of boyfriends in college. But something told her she had just moved into a higher league.

CHAPTER 15

Las Vegas, Nevada

When Cate opened her eyes the following morning, it was practically pitch dark. The only light came from the digital clock on the nightstand that told her it was ten o'clock. She could see the vague outlines of the hotel furnishings and it slowly dawned on her where she was: at a resort hotel in Las Vegas, of all places. She sat up and rubbed her face. She was still dogged tired.

She went to the window and pulled at the blackout blinds. Sunshine poured through the small opening and a dazzling deep blue sky greeted her.

"Cate?" A groggy voice mumbled her name from under a pile of pillows.

"Hey, sleepyhead. Rise and shine."

"What time is it?"

"Ten o'clock."

A tousled blond head popped up and looked around. "Well don't that beat all? I slept like a log."

"Me, too. But now we need to get up and decide what to do."

"Right," said Victoria. "I'll make some coffee." She stumbled over to the coffee maker and grabbed the pot to fill with water. Cate took the opportunity to grab a quick shower.

When she emerged, Victoria looked her over with a frown.

Cate glanced down at her sad attire—a pair of wrinkled capris and a faded cotton top, the same clothes she had donned the evening before. "It's all I brought."

"Hm," said Victoria and handed her a cup of coffee.

There was a small table in the corner and they sat down across from each other.

"So, what are we going to do?" Cate asked.

Victoria took a sip of coffee. "I don't know. You reckon we ought to give it up? Pack up and go home? Are we in any danger?"

"Maybe. I wish I knew if there was any kind of connection between our visit to Mr. Peterson and those thugs back in Prescott." She thought for a moment. "I'd like to see if Mr. Peterson made it through the night."

"Yeah. If he's conscious, we might be able to get some information. Then we might have a better idea what our next step is."

"Right." Cate stood up. "No time like the present. Which hospital did you say he was at?"

* * *

The hospital was a mile from the resort. Cate drove and Victoria navigated. When they approached the front desk, the receptionist told them that Mr. Peterson was still in ICU. Only family members were allowed.

"Is he conscious?"

"I'm sorry ma'am. I can't give out that information." She was a large woman with dull brown, stringy hair, a slight mustache on her lip, and a dour expression.

"I see," said Cate. "Well can we at least give him a card?"

The woman's expression softened for a moment. "I don't see why not. You can leave it here at the front desk and someone will see that he gets it."

"Why thank you, Ms. Wilson," Victoria said, looking at the woman's name badge. "We'll do that."

Leaving the hospital, they headed for the parking garage. They trudged up the stairs and turned the corner onto the second floor where their car was parked. They were about halfway to the car when suddenly, Victoria grabbed Cate's arm and pulled her into a row of parked cars.

"What are you—" But before Cate could finish her sentence, Victoria pressed her hand over her mouth and pulled her down to squat behind an SUV.

"Hush," she whispered. "There are two guys over there, next to that police car." She nodded her head towards a row of parked cars. "Recognize them?"

Slowly, Cate raised her head and peered through the window of the SUV. She spotted the two men not more than twenty feet away in the next row of cars. She recognized one of the men immediately. It was the detective with the bushy eyebrows: Lawes. She ducked back down and turned towards Victoria.

"That's Detective Lawes. But I don't recognize the other one."

"Me neither," Victoria said softly. Then she rose up until she could see the two men through the SUV's window. Cate joined her, counting on the vehicle as a blind.

The detective was speaking to a tall man with slender build. He wore a cap pulled low over his brow. His face was turned away from them.

But the detective's face was clear. It was flushed red. His thick eyebrows were drawn together, and his features were taut with fury as he spoke. "Where's the package?"

The taller man hunched his shoulders defensively. "We never found it. The man wouldn't tell us anything. Trust me. We tried." His voice was high, whiny.

"And then you shot him? How could you be so stupid?"

"What do you want, man? We did what we had to do."

"Yeah, right. Sure, you did. Well you just better hope that man doesn't live to tell about it."

"It's not our fault the package wasn't there. Now what about the money?"

"You'll get the money when I see the goods. Now get out of my sight." With that, the detective yanked open the police car door and slid inside. He backed the car out with tires squealing, then roared out of the garage.

The taller man stood in the empty parking space and stared after the car as it descended down the ramp. He jerked his cap off and ran his fingers through his hair. It was lank and greasy, hanging to his shoulders. Without the cap, Cate could see his face. It was pimply. Except where the port-wine stain covered half of his cheek and brow.

Victoria gasped. The man jerked his head around. She pressed her hand to her mouth. The two women slowly sank further down behind the car. Then they heard his footsteps. He was walking methodically down the row of cars. Every now and then his footsteps paused.

As he got closer, Cate motioned for Victoria to follow her. She duck-walked around to the back of the SUV just as he reached their hiding place. Cate held her breath and willed Victoria to do the same. When he moved on to the next car, the women slithered around to the opposite side of the SUV.

A service stairway lay just beyond them, kitty-corner from the front end of the vehicle. Cate glanced at Victoria, who nodded. Then she got down on her hands and knees to peer under the carriages of the cars. When she could see by the angle of his feet that the man was turned away, she crawled, still on hands and knees, to the stairs and slipped into the stairwell. Victoria scampered after her.

From their new vantage point in the shadows, they could see him without being seen. Black eyes in a ferret-like face gazed slowly around the garage as he carefully canvassed the area. He held a firearm in one hand.

Eventually he stopped moving and stood stalk still. Seeing and hearing nothing, he shrugged and pulled his cap back over his head, hiding most of the livid birthmark. Tucking his hands in his pockets, he took one last look around, then sauntered to the pedestrian exit.

When they were sure he was gone, Victoria took a deep breath and let it out. "Holy Mother of God. I thought we were goners for sure."

"You and me both," Cate said. "Come on. Let's get out of here."

As they returned to their car and pulled out of the parking garage, Victoria said, "I recognized him. He was one of the guys running from Peterson's house. I could tell by the birthmark."

"Wait. You saw the perps leaving the house?"

"Well, I didn't know that then, did I? It all happened so fast. But now I remember. It's him. I know it is."

* * *

By the time they returned to the resort, it was early afternoon. They both kicked their shoes off and flopped on their beds.

"So now what?" Victoria asked.

"I have no idea."

"Well I have one." Victoria stood up and grabbed her handbag. "Come on. Let's go."

"Go where?"

"Shopping. Honey, we can't have you traipsing all over Las Vegas looking like that."

They found a shopping mall in downtown Summerlin. It was no surprise to Cate that Victoria was a veteran shopper. Before Cate knew it, she was ensconced in one changing room after another trying on a variety of shirts, cropped pants, and dresses. They settled on a nice assortment of casual, but smart clothes at a surprisingly reasonable prices.

Then Victoria dragged her into a high-end dress shop. When Cate tried to object, Victoria raised one plucked eyebrow and that settled the argument. Selecting an assortment of dresses, she pushed Cate once again into a dressing room. Cate tried on and discarded all of them as either to frilly, too large, or too flashy.

Finally, Victoria found what she was looking for. When Cate tried it on, she had to admit that Victoria was on the mark. It was a simple sleeveless dress in black raw silk that fit Cate's slender shape to perfection.

"Well?" said Victoria from behind the door. "Let's have a look."

Cate stepped out and turned slowly in front of a three-paneled mirror.

"Perfect," Victoria purred. She handed Cate a metallic-sequined bolero jacket.

"Oh, no. This is way too dressy for me."

Another raised eyebrow from Victoria had Cate shrugging dutifully into it.

"Perfect," Victoria said again. "Don't tell me you can't afford it because I'm buying."

"But Victoria, when will I ever wear something like this?"

"You never know. Every woman should have a little black number, just in case."

By the time they finished, the afternoon was waning, and Cate wanted nothing more than to go back to the hotel room and sit in front of the television and think about their next move.

But Victoria, it seemed, had other plans. The next thing Cate knew, she was sitting in a hair salon listening to the stylist and Victoria talking over her head. A shampoo, cut, and blow dry later, she looked in the mirror in astonishment. Her hair had been trimmed and layered to frame her oval face, bringing out a natural wave and stunning shades of blond she never even knew she had.

When they returned to the resort, Victoria insisted that they pull up to the front to avail themselves of valet parking. They had too many packages to try to lug them all the way from the parking lot. This way, they could haul everything in through the front door. Cate thought this was pretty extravagant, but she was too tired to argue. Shopping was hard work.

As the valet pulled away, a man with a baseball cap started to follow the two women in. The doorman nodded at a security guard who intercepted the man in the cap.

CHAPTER 16

Las Vegas, Nevada

Sam got a call late in the afternoon. When he learned it was Michael Connelly on the line, he was pleasantly surprised. Sam had been friends with Michael from way back. They trained at the Academy together and a few years later ended up at the same field office for several years.

"Michael, how are you? Is there something I can do for you?"

"Maybe. I hope so. It seems my sister is in Vegas. She witnessed a shooting."

Sam sank down into his chair. "You don't mean Caitlin Connelly, do you?"

"Yes. I take it you know something about this?"

"I know she was involved in a recent shooting of a retired FBI agent, but I didn't make the connection to you."

"Yes, my baby sister. What can you tell me?"

Sam took a moment to absorb this new information. Then he settled in to advise his old friend what he knew. "Hell, Michael, I understand your concern. Quite honestly, when I heard about Peterson getting shot and that two women were involved, I was uncomfortable with the situation. My sources told me that these women were looking into an old child trafficking case. Some of the players may be involved in a case I am working on now. So I thought I just might check out the situation."

"And?"

"I saw them last night. They were having dinner at the resort where they were staying. They were an odd pair. One was small, a little on the plain side, the other was drop-dead gorgeous."

"The plain one would be my sister."

"I see. And the other one?"

"Her sister."

Sam scratched his head. "What? You only ever mentioned one sister."

"Because Cate is our only sister. But she was adopted. You know that Cate was rescued during that old bust. Maybe there was a sister as well. She claims to have a DNA report showing they are sisters."

"So that explains why they are both here in Vegas. My contact told me they were looking for their birth parents. Anyway, they both seemed quite okay under the circumstances. I didn't actually talk to them, since I am undercover. But your sister seemed to be pretty level-headed."

"Whether she is or not, I don't like it. My sister decides to pay a visit to Peterson, the SAC on that child trafficking bust. The one that likely brought her into our family. And then she stumbles on a robbery at Peterson's house. Now he's in a coma in intensive care."

"Yeah. Too many coincidences."

"It sounds like she may have stirred up a hornet's nest. So can you help me out here?"

"What would you like me to do?"

"Track her down and tell her to go home."

Sam thought for a moment. "Let's say I did that. What do you think her reaction would be?"

"She'd be mad as hell. Probably dig her heels in even more, if that's possible."

"Yeah. And I would risk blowing my cover."

"Well, damn it, Sam. Is there anything you can do?"

"I've put out the word."

"What do you mean?"

"Michael, this is Vegas. Everyone has their network. You know, doorman, valets, waiters, policemen. They watch each others' backs. I let my people know to keep an eye on the two women. At the moment I can tell you they're safe and sound at the resort."

* * *

Despite reports by his network that the two women were okay, Sam never-the-less decided to check on them that evening. He returned to the same bar and took the same seat as the night before.

Just as his drink arrived, the two women entered. Sam did a double take. He recognized Victoria. She was hard to miss. But the woman with her . . . was that Cate? Whatever she had done to her hair was stunning in its effect. And her clothes. They were new and gently hugged a very slender, but perfect form. Gone was the waif, replaced by a . . . beautiful woman.

He watched as the two sisters crossed the restaurant to a table on the far side of the room. As before, Victoria ordered a bourbon on the rocks and Cate ordered a beer. At least that hadn't changed, Sam thought. The women smiled at each other and raised their glasses.

Sam settled in for his drink and a bit of surveillance. As he allowed his eyes to wander in their direction every now and then, he had to admit that he was intrigued by Cate. The night before, his concern had been strictly professional, although that blush when he caught her looking at him had pulled at his male vanity. But tonight, things were taking a new turn. He hadn't registered the fact that she was the sister to his very dear friend. That made it all the more personal.

And now that she'd cleaned up, she was very attractive. Not like her sister. Victoria was stunning, elegant. Cate was like a gamine—a slim, petite young woman . . . and sexually very appealing—not even aware of her own charms. He longed to get to know her and cursed the fact that he had to keep to his cover.

CHAPTER 17

Las Vegas, Nevada 1985-1993

Janet and Art became a number in the glittering town of Las Vegas in the next few months following that first date. Art introduced her to his colleagues, all of whom were involved in the entertainment industry in one way or another. They attended cabarets, dined at fine restaurants, and enjoyed the many private parties put on by friends and colleagues. When they finally found themselves alone in the bedroom, they lit each other on fire with passion.

Six months after they began dating, they married. Janet wanted something simple, perhaps at the ranch with family and a few friends. Art convinced her to hold the wedding in Las Vegas. When she balked at the cost, he assured her that he would pay for it. It was a large and glittering affair typical of all Las Vegas events. Three hundred guests were Art's friends and associates. A few dozen came from Janet's family.

They settled into Art's townhouse where he encouraged Janet to make herself at home. With his approval, she redecorated, turning the bachelor pad into a charming place suitable for entertaining as an up and coming couple.

Janet continued to pursue her freelance photojournalism career and Art continued to network with the VIPs—those above board and those in Las Vegas's seedy underbelly. At his insistence, they attended the most important functions together, but she soon grew tired of glitter and glitz. She was feeling her biological clock ticking. It was time for babies. Art was more than happy to oblige.

But Janet's flow came regularly every month like clockwork. She tried not to let herself fall into despair, but each month it got a little harder. A year passed. Their marriage became strained. When she tried to find comfort in Art, he started to rebuff her entreaties. Finally, they decided it was time to see the doctor, who referred them to a fertility specialist.

"People are always surprised to find out how bad humans are at reproduction," he told them. He was in his mid-forties and radiated kindness. Janet immediately felt comfortable with him. "Not all eggs are normal," he went on. "Not all normal eggs implant. There's actually only about a fifteen to twenty percent chance in any given month that a couple will conceive. I know that's not much comfort to you, and as you have been trying for a year, we are going to run some tests. Okay?"

The tests all came back normal. For the next two years, they went through the whole fertility treatment regime: Janet taking hormones and her basil body temperature every month. Sex became a command performance. But still no babies.

Meanwhile, Art began to pursue in earnest his candidacy for Clark County Commissioner and in 1989, he won. Janet tried to be happy for Art. She kept her chin and her career up. But she yearned for a child.

Then one day, Art came home with a precious bundle in his arms. The baby wasn't more than a month old and was crying its lungs out. Janet, who grew up on a ranch where children came along on a regular basis, swept the child into her arms and held it close. She took some formula that Art had in a carryall and warmed it up. The baby's tiny fists clutched at the bottle and he sucked it down.

When he finally fell asleep, she asked Art, "Where did this child come from?" He told her that he had been removed by Child Protective Services from an abusive family. They could foster this child, he told her, and even adopt him.

Janet studied the child's tiny sleeping face, his delicate fingers that kneaded the flannel blanket, a precious bundle wrapped in swaddling. Tears swam in her eyes and spilled over onto her cheeks. She wanted this child in the worst way.

Art took care of the paperwork. He soon came home with a birth certificate showing Janet and Art as his parents. They named him Ben after Janet's father. A year later they adopted their second child. They named him James after Art's father. In 1992, they adopted their third child. They named him Carl.

A year later, Las Vegas was rocked with a major bust-up of a child trafficking ring.

* * *

Janet read the newspaper article about the bust. She learned that these children were purchased for all kinds of things: to be photographed in suggestive poses, paraded at auctions to be sold to the highest bidder, or sold out of hotel rooms and truck stops to any man with the money and the desire to buy sex. Boys or girls, it didn't matter as long as they were young.

She beheld her own children, the oldest only four years old, so innocent and helpless and her heart broke at the thought of what could happen to children. When Art came home that evening, she hit him with a barrage of questions. How could this happen? How long had it been going on? What would happen to those children now? Art did his best to comfort her, to reassure her that the children were being well taken care of, that such activities seldom happened in Las Vegas.

Janet tried to find out more but despite the scandalous nature of the bust, very little appeared in the local news reports —just the initial report featured on the front page, then a smaller article buried on page three stating that the children rescued from the bust were nowhere to be found. How was that possible, Janet thought. They couldn't have just disappeared. When she asked her husband about it, he lost his temper and told her to leave it be.

CHAPTER 18

Las Vegas, Nevada

The next morning, Cate and Victoria checked out of the hotel. There was no such thing as cheap at the resort where they had spent the last two nights and it was putting a dent in Cate's pocketbook. Even breakfast was enormously expensive. They located a coffee shop a few blocks away and tucked into a hearty breakfast of bacon and eggs.

As they were enjoying a second cup of coffee, Victoria said, "I've been thinking. We need to find a way to get in to see Peterson."

"Yeah. But how?"

Victoria patted her lips daintily with her napkin. "We need to get a sympathy card."

An hour later, they returned to the hospital. Cate sat in the waiting area and watched as Victoria approached the front desk. She couldn't believe their luck. Instead of yesterday's dour-faced woman there was a young man at the helm. Victoria shot a smug glance at Cate and nodded, then turned her attention to the young man.

She waited until he finished entering something in the computer then looked up. "May I help you?"

"I surely hope so." She gave him a pitiful look. "I was hoping to be able to see Mr. Peterson today."

The man checked the hospital inpatient records by clicking a few keys on the computer. "I'm sorry ma'am. He's not receiving visitors at this time."

Victoria dropped her eyes, looking discouraged. "I see. Same as yesterday, huh?"

The man looked at the screen again. "Well, it does say here that he's conscious. They moved him out of ICU and into the telemetry unit."

"Telemetry unit?"

"That's where they put patients who aren't completely out of the woods, but don't need the same level of care as ICU."

"Oh, my goodness. Why that is wonderful news." Victoria beamed at the young man and Cate watched him blush.

"Yes, it is," he said. "But they still aren't allowing visitors. I'm not sure why. Hospital policy generally allows short visits in that unit." He gazed once more at the computer screen. "Ah yes, here it is. By order of the sheriff's office."

"Well now, that is strange. I hope he's not in some kind of trouble." She shook her head pensively. "But I did bring him a card. If I give it to you, will you see that he gets it?"

"Of course." He took the card, wrote the room number on the envelope, and dropped it into the internal mail tray.

"Why, thank you, young man. You are so very kind." As she sashayed through the waiting area and out the door, Cate could see the man's eyes follow the sway of her shapely hips.

* * *

They skirted by the reception area and headed straight to the elevators. Using the printed schematic provided to visitors, they found their way to the telemetry unit. It wasn't hard to find the room number. The door was closed. With a nod from Victoria, Cate pushed it open slowly. Mr. Peterson was lying flat on his back. His head, swathed in gauze, was practically swallowed up by the large white pillow. A monitor measured his vital signs.

Victoria stood guard at the door while Cate approached the bed. "Mr. Peterson, can you hear me? It's me. Cate Connelly."

The man's eyes opened slowly. He gazed at her for several minutes and she could see that he was slowly regaining his memory. "Cate. Is that you?"

"It is."

He lifted his hand. Tubes ran from his veins to a couple of bottles hanging beside the bed. "Thank you. Thank you for saving my life."

Cate felt her eyes water and gently took his hand. "You're welcome, Mr. Peterson."

"Jim," he said faintly. "Call me Jim."

"Yes, Jim."

He closed his eyes and Cate felt a moment of panic. Was he going back to sleep? Then he opened them again and turned his head towards her. "Tapes," he mumbled. "You need to find the tapes."

"Tapes?"

"FBI surveillance tapes."

"Where would they be?"

"At my house. In my office."

"Okay, Jim. We'll find them."

Jim nodded. "Very important. In case of my death. Get them and keep them safe."

Cate felt a lump form in her throat. "Jim, you're not going to die."

Jim's eyes fluttered and one of the machines began beeping more rapidly. "Just get those tapes. Bottom . . . desk drawer."

"We will."

Suddenly the door opened, and a nurse entered. "Just what do you two think you're doing in here?"

"Ah, visiting Jim?" Victoria said.

"This patient is not allowed visitors. Family members only." She tapped the chart. "Now which one would you be?" she glared at Victoria. "John or Bill?"

"Why, we're so sorry," Victoria drawled. "We thought it would be okay, you know. If we just popped in for a minute. We'll just be leaving now."

***

Fifteen minutes later, Cate and Victoria pulled up to the front of Jim's house. There was crime scene tape plastered across the front door.

"Are you sure we should be doing this?" Victoria asked.

"Yes."

"But what happens when you cross over that tape?"

"We can be arrested for interfering and hindering an investigation, not to mention opposing a police officer for crossing a police line. That charge carries a maximum possible sentence of two years in prison."

"But I don't see any police officer."

"Exactly. Something seems strange about the whole scene. They should have finished up any investigation by now if it was just a simple robbery gone bad. So why haven't they removed the crime scene tape? And if they haven't finished collecting evidence, why isn't there an officer at the scene?"

As Cate reasoned through it, her expression darkened. "And think about it. We know that at least one of those investigating officers wants something that Jim has. Probably those tapes. We need to do this."

As they got out of the car, Cate grabbed her backpack just to be sure she would have whatever she needed. Then she glanced up and down the street. It was pretty quiet; a lone car passed slowly by, and she could see a neighbor walking her dog a few houses away. Still, it might be just a bit conspicuous if they tried to break into a house covered in crime scene tape. "Let's check around back. Hopefully, we can get in without anyone seeing us."

They followed a meandering flagstone walkway that led from the porch across the front lawn to the back. There they found a large, covered patio with a barbeque, picnic table, and some padded outdoor seating. Oleander and bougainvillea surrounded the perimeter in a lovely, scented hedge. Cate had no trouble imagining neighbors or family gathered there on the many warm evenings, drinking a few beers and cooking up hamburgers.

She slipped across the patio with Victoria close on her heels and approached the door cautiously. Cupping her hands to block the glare, she peered inside. As expected, the place was empty. The living room was just as she remembered it—a large, comfortable-looking couch, a couple of easy chairs, a flat screen TV. A book lay on the end table and several newspapers were strewn across the coffee table.

She pulled two pairs of disposable gloves from her backpack and handed one to Victoria. Donning the other pair, she tried to open the patio door. No surprise there. It was locked.

"Now what?" Victoria asked in a hushed voice.

"Shouldn't be too hard to break in," Cate said. She pushed against the door, then using pressure, lifted and dropped the door a few times. Only a few seconds later, the lock slipped and failed.

"Oh my God, that was easy," Victoria spoke softly.

With a satisfied glance at Victoria, Cate slid the door open. As she stepped inside, she held her finger to her lips and signaled for Victoria to wait. They stood for a moment listening for any sign of life. A wall clock ticked off the minutes. The air conditioner came to life, spilling cool air down through the vents. Cate gave a sweeping but thorough glance around the room. Satisfied that they were alone, she let her shoulders relax.

Then she pointed out a metal bar lying next to the sliding glass door. It fit into the track to prevent a break in. "That's why people use these things," she said. "I imagine under normal circumstances, Jim would have secured the door. But of course, he left in an ambulance."

They made their way to the study and paused at the doorway. The place was every bit as much of a disaster area as the first time they saw it. Only now everything was covered in a fine layer of black fingerprint dust—the desk, the overturned office chair, the bookcases, and files whose contents were strewn across the floor.

Cate pulled two pairs of crime scene booties out of her

backpack and handed one pair to Victoria. Victoria watched as Cate slipped them over her flat-heeled sandals. "You're going to have to take those off," she said, gesturing to Victoria's very stylish-looking pumps.

"Hmph," Victoria said as she slipped out of her shoes and slipped on the booties.

They stepped carefully around the books scattered across the floor, pushing them aside as necessary, and made their way around to the front of the desk. It was an antique made of solid oak with ornately carved inlays on the legs and sides. There were but two drawers across the top.

"Didn't Mr. Peterson say the tape was in the bottom desk drawer?" Victoria asked.

"He did. I don't get it."

"Me neither." Then she gestured at the desk. "Anyway, I guess we should have a look."

Seeing Victoria's moue of distaste at all the black powder, Cate did the honors. With gloved hands she pulled open one of the drawers. It was shallow, only deep enough to hold stationery and pens and other small items. It was empty; its contents no doubt lay in scattered piles mingled with the books and files. She pulled open the second drawer. It, too, was empty, its contents having suffered the same fate as the first.

They turned and gazed in dismay at the jumble on the floor. The thought of pawing through all the books and papers, covered as they were with fingerprint dust, seemed a daunting task.

"Land sakes," said Victoria, "how are we ever going to find these 'tapes' in this mess?"

With a sigh, Cate turned back to close the desk drawers. The first one slid in with ease; the second one got stuck half-way in.

"That's strange," Cate said. "I didn't have any trouble opening it." She pulled it open a bit and then tried to ease it closed. Again, it jammed. So she pulled it all the way out and set it on the desk. She knelt and peered into the opening. She couldn't see any obstruction. Then she straightened and they stared at the drawer.

"Didn't Mr. Peterson say 'bottom desk drawer?'" Victoria asked.

Cate glanced at her sister, then back at the drawer. Carefully, she lifted it and flipped it over. There, in the slightly recessed wooden liner of the drawer was a long flat package attached with packing tape.

"Victoria, you are a clever girl."

"My mama didn't raise no fool," Victoria chortled.

Cate tried to prise the tape loose with a stubby fingernail but the tape stubbornly stuck to the surface.

"Girl," said Victoria, "move aside." In contrast to Cate's short, scruffy nails, Victoria's were long, perfectly manicured, and smoothly polished. She ran one nail along the edge of the tape and eased back a strip just large enough for Cate to grab a hold and rip it off.

The package was covered in plastic wrap and sealed with several layers of masking tape. There appeared to be three cassette tapes under all the wrapping. Cate started to tuck them into her backpack when they heard voices.

Someone at the front door. They heard the rasp of a key sliding into the slot. The rattle of a doorknob.

Quickly, Cate slid the drawer back into the desk. She looked around for an egress just as the front door opened.

There was but one window in the study tucked into an alcove with a cabinet beneath it. She hurried over to the window and slid it open. "You first," she said, turning to Victoria.

Cate gave her a hand up onto the cabinet. It was a tight fit through the window, but Victoria managed to shimmy through and drop to the ground. Then Cate hopped up. She was just about to squeeze through when a voice spoke. "I don't see why we have to do this again. We've already looked twice. There's nothing here."

Cate felt a frisson run up her spine. She recognized that voice. It was high and whiny. The man with the port-wine stain birthmark.

She turned to squeeze through the opening just as he reached the study's entrance. "I mean, look at this mess. You're telling me Lawes expects us to search through it all again?"

The two men stepped into the study and spotted Cate just as she was sliding through the opening.

"Whoa," one of the men said and ran to the window. He stuck his head out in time to see Cate fall to the ground.

"Hey. What the hell?"

Victoria grabbed Cate's hand and helped her to stand up.

"Run," Cate shouted. With Victoria helping Cate, they made a mad dash towards their car parked in front of the house, then tore across the front yard and scrambled into Cate's jeep. When the men realized where the women were headed, they turned back to the front of the house. Just as they came charging out the front door, Cate sped down the street and took a quick right turn.

Victoria held onto the back of her seat for dear life gazing behind them as Cate careened down one block then another.

"I think we lost them."

"Good."

"So, you might want to slow down just a tad. I'd hate to see you get pulled over for speeding."

CHAPTER 19

Las Vegas, Nevada 1998

Five years had passed since the child trafficking case. Janet's youngest child was now six years old. As she took up a fulltime job as a mother, thoughts of the poor children rescued during the bust slipped to the back of her mind.

Then Art decided to run for mayor. It meant that Janet had to attend tedious luncheons and dinners where she was expected to listen to Las Vegas's very important persons praise Art for his work as commissioner and endorse his candidacy. Janet chafed; all the social schmoozing was tedious in the extreme.

Still, when Art asked her to attend a function, she dutifully put in an appearance such as one occasion at the Four Seasons Hotel, an elaborate luncheon filled with many very important people in Las Vegas.

She took her assigned place at the table and smiled graciously at her table mates. But she wasn't hungry and found herself picking at her plate of salmon, potatoes, and salad—or as described on the invitation, smoked salmon, Hasselback potatoes, and three pepper salad. The man on her left initiated a conversation. He was remarkably short with graying hair and a mischievous grin. He spoke to her softly. When she noticed a slight accent, she asked him where he was from.

"I am from Poland, but I used to work in Latin America."

"Oh? What kind of work did you do?"

"I worked for your government. It was all very hush-hush, you know."

Janet smiled politely. "Really? So you can't talk about it, then?"

He nodded. "A lot of corruption."

"I see." She was beginning to regret the conversation. What kind of a nutjob was he? She thought to change the subject. "So . . . what brings you to Las Vegas?"

He quirked a bushy eyebrow at her. "A lot of corruption."

Janet glanced from her plate of salmon to his face. She could see a veiled smirk and felt a little uneasy. "Yes, I suppose you're right," she said. "We have our fair share of corruption right here in the U.S."

He grinned at her slyly. "Not in the U.S. Right here in this room."

Janet eyed him indignantly. "Just what are you implying?"

The grin slid from his face. He turned his attention to his food. "Sorry, Mrs. Townsend. I may have spoken out of turn."

"I should say so." She took a stab at her salmon and tried to pretend the man wasn't there.

Then he said, "How are your boys, by the way?"

Janet felt heat flush her face. "My boys?"

"I believe you have three adopted, no?"

"Yes, but what are you saying? About my boys?"

"Nothing. Your husband speaks of them often. That is all. The fish is very nice, don't you think?"

Before she could query him further, the first orator stood at the podium. As he heaped praises on Art, Janet stewed. What was this man sitting next to her alluding to? She had no doubt that that comment about her sons wasn't just casual conversation. No, he knew something. But what? Was she meant to know what he was referring to, like a co-conspirator? Or was he baiting her, somehow? The conversation made her feel . . . dirty. And afraid for her sons.

When speeches ended, she turned to quiz the man sitting

next to her. But he was gone. What could the man possibly be alluding to? Her sons were adopted, but there was nothing unusual in that. Or was there? It had never occurred to her to question Art regarding the adoption, but now she wondered. She decided a little snooping was in order and slipped out as quickly as she could. If she hurried, she could get home long before Art.

She returned to the house and headed to Art's office. The house was large and his office was on one end, hers on the other. It was rare that she paid his office a visit. Now she stood and gazed around her. Like her husband's taste in all things, it was opulent.

Tall bookcases extended from floor to ceiling in dark mahogany. Every shelf was filled end-to-end with hardbound books, many of which were first editions. She figured that was for show, as she seldom saw Art read anything but the newspaper. The room had that unique, somewhat musty smell of a library that housed old books.

Art's large oak desk took center stage. Janet walked around it and sat in his leather office chair. The desk had pedestals on either side where she knew he filed his most important documents, like birth certificates. She pulled on one of the drawers, not surprised to find that it was locked. She searched for the key. It was possible he had it on him, but she doubted it. Eventually she found it tucked in the back of the large central drawer.

The files were well-organized. She expected nothing less. Her husband was meticulous. She easily found the manila folder labeled "birth certificates" and pulled it out. All three certificates were there. Her three beautiful boys. She had used the certificates to enroll the boys in school, but had never looked very closely at them, only to see that Janet and Art were named as parents. She stood to take the folder to her office when she heard her husband's voice. He was talking to Rosa, the housekeeper. What was he doing home so early?

Hastily, she pushed the desk drawer closed and started to leave the office when she heard his footsteps approaching. She stuffed the folder into the seat of her pants and pulled her blazer down over it. Quickly searching the bookcase, she picked up a book about early architecture in Las Vegas. She turned as he entered.

"Well, hello Art. What brings you home at this time of the day?"

"I had to get away from everyone." He scowled. "This campaigning business is wearing me out. But what are doing in my office?"

"Oh, I just wanted to look at this book. It's for a project. The old and the new Las Vegas. I thought I'd see what kind of photos I could find."

He reached up to caress her cheek affectionately. She wanted to shrink from his touch and sweat trickled down her back. As she slid around him to the door, she said, "Well, I will leave you in peace. See you at dinner."

She needed to hide the folder, but where? Then she realized that one of the few places her husband almost never visited were the children's bedrooms. Quickly, before the boys got home from school, she tucked it into the top shelf of the closet of her youngest son's room

All that afternoon and into the evening, she thought about the file she had hastily hidden in the closet. At bedtime, as she kissed Carl, now six years old, and pulled his covers up around his neck, she fought the urge to take the file out and look at it.

* * *

Morning brought its usual chaos as she readied the boys for school. Art was the last one out the door. She would be working from home, she told him. She smiled, kissed him, and closed the door behind him. And blew out a huge sigh of relief. She wasn't used to dissembling; she was sure she caught her husband giving her a puzzled glance or two. What saved her, she was sure, were his own distractions over the campaign.

She hurried into the boy's room and retrieved the folder, then settled into her own office after telling the housekeeper that she was not to be disturbed. She had already worked out who she was going to call: the mother of her son Ben's best friend. She had become very close to Diana since the two boys enrolled in pre-school together. Diana worked in Vital Records.

"Hi Diana," she said when she was transferred to Diana's desk. "This may sound like a strange question—"

"There's no such thing as a strange question at Vital Records. What did you want to know?"

"Well, I . . . did you know that Ben and his brothers were adopted?"

"No, I didn't. Not that it matters one wit to me. But do they know?"

"No, we never told them. It just didn't seem, well, what would be the point?"

"I understand. Adoption is a very private, personal matter."

"Yes, well, that's why I'm calling. I was wondering about Ben's adoption records. I assume they are kept with your department?"

"Yes, all adoption records are kept here, but access is often limited. Let me just see what we have for Ben." Janet waited for several minutes until Diana came back on the line. "Janet, this is strange. I don't see any records for the adoption. I can find his birth certificate, but nothing on adoption."

"Are you sure?"

"Yes, I'm . . . I just don't understand it."

"What about James? Can you find his records?"

Another long pause. "Janet, there's nothing here on James or Carl either. Are you sure they were adopted in Nevada?"

"Absolutely."

"Well then, I just don't understand it."

"I don't either. Look, Diana, I need to think about this, what it means. Can you do me a huge favor and keep this to yourself?"

"Of course. Oh, absolutely. All inquiries made in this office are confidential. Just let me know if you need anything else."

Janet hung up the phone and stared out the window. What had that man at yesterday's event said? The conversation turned from corruption to her boys in a matter of two sentences. Why? And who was that man?

She hurried out to the front hall, grabbed the local newspaper, and returned to her office. Yesterday's event was in the society pages. As luck would have it, Mae Bennett had covered it. Mae was one of her closest associates at the paper. They had worked together on many stories back in the day when Janet was still freelancing.

She picked up the phone. "Hi Mae. This is Janet Townsend."

"Oh hi, Janet. I saw you at yesterday's event. Sorry I never got a chance to say hello. I was going to, right after all the speeches, but when I looked for you, you were already gone."

"Yes, I had something pressing I needed to take care, so I scooted out as soon as I could. Anyway, I have a question about that event and I thought of you."

"Tell me, my friend."

"I'm wondering about the man seated next to me. You don't happen to know who he is do you?"

"Hang on. Let me look at some of the photos . . . There you are. Sitting next to Joe Hodak." Mae chuckled. "Lord what a character."

"Oh? How so?"

"Oh, I don't know. He's been part of the scene here in Las Vegas for at least ten years. But he's very elusive. Sometimes he shows up at these official functions like your husband's yesterday. But I've heard people say they have seen him in Las Vegas's underworld as well."

"He's not, like a detective or something, is he?"

"Hodak?" Mae chortled. "I don't think so. You know what I think?"

"Tell me."

"I think he's a henchman for someone. When you've been working the social scene here in Vegas as long as I have, you get to know all the characters, the good, the bad, and the ugly. So tell me, what's your interest?"

"Um, I'd rather not talk about it over the phone."

"Okay . . . Tell you what. Give me a day or two to see what I can dig up. How about lunch on Friday."

"You got it."

* * *

"So, Joe Hodak," Mae said after they had given the server their order. As usual, she was dressed flamboyantly, in a short red and gold dress that shimmered when she moved. This week her hair was dyed nearly platinum blond. Blunt bangs accented heavily mascaraed eyelashes and sparkling eye shadow. Janet knew it was all for show. When she got home to her three children and husband in the evening, she would scrub her face clean and don a t-shirt and shorts.

"I had to do a little digging on this one. Everybody seems to know him, but they don't like to talk about it. I finally squeezed out some information from one of my CIs."

"CIs?"

"Confidential informants. The police aren't the only ones who have them you know. Why, we'd never know anything going on in this town without a few spies," she said, batting her lashes.

"Okay. I believe you. But after all this time freelancing, how come I never heard of them?"

"Darling, you just don't run in the right circles." Mae grinned. "Anyway, it's just what I thought. He is the henchman for the owner of one of the biggest strip joints in town. See, what he does is, he sees to it that city officials look the other way, if you know what I mean. My CI tells me Joe has been asked to fund everything from tuition for kids' private schools to upcoming election campaigns."

Suddenly, Mae's face turned as red as the red in her dress. "Shoot, Janet, I didn't mean to imply . . ."

"It's okay. Really. It's entirely possible that Art has received donations of this kind. That's not what I am worried about."

"No?"

Janet glanced quickly around the room, then bent her head

towards her friend. "I need you to keep this totally under your hat."

"Of course."

"No really. You must never speak of this conversation to another soul."

"Got it."

"It's about my kids' adoptions. This guy, Joe, who was sitting next to me at the fundraiser? He brought up corruption and my sons in the same breath. I was so stunned I didn't know what to think. But I've done plenty of thinking since. That morning I called you, I had just spoken to a colleague at Vital Records to look into the boys' adoption records."

"And what did you find out?"

"Nothing. They couldn't find any records."

"No kidding?"

Janet shook her head slowly. "Tell me something. Those city officials you mentioned, taking bribes. Do they include Clark County Commissioners?"

"But you don't think . . ."

"It makes me sick to think about it, but now that the thought is out there, I can't put it back in the bottle. Do you remember that child trafficking ring about five years ago?"

Mae stared at her friend for a long moment. Janet could see the wheels turning. "You're thinking Art was part of it?"

"I'm thinking he got our boys through that organization. Like a payoff. Think about it. He's a commissioner. And Las Vegas was undergoing a huge makeover."

"I remember. Word on the street was that commissioners were accepting all kinds of bribes from contractors to help them procure lucrative contracts, speed up inspections, get payments more quickly, whatever."

"What if, instead of money, Art accepted babies."

"No. No way." Mae frowned and stabbed a piece of salad onto her fork. She looked at her friend. "Even if it's true, what are you going to do about it?"

Janet gazed grimly at her salad. "I don't know. I need to think about it. I know one thing. Protecting my sons is paramount."

CHAPTER 20

Las Vegas, Nevada

Having eluded their pursuers, Victoria and Cate drove aimlessly, waiting for their hearts to slow down. Eventually they pulled over so that Victoria could retrieve another pair of shoes out of her luggage. All the while she bemoaned the loss of the ones left behind, very expensive and one of her favorite pairs. They decided to look for a motel on the outskirts of town.

Cate, who was looking less the worse for the wear than Victoria, checked them in. They dropped their bags on their beds and Victoria headed straight for the bathroom. While Cate waited her turn, she pulled the package they had retrieved from Peterson's house out of her backpack.

It was carefully wrapped in plastic and covered in several layers of packing tape. Cate rummaged around in her pack until she found her pocketknife in the bottom. She carefully cut away the packing tape. There were three cassette tapes inside, each contained in its original plastic box. They were labeled with dates covering the period 1990-93. They looked very well preserved. But she hadn't seen a cassette player in years. Did they even make them anymore?

"What do you think, Victoria," she asked when her sister emerged from the bathroom freshly washed and dressed in a clean pair of jeans and button-down shirt. "Can we find something to play these on?"

Victoria sat next to Cate and picked up one of the cassettes. She examined it, turning it over a couple of times. "Well, I'd say they are in excellent condition. Let's check online and see if we can get a cassette player." She did a google search on her iPad, then said, "It looks like we are in luck. You can buy them at Walmart and Best Buy and Target."

"Great," Cate said. "Let's do that first thing tomorrow. Just now, I am going to see about getting rid of all this . . . dust. Even my teeth feel gritty." When she emerged from the bathroom, she found Victoria once again on her laptop pouring over the reports from Peterson.

"I'm still puzzled over these intake reports. I mean, why isn't there a report from the night of the bust? It makes no sense." She pushed the laptop aside in disgust. "I mean if they rescued twenty-three children, where else would they take them?"

"Yeah, it should be there. So why isn't it?"

"Because they are a bunch of incompetents?" Victoria grumbled.

"Or maybe they never filed a report."

"Why on earth wouldn't they have?"

Cate stood and began pacing the room. "I have a bad feeling about this."

"Like what?"

"What if the CPS was in collusion with the child traffickers? Maybe they were even supplying children. It wouldn't have to be the whole organization. Just a few evil people. There's virtually no oversight of the CPS."

Victoria stared at her sister. "Hang on a minute. Just what are you saying? That Child Protective Services is involved in child trafficking? Surely not."

"I know it's hard to believe. But the foster care system is one of the greatest intersections with one of the worst crimes—human trafficking. I saw one report that said that sixty percent of human trafficking victims in the U.S. were involved in the foster care system at one time."

Victoria scowled, then thought for a moment. "Okay, so let's say you're right. The CPS never filed a report because they were in on the whole thing. Where does that leave us?"

Cate stopped pacing and slumped onto the edge of the bed. "I don't know."

"Well, there is one thing we can try."

"What's that?"

"A visit to the CPS. What's the worst that could happen?"

* * *

The next morning, they drove over to the office of the CPS in downtown Las Vegas. An enormous woman who looked to be in her sixties waddled up to the counter and shoved a visitors' log at them.

"You need to sign in," she said. Cate grabbed a pen and scribbled her name, address and telephone number into the log.

When she finished, the woman pulled the book back and glanced it. "What can I do for you, Ms. Connelly?"

They told her what they were looking for. Her triple chin waggled and her eyes, buried in flesh, turned to flint as she shook her head. Records were not accessible that far back and, in any case, were only made available to law enforcement, she told them.

As they left the building and made their way to the car, Victoria sputtered. "Where did they find that . . . woman?"

"I don't know, but I sure wanted to . . ."

"Shoot the bitch?"

Cate shot her sister a look and then they both burst into laughter. "You took the words right out of my mouth."

"So, what now?" Victoria asked.

"Hell, if I know." Cate leaned against their car and thought for a moment. "I think we're missing something. I mean why did Peterson keep all that stuff if there wasn't something important about it?"

"The tapes," Victoria said. "We have to see what's on those

tapes."

* * *

Cate and Victoria found a Best Buy where they were able to purchase a tape player, then made their way to their motel room in the late afternoon. Just as they arrived, Cate's cell phone chirped. She looked at caller ID.

"It's Liam," she said to Victoria.

"Well then I suggest you answer it. The poor man is worried."

Cate sighed. "You're right." She answered the phone with a cheerful "Hello Liam."

"Cate, is it true that you were there when Peterson was shot?"

"Oh, you heard about that."

"Of course I heard about it. It was in our police reporting system." Cate knew he was referring to the regional information sharing system, a nationwide network to facilitate law enforcement communications. She should have known he would find out sooner or later.

"So what in the hell were you doing there?" he demanded.

"I told you, Liam. Looking for my birth parents."

"But don't you see how dangerous this is?"

"It's a little too late to be worrying about that, Liam. Our only option now is to go forward."

"But what do you think you'll accomplish besides getting yourself killed?"

"Liam, I'm being careful, okay? I just have to finish this."

"Come home, Cate."

Cate sighed audibly. "Soon, Liam. Victoria and I have a few more leads to follow."

Finally, after several more reassurances that she was fine and she would be careful, she ended the call.

When she glanced at Victoria, she saw concern in her sister's eyes. "What? I did what you told me to do. He's just a worrier."

"Yes. Yes, he is. And maybe he's right. Maybe we should just give this up and go home."

"Look, I will understand if you want to drop this thing. But don't you see? Peterson entrusted me with his evidence. I feel a certain . . . I don't know, obligation to see this through."

"You're right. I know you're right. And darn it, I want to know what happened to us. Was my father involved? If so, what did he do? How low would he stoop? If I don't get to the bottom of this, it will just eat away at me. Besides, I'm certainly not going to let you do this alone."

Cate glanced at Victoria feeling grateful. In truth, she wasn't sure if she was really up to following this thing without the support of Victoria, who was proving to be bold, smart, and steadfast throughout their ordeal.

"Thanks, Victoria."

"We're in this together, girl. Liam will just have to cool his jets." Then she smiled slyly.

Cate glanced at her. "Victoria?"

"Hmm?"

"Are you? You are, aren't you? You're interested in my brother."

"Well," she drawled, "he is one of the best-looking guys I've seen in a long, long while."

Cate allowed herself to speculate for a moment. "I guess, now that you mention it, he is that." She grinned at Victoria. "I suppose you could do a lot worse than him. For sure, whatever woman captures his heart will be cherished and protected for life."

When they got to the room, they dropped their package on the bed. Thoughts of Liam took a back seat to their mission. They grabbed one of the tapes and pushed it into the player. They heard a moment of scratchy silence, then a man's voice, soft and rough, cut into the static:

You got something for us?

Yeah. Some really good stuff. Our client's definitely going to like it. This voice deep and husky.

Okay. Let's plan to meet up at—

At that moment Cate's cell phone chirped, and they paused the player. The number had a Las Vegas area code. She didn't recognize the caller.

"Hello?"

"Is this Caitlin Connelly?" It was a woman's voice, husky, abrupt.

"Speaking."

"You were asking about a CPS report."

"Yes. Yes, I was."

"I might have some information for you. Meet me at Javier's at five o'clock."

"Wait, who is this?" Cate demanded, but the call had already ended.

* * *

When they entered Javier's restaurant, the smells of chili's, marinated meats, and fresh tortillas surrounded them, and Cate's stomach growled noisily. As they waited for their eyes to adjust from the intense brightness of the desert sun to the dimmer interior, a woman approached them. She was a plain Jane with a round pleasant face, hazel eyes, and hair halfway between brown and blond generously sprinkled with grey.

"My name's Carol. I have a table over there." They followed her to the back of the room where she took a seat with her back to the wall. The sisters took a seat on either side of her. As they settled in, a waitress came to take their drink orders. Victoria ordered a margarita and Cate ordered a Corona. They made small talk as they waited for their drinks to arrive. The woman responded in monosyllables as her eyes flicked nervously about the restaurant.

When the drinks arrived and the waitress moved out of hearing range, Cate asked, "What's this all about?"

Carol leaned in close and spoke quietly. "I work at Child Protective Services. I saw you when you came in. I heard you asking about that intake report, the one following a major bust of a child trafficking ring in 1993."

"That's right."

"Why were you asking about it?"

As Victoria opened her mouth to speak, Cate touched her hand to forestall her. "Why do you want to know?"

Carol's eyes darted from Cate to Victoria and back. "You won't find it."

"Why not?" Cate asked.

"That report doesn't exist. See, I'm the records clerk in the state office. One of my duties is to file all screening and intake reports for all counties in the state. When I overheard you asking about that report, I thought I'd take a look. There are no intake reports for that date."

"So . . . why are we here?"

"A missing report, especially that old is not so unusual." Carol continued without answering the question. "We only started keeping better records about twenty years ago. Now we have a database where all cases are logged in and reports are stored electronically. That's one of the reasons they hired me—to develop and maintain the system." Her eyes shone with pride for a moment before she continued.

"Reports back in those days are kept on microfiche. You have to go down to the basement to look them up. Which is what I did. You know, went down to the basement to find your report."

"That was really kind of you. But why go to so much trouble?"

Carol looked around her furtively. "Things have gotten real weird at the office these days. One of things I always loved about my job was knowing that, in my own small way, I was helping children in need. Now, I'm seeing a lot of meetings behind closed doors, people coming to the office that don't look like they belong."

"How so?"

"See, you got your caseworkers and your attorneys and your parents looking for their children. But these other people, they sure don't look like any of them. They look . . . I don't know . . . slimy.

"So, then you two come along and ask about a report on a case from way back when. It made me curious. When I couldn't find it, I thought maybe it was misfiled under the wrong date or something. So, I started digging around. That's when I noticed something was off. A lot of the cases back then were missing the screening reports."

At their puzzled looks, Carol said, "See, someone in the community has to file a report to the CPS alleging child abuse. A caseworker must then decide if the allegations look legitimate. If they do, the case is screened in. The next step is to open an investigation. Then, if child abuse is determined to have occurred, the caseworker takes the child from the family and prepares an intake report.

"That's where I noticed a problem. In a lot of those cases back then, there was no screening report. I might not have thought too much about it except that now I'm seeing it again. No screening reports."

"But I still don't see why that's a problem," Cate said.

"Think about it. How does a child end up under CPS protection? Someone makes a report to the police or the CPS. That triggers an investigation and a screening report. If they don't find any evidence of misconduct, they throw the report away. But if they do find something, why they take the child and issue an intake report. So why would there be so many cases that don't have a screening report?"

"Because no one reported the case?"

"Exactly. And that's where I ran into a problem. See the computer system is set up so that a number is assigned with the screening report. I can't file intake reports without this number. When I started asking around, they told me the reports probably got lost. When I asked how I was supposed to enter the case into the system without it, they told me that was my problem and asked me if I wanted to keep my job."

"Hang on," said Victoria, "Who are 'they?'"

"Those same ones that hold meetings behind closed doors and receive strange visitors. They're pretty senior and I don't doubt for a minute that they would find an excuse to fire me."

She glanced at Cate, then Victoria. "So, I started improvising. I just made up dummy screening reports. But I kept track of the intake reports that went with them."

She leaned down and pulled a large manilla envelope from her shoulder bag resting by her feet. "Here are copies of those reports. You'll see that only a few caseworkers under these supervisors are involved."

"Why are you giving them to us?"

Carol glanced around the restaurant furtively. Only a few tables were occupied and they were not within hearing distance. "Does the name Victor Belinsky mean anything to you?"

Cate drew her eyebrows together. The name did sound familiar, but she couldn't place it.

Seeing her puzzled look, Carol said, "He headed up the operation that got busted that you're so interested in. Spent twenty-five years in prison. Got out three years ago. Then about six months ago, he started visiting the CPS."

"Are you saying he's started up again?"

Carol shrugged. "It fits. Just like back then. From what I'm seeing, children are being taken from their parents when a complaint hasn't been issued. Why? Who are they? I think they're being 'kidnapped' for sale to child traffickers."

"Wow," Victoria said, "that's quite some accusation."

Carol nodded her head vigorously. "And I hope I'm wrong. But what if I'm not?"

"Well, what do you expect us to do with this information?"

"I don't know. But I've been looking for someone outside of the CPS to give those reports to. Maybe you can them pass on to someone that could take a look."

Cate took the package. "You do realize that this is pretty circumstantial. I mean, all you have are missing reports and strange meetings."

"But now I have you. Maybe you can try to find one of the families in one of those reports. See for yourself if the case seems legit."

***

Cate and Victoria were pensive as they drove back to the motel room.

"I don't know, Cate. Do you really think she's onto something?"

"Maybe."

"We don't know the first thing about child abuse investigations."

"No, we don't."

"If she's right, it could even be dangerous to go snooping around. Look what happened to Peterson."

Cate nodded. "He got shot."

"And anyway, how would we go about it? Go knock on the door to one of those families? What would we even say?"

"I don't know."

"Then again, if she's right, those poor children are in a heap of trouble."

"True."

"You think maybe we should at least take a look at those reports?"

"Yes, I do."

When they reached their motel room, they noted that there were two sets of reports: one from the early 90s and the other from the last few months. Cate zeroed in on the old reports and Victoria took a look at the recent ones. As they began reading, Cate noticed the Victoria's pallor had faded to a sickly grey. "Cate, these children. Why some of them are just babies . . . I think we need to hand this stuff over to the authorities."

Cate nodded her head. "I agree. The problem is, which authorities? Seems like there is a lot of corruption in this town."

"So, we just do nothing?"

"Not nothing, no. My brother's in the FBI, remember? Maybe I can call him and see if he can recommend someone in Vegas we can trust with this information."

CHAPTER 21

Las Vegas, Nevada 1998

When her husband won the election for mayor, Janet announced that she was ready to go back to work. Now that little Carl was well settled in the first grade, there was no need for her to stay home. She didn't mention that she needed work to get out of the house and away from her brooding thoughts about a man she had once trusted so absolutely.

Ever since she began to suspect what Art had done, her repugnance of the man had grown. She began to sleep poorly and used it as a perfect excuse to sleep in another bedroom. He rarely demanded his marital rights. When he did, she faked it. When he felt her shudder, he thought it was desire. It was loathing. She learned to keep her thoughts and feelings to herself. For the sake of the children. She figured he was getting it elsewhere. He had plenty of women to choose from in Las Vegas. She was grateful to them, whoever they were.

She was happy to learn that getting freelance work was not a problem. The city was growing rapidly, bursting with activity; there was no end to news, entertainment, politics, and opinion. She quickly got swept up in the entire Las Vegas scene, a city that was morphing from the Gambling Capital of the World to the Entertainment Capital of the World with the rise of variety shows, magicians and circus performers bringing in families and visitors of all ages.

Unlike her first foray when she was innocent and starry eyed, this time around, she was more in tune with the nuances of Vegas's entertainment industry. People tended not to notice the face behind a camera, and she used it unabashedly as a blind behind which to learn the name of every mover and shaker, and to listen in on their conversations. It didn't take long to get to know the players, how they made the great entertainment machinery work like a well-oiled machine. If some of that oil came from bribes and payoffs, well it was all part of the business.

She finally understood a comment her husband had made on their very first date: the Clark County Commission was *the* most powerful governmental body in the state of Nevada. Her husband had been a commissioner for eight years.

He had never been caught in any wrongdoing and part of her wanted to bury her head in the sand, pretend Art was the honest, hardworking man she had always thought him to be. But another part of her knew she was deluding herself, ever since she learned that something was off with the adoption of her children. That side of her just couldn't seem to let go.

If Art was taking payoffs, where was the money going? They lived well, could afford to put their kids in private school, had a housekeeper who also minded the kids as needed. They had a nice large house with a swimming pool and an outdoor entertainment area where they hosted barbeques and parties for Art's colleagues. Was there more to those events than simple networking? Suppose that Art was getting kickbacks? Did they amount to a lot of money? If so, where was the money?

She thought about the birth certificates that were locked in his desk file. Maybe there were other things in there like bank statements or records of other assets she never knew about. She bided her time until she got an opportunity to snoop. It came a few weeks later.

The kids were in school, her husband was at the office, and the maid had called in sick. And Janet had no work assignments that day. By eight that morning, the house was silent, empty. As she made her way to her husband's office, her footsteps echoed in the hallway. With hammering heart, she unlocked one of his desk drawers. The first thing she found was a bank account in the Cayman Islands. When she saw the balance of several million, she about fell over.

As she thumbed through the files, she discovered that Art held equity in numerous resorts around town, owned several timeshares in California and Hawaii, and had a healthy stock portfolio that she had never seen. Slowly, anger overcame shock. She had no idea what she was going to do with this information, but she determined to keep her own records. She spent the rest of the day photographing each and every document. By the time she was finished, hot-blooded anger had turned to cold rage.

She carefully returned the files and folders and locked the drawers. She would make copies of her photographs. And then she would give one copy of the photographs to her friend Mae for safekeeping. After that, she would confront Art.

* * *

"Janet, Janet, Janet." Art looked at her in a pitying way. "It's the system and everyone knows it. It's how things get done in a town like Vegas. What do you think happened when I was elected to the commission? Surely you didn't think I would watch everyone else with their palm out and not put mine out as well. How long do you think I would have lasted if I didn't play the game?"

"And the boys?"

"What about them?"

"I did a little checking. There are no records of the boys' adoptions."

Art's patronizing smile slowly faded. "Those adoptions were done privately."

"There still should have been records, even if they were sealed."

"Janet, what are you getting at?"

"They were adopted right around the time of that child trafficking bust."

Art's face flushed a dull red. "Now hang on, Janet. One has nothing to do with the other."

"Do you honestly expect me to believe you, when you have been lying, hiding things from me all this time? Tell me something, were those boys a payment, a bribe?"

His eyes narrowed angrily. "I did that for you. You couldn't have children, so I fixed it."

Janet felt a slow burn of rage. "Where did they come from, Art. We're they part of that child trafficking scheme? Were you part of it?"

Art sneered. "What do you care? You have your boys."

"But it's so . . . evil."

"Is it? How do you know they wouldn't have ended up in a far worse place? Do you know what they use these young kids for? Child pornography, prostitution, satanic rituals."

"No."

"Yes, Janet."

"But you, you could have stopped them."

Art sniggered. "Oh, Janet. You're so wonderfully innocent. Do you think I'm some kind of superhero? I was a commissioner. If I had tried to stop them, I would have been a dead commissioner. Don't you see? I played the game, kept my head down. That's how I survived."

"I'm going to report you. I'm going public with what you did."

"Right. That's an excellent idea. What do you think would happen to your darling boys?"

"They're not just my sons. They're yours as well."

"No, they're not. I brought them home for you. But they are not, and never will be, my sons. So, here's what you are going to do. You are going to be a dutiful wife and raise those boys. And we will never talk about this again."

CHAPTER 22

Las Vegas, Nevada

Sam and his partner paid yet another visit to "Ramon's". They took a table and ordered two scotches neat. As they nursed their drinks, they watched a girl writhe on the pole nearest their table in a fairly decent parody of lust. She was young, her bare breasts were pert, her legs long and lithe. But she was too thin, by Sam's standards. Her eyes sparkled; they hadn't acquired that vacant look of so many strippers in the seedier joints of Vegas.

That's because this particular strip joint stood out among its more than two dozen competitors as the biggest and best in town in a palace just off the Las Vegas Strip. It was the only one of its size.

It also blatantly ignored Las Vegas's regulations. For some inexplicable reason, there were those in the mid-90s that decided no one should be able to enjoy both alcohol and full-nude erotic dancing. Laws also limited how dancers and patrons could touch each other. "No dancer shall fondle or caress any patron, and no patron shall fondle or caress any dancer."

Despite these regulations, this place offered fully nude dancers, alcohol, full-contact lap dances, and no ban on gawking patrons placing tips in dancers' G-strings. The owner, Ramon Swanson, tossed bags of cash around to put politicians and city commissioners in his pocket; if some of the practices were outside the bounds of the rules, they looked the other way.

He also made it a policy to retain only the freshest talent. Young, nubile strippers vied for a spot at his club where men paid handily for a good performance, on stage and off. Ramon made sure the girls were healthy but wasn't beyond offering a little performance enhancing substances. Sam was sure that's what put the sparkle in the stripper's eyes.

The problem with providing only the freshest girls was what to do with the older, worn-down women who had loyally worked for him. That's why Ramon had purchased a couple of joints from his competitors. Rather than throw them out on the street, he gave them the opportunity to continue their trade for a few more years.

Between the bribes and his compassionate treatment of his girls, Ramon enjoyed a level of loyalty that kept people from talking. That made Sam's job all the more difficult. He knew that even seedier enterprises took place under Ramon's sphere of influence. Which is why he and Kyle had taken to frequenting the place. They tossed plenty of money around. The girls took note. Lately more than one offered to give them a lap dance.

They never took the bait. They wanted more, they said. A whole lot more. And younger. Surely someone in the joint knew where they could find truly fresh, untouched meat.

Ramon got the message. One evening he joined them at their table. There were some establishments he told them that made available very young girls, or boys if they were so inclined. But of course, given their scarcity, the price ran high.

Sam took a big gulp of his drink and leaned into Ramon. "What about virgins? Got any of those?"

"Well, now, that is another commodity altogether. They are scarce indeed, being as how a virgin is a one-shot deal, so to speak. But young, slightly used girls and boys are not quite so scarce. You interested?"

Sam's gaze turned icy. "I might be."

Fortunately, Kyle chose that moment to intervene. Ramon

may have mistaken that look on Sam's face for drunken lust, but Kyle knew otherwise. He brought his hand down on Sam's shoulder. "Come on, now, Sam. I think you've had enough for tonight."

"But what about those girls?" Sam slurred.

"We'll come back another time." Kyle guided Sam to his feet and, with an apologetic nod at Ramon, hustled Sam out of the place.

"He's got some hinky business going on. I know it," Sam said soberly when they were safely away from the neighborhood.

"Yeah. And if he's working with Victor Belinsky, I can just bet what it is."

"He's a cautious one, though, isn't he? I bet right now he's putting out feelers about us. Let's hope our cover holds."

* * *

The next morning, Sam arranged to meet Jamie. He found a vacant table at his favorite café and took a seat. The bright sun shone into the windows of the homey place, which boasted a handful of booths and as many tables. The proprietor's husband hustled over with a smile and a pot of coffee.

"Good morning, Sam," he said warmly and poured the rich black liquid into a cup in front of him. "¿Cómo estás?" How are you?

"Muy bien, ¿y usted?" I'm fine. And you? Sam responded in kind. His Spanish was rusty at best. He would not have been able to carry on a sustained conversation, but it was their ritual to start the day with a few words.

"Will you have the usual today?"

"Yes, please. And Jamie's coming. He should be here any minute now."

As if on cue, a man in his mid-thirties entered the café and joined him. With his clean-cut look—short, light brown hair and regular features—he had a face people trusted. Victims loved him. Perps were often misled by his gentle demeanor. He was dressed in a casual button-down shirt and a pair of khakis, an attire suitable for the kind of investigations he normally conducted in the white crime division of the FBI.

Sam greeted him without standing up. "Jamie, good to see you."

"Hey, would I turn down a chance for breakfast at the café?"

Just then the proprietor, a short woman with unruly black hair tied back in a large clip, approached them with coffee pot in hand. "Hello, my young friend," she said to Jamie in heavily accented English patting him on his shoulder. "What will you have this morning? Bacon and eggs? An omelet? Or maybe huevos rancheros?"

Jamie grinned up at her then took a sip of coffee that she had just poured. "Mm. It all sounds good." He thought for a second. "How about a Spanish omelet?"

"You got it."

When the woman left, Sam said, "So tell me what happened yesterday."

"The two women went to Jim Peterson's house. They went around back and broke in through the patio door. They were in there I'd say about a half an hour. Then, a couple of guys came up to the front door. They had a key and went right in."

"What did they look like?"

"I don't know. Like day laborers, maybe. Jeans, work shirts, you know the type."

"Okay, so then what happened?"

"Well, I was real worried about those women and was about to go in after them. Suddenly, I heard this crash and the women came around from the back of the house. They got to their vehicle and took off. A second later, the two men came running out of the front door after them. But the women were long gone by then. I tell you, that woman, Cate? She drove like a bat out of hell. There was no way to follow them." Jamie shrugged. "I'm sorry. I lost her."

"Well, it's not really your fault. A one-man tail is difficult. So where do you think they went?"

"I think they left Las Vegas. I have put out feelers all over town." Jamie shook his head. "No one has seen them."

CHAPTER 23

Winnemucca, Nevada 2000-2007

Janet decided to retreat back to her home on the ranch in Winnemucca. Much as Janet despised Art for what she now knew about him, she realized he was right about one thing. She had a duty to raise her boys.

In public, she kept up the charade of loving wife. At home, she avoided Art as much as possible. It wasn't difficult. Art spent most of his time at work. When she wasn't freelancing, she spent most of hers helping the children with homework, participating in the PTA, attending their school science fairs and sports events.

Thus when the children were released for summer vacation, she packed them up and brought them to the family ranch in the northern part of the state. She wanted to give the boys a chance to experience a life outside of the glitter of Las Vegas.

As she headed out of the city past the last of the residential neighborhoods and into the dessert, the azure skies stretched into infinity over the untouched desert terrain. For the first time since her tête-à-tête with Arthur, her heart lifted; the dark oppression that had weighed her down dissipated like a fog burned away by the sun.

Her boys gazed out the window in fascination. Soon the terrain grew rougher as they gained altitude. Undulating hills sprinkled with sagebrush and pine dotted with rocky promontories, sweeping valleys with spring green grasses where antelope gathered in large herds. In the distance rose majestic snow-covered mountain peaks.

Finally, they descended into a big, flat sagebrush valley. Home, Janet thought joyfully. The minute she pulled into the driveway, the boys scrambled out. The rambling single-story wooden house had sheltered three generations of Jones's. A porch ran the length of the front; some of its spindles were broken. The yard consisted mostly of scraggly crabgrass giving way to vast acres of sagebrush that surrounded it in all directions.

Janet's mother rushed out the front door to greet them. A huge smiled creased her careworn face. She pushed errant wisps of gray hair caught by a gentle breeze out of her eyes, eyes that shone with the excitement of seeing her grandchildren.

"Hello, my young lads," she said, smothering each one with a huge bearhug. They hugged her back shyly. Then she said, "Well, now. Have you all eaten?"

"Yes, ma," Janet said. "We had lunch in Austin."

"Well, all right, then. What would you boys like to do?"

"Can we see the rest of the yard?" James asked.

"Good heavens, yes. But you must promise me you'll stay within shouting distance."

* * *

That evening, Janet's mother put on a huge supper. Janet's brothers, Will and Pat, arrived with their families an hour before. The women gathered in the kitchen to help with the last-minute preparations. They inserted the two leaves into the dining room table, so that it extended into the very ends of the large dining room.

As the women worked in the kitchen, Janet's sons became acquainted with their cousins—three girls, ages five through thirteen, and four boys, ages seven through sixteen. The place resonated with the shrill screams of the girls and shouting from the boys. Soon, Will, Pat and Grampa dragged the whole pack outside to play.

When Janet stood on the porch to announce that supper was ready, they came tumbling back in. The boys vied for position next to their new-found cousins until Pat sorted them out. It was a loud, boisterous affair as they passed plates until they were filled to overflowing. Lamb shanks, mashed potatoes, green beans tossed salad, and buttery rolls, to be followed by two large chocolate cakes and rainbow ice cream. It wasn't until their bellies were full that the children settled into a satisfied stupor.

***

The boys were quickly inculcated into ranch life. Like all of its neighboring ranches, the J&R ranch was big by necessity. Raising cattle in the arid, high desert climate of the Great Basin, which spanned most of Nevada, required at least ten acres per cow. And much of the work tending cattle was still done by horseback. The older boys learned to ride and herd the cattle. Even Carl was given jobs to do, starting with collecting eggs and feeding the pigs.

For the next few summers, Janet returned to the ranch with her sons. Life in Vegas had become suffocating and she felt the need to recharge where she could breathe freely under the endless skies in the high desert. But as the children grew older, they began to balk. They had their life and their friends in the city. Finally, when her youngest was fifteen, Janet relented. But her decision had nothing to do with their entreaties. Rather something happened that shook her to her core.

She had gone into town to run errands at the local Farm and Fleet for her mother when she heard someone call her name.

"Janet, is that you?"

Janet turned and gazed at the woman standing with her husband behind her in the checkout line. The woman greeted Janet with a kindly smile, not the effervescent greeting she had become accustomed to in Vegas. It took Janet a minute before she recognized her. She was Susie from the neighboring farm.

They had grown up together, gone to school together, graduated from high school together. Susie was with her husband.

But Susie had aged. Her hair had turned grey and deep lines scored her forehead and carved a permanent frown around her mouth.

"Well, hello Susie. Gosh I haven't seen you in . . . I don't know. Fifteen years?"

"I reckon," she nodded slowly. "I hear you married and moved to Vegas."

Janet flashed her a rueful grin. "It's true. Yup. We live in sin city. Which is why I try to come back here when I can. Recharge my batteries with country air."

Then, as she gazed at her childhood neighbor and her husband, she felt a jolt run through her. Suddenly, she needed to get away from them. Not caring how it looked, she abruptly made her excuses and practically ran to her car.

When she got a good ten miles out of town, she pulled her vehicle over and took a deep breath. Her hands shook with the sudden realization. For when she had looked into the face of Susie's husband, she saw her own son Carl. The likeness was unmistakable, right down to his deep cleft in the chin. Her shock was so great that she couldn't fully process it.

She gazed around her, at the high desert that had been her home. A car passed, stopping to see if she was okay. Realizing that stopping on the side of the highway was drawing unwanted attention, she pulled back onto the road and headed back to the ranch.

As she drove, she reviewed what she had said to Susie. She was pretty sure she hadn't mentioned the boys, thank goodness. But what did it mean that Carl was the spitting image of Susie's husband? Could he be theirs? Art said the sons they adopted had been removed from homes where the parents were unfit. Could Carl have been removed from Susie and her husband by the CPS? But no, it couldn't be. There was just no way in hell she believed that they hadn't been good parents. Susie was always one of the kindest girls in their class.

She pulled up to the ranch house and began unloading supplies. Her mom came out to help. The boys were out riding herd.

"Guess who I saw in town today, Ma? Susie Zambrano. Although I guess she has a different last name now."

"Oh yes. Susie Jaso. Poor woman."

"Why do you say that?"

Her mother sighed as she grabbed a bag of groceries. "They took her kids away."

"Who did?"

"Those government people. So-called protective services. Said they didn't have a decent place to live. Well, okay so they were living rough, but only until they could get their house built."

"Hang on, Ma. Are you saying the CPS took away their kids?"

"Yup. It was back some thirty years ago now. The daughter was only four years old. And their son was just a baby. It just about killed both of them. They tried everything they could for years to get those children back, but I guess the CPS is law onto itself. Meanwhile, they had some more kids. Six, I think. Still not a one of them can replace those two they lost."

* * *

Janet gathered up her three sons and returned to Vegas that very next week. She couldn't bear the thought of running into Susie Jaso again. God forbid that she and her husband saw Carl. She was so sure that they would recognize him. Better to stay in Las Vegas where the crowds provided a shield of anonymity.

And then another bombshell dropped. On the very week she returned to Las Vegas, her husband announced that he was running for governor. As part of his campaign, he planned to play up his image as a loving husband and father to three boys. His campaign director came to visit the house, to see Art's family. Indeed, they would make for some beautiful photo ops in the months to come—the lovely wife and three very handsome blond haired, blue eyed boys.

Janet was horrified. The last thing she wanted was for the spotlight to be shone on her boys. She knew the chances were infinitesimal that Carl or any of them would be seen as anyone but the children of Art and Janet Townsend. But the guilt ate away at her. Even if no one else knew, she did.

Her nerves began to fray. She lost her appetite. She couldn't sleep for more than a few hours at a time. On more than one occasion, Art found her in the garden in the middle of the night, a glass of wine in hand.

One night he approached her. She didn't see him come up from behind. "Janet?"

She jumped, spilled her wine. Her hand shook as she turned towards him. He tried to pull her into his arms, but she resisted, stepping just out of reach.

"Janet," he said softly, "is something bothering you?"

She looked up at him, his face masked in kindness. But she knew it was a facade. Under that mild look was an amoral man. A man without a conscience.

She pulled her own shield around herself, the one she had been perfecting for years. "I'm fine Art. Just a little nervous, I guess, at the thought of another campaign."

"It will be fine, Janet. Trust me. We'll get through it and then you can move into the governor's palace. Won't that be grand?"

"Yes, Art," she pasted a smile on her lips. "Grand. Now if you'll excuse me, I think I'm ready to go back to bed."

***

The next day, the official launch of Arthur's campaign began with a huge rally at the Las Vegas Convention Center. At the insistence of Art's campaign manager, the sons were cajoled into putting on sports jackets and stood ready to be paraded on stage. But first would be Janet's command performance. On que, she mounted the steps to the stage and turned towards the audience, preparing to smile and wave.

As she looked out into all the smiling faces, the cream of Las Vegas society, her visions started to fade in and out. Then she fainted. When she came to, she was in an ambulance. The medical staff at the emergency room noted that she was severely underweight, and her blood pressure was through the roof. The family doctor was consulted. He recommended that she be admitted to a private clinic for an extended rest. And he prescribed Xanax to treat her anxiety.

CHAPTER 24

Las Vegas, Nevada

When Victoria woke up, she found Cate hard at work shuffling through the reports from Carol. There were now several stacks on her bed. "Cate, what are you doing?"

"I was just thinking, maybe there's no intake report following the bust, but what about before the bust? Which is what I'm looking at now. And I noticed something. There seem to be a lot from Humboldt County."

"Humboldt County. Where is that?" Victoria grabbed the map of Nevada and spread it out. "It's in the middle of friggin' nowhere."

"Exactly." Cate grabbed the laptop and typed in a Google search. "It says here that the population of the entire county of Humboldt is only eighteen thousand souls. I figure there's a few too many cases for such a small area. So I have been sorting them out by county, just to check."

"Good thinking. Let me grab some coffee and I'll help."

An hour later, they had sixteen stacks sorted by county. Three were significantly taller than the rest: Clark County, home of Las Vegas; Washoe County, home of Reno; and Humboldt County.

Cate pulled the stack of reports from Humboldt county

closer and shuffled through them, her hands trembling with excitement. "Look at these reports. I count at least forty cases in the county in the early 1990s."

She was thoughtful for a moment. Then it hit her. "Victoria, didn't you say your genealogy report showed a high percentage of Iberian Peninsula heritage."

"Yeah. So?"

Cate jumped up. "Hang on. I remember passing one of those displays in the lobby, you know with brochures telling visitors 'what's happening around town.' I'll be right back."

She returned a few minutes later. Her eyes were sparkling with excitement. "Look at this. 'Basque Festivals in Nevada.'"

Victoria took the brochure from Cate's outstretched hand. "Okay?"

"Don't you see? I think the Basque country is located on the Iberian Peninsula. People in this part of Nevada are of Basque descent."

Victoria's face lit up. "By George, I think you're onto something. What do you say we drive on up there and poke around?"

* * *

The drive to Winnemucca took over seven hours. There was little traffic and Cate found she could put the pedal to the metal. As they ate up the miles, Victoria started playing one of the tapes. It seemed to be a voice activated kind of thing. There would be a conversation followed by a short pause, then another conversation. Sometimes, they heard music or a television in the background and they had to strain to hear the voices cutting through it.

The voices talked of deliveries, places and dates, money. Money came up a lot, usually in the hundreds, sometimes in the thousands. Some of the voices were women, but most were men. Some were old and scratchy, some strident and demanding, some guttural. But there was one voice that consistently came in and out of discussions. It was deep, resonate.

When they were halfway through it, Victoria turned it off. "What do you think, Cate?"

"Peterson said they were surveillance tapes."

"So who were they recording?"

"Hard to say. Maybe they bugged an office somewhere."

"Sounded like a lot of deals were being made."

"Yeah. Welcome to Las Vegas," Cate said. "I sure would like to know who belongs to that one voice, the deep one."

"Yeah, he seemed to be in the thick of it all."

Victoria began playing the tape again. Like before, there was a lot of static. As near as they could tell, deals were being cut by every business in town—building contractors, casinos, strip joints—you name it. It was somewhat mind-numbing and after a while Victoria drifted off to sleep. Then Cate heard a conversation that caught her attention. Two men were talking in hushed voices. One voice was husky; the other, deep and resonating that by now was sounding quite familiar.

As she listened to it, Cate clutched the steering wheel. "Victoria, wake up. Listen to this." They had to replay it twice more before they could catch all the words and realize what it was that they were hearing.

Deep voice: *You know my wife. She wants a child. But she can't seem to get it done.*
Husky voice: *Is that right? Such a shame. Maybe I can help you out.*
Deep voice: *Oh yeah? How's that?*
Husky voice: *Well, you know, there are children in this town, orphans and the like.*
Deep voice: *I don't want someone else's sickly child.*
Husky voice: *I hear you. But maybe I can find a nice healthy baby for you. Let me see what I can do.*

They continued listening, hoping for something more. But the conversations had returned to stuff that did little to hold their interest. Victoria was just drifting off when the topic came up again and Cate nudged her awake.

Husky voice: Listen I got some good news for you.
Deep voice: I could use some good news.
Husky voice: What if I told you that I could get you a nice, healthy baby boy?
Deep voice: Yeah? Just where are you going to find one?
Husky voice: Already have. And this boy? He's got blue eyes and blond hair. Just like your wife's.
Deep voice: Okay, what's the catch?
Husky voice: No catch. I'm just doing you a favor. Know what I mean? Of course, there are a lot of expenses involved.
Deep voice: How much?
Husky voice: Say, fifty grand.
Deep voice: That's pretty steep.
Husky voice: Look, normally we can fetch as much as a couple hundred thousand. But for you we're giving you a good price.
Deep voice: I'd have to see the goods first.
Deep voice: No problem. But be sure to bring your money. These babies are, you know, perishable goods. We try to bring them straight from the mom to the adoptive parent. If you like what you see, you take it home with you.

Victoria stared at Cate, round-eyed. "Holy crap, Cate. That man just bought a baby."

"Sure sounds like it."

Victoria stared at the road, thought a moment. "Let me see that package we got from Peterson." She pulled it out and shuffled through it until she found what she wanted. "These birth certificates. Do you think they're connected to this conversation?"

"I'd bet the family pub on it."

"It says the parents' names are Arthur and Janet Townsend. Arthur Townsend. Who is he anyway?" Victoria grabbed her iPad and started googling. "Geez Louise, Cate. Arthur Townsend is the governor of Nevada."

Cate glanced at her, then turned her attention back to the

road. "Supposing," she said pensively, "he did buy his babies. Can you imagine what it would do to his career if it ever came out?"

CHAPTER 25

Winnemucca, Nevada

They continued to listen to the tapes but heard nothing of note. Just more Las Vegas business deals. As they got closer to their destination, the day grew more and more dreary. The road ran straight across a desolate landscape of scattered sage brush and barren earth that was all brown and foreboding. By the time they reached Winnemucca, an enormous cloud of black, gray, and wintery white, had gathered on the horizon.

Just as they reached the town, rain started to splatter their windshield. Soon the clouds let loose in a steady downpour. They drove down Main Street, which consisted of a collage of streetlights, casinos with bigger-than-life signs boasting "Winners", and a smattering of hotels, bars and fast-food restaurants. Mountains rose in the distance on the far horizon. Snow left over from the winter storms still capped the highest peaks.

Victoria felt the gray press in all around her and wanted nothing more than to turn tail and head back to the bright sunshine of Las Vegas. They found a motel on the main drag. It was one of those fifties era types with a neon sign out front and rooms arranged in a long row with parking in front.

When Victoria entered the reception area, a bell tinkled, and a man stepped out from the back. He was of Asian descent, looked to be about fifty. "Yes," he nodded affably, "I have a very nice room for you two young ladies. Very clean, two nice comfortable beds."

"That's all we need," Victoria smiled.

He handed her two keys—not key cards, but good old-fashioned keys. When he saw her smile, he said, "Well, you know, one of these days I might modernize a bit. But now don't you worry, you will be perfectly safe. This is a good neighborhood."

"Thank-you," Victoria said. "I'm sure we'll be perfectly fine. By the way, can you recommend a good restaurant?"

"Well, there are plenty of them around. What kind are you looking for? Steak house, hamburger joint, Chinese? Or maybe you'd like to try our local fair. We have a couple of Basque restaurants. But for those you need a reservation."

"Oh, well a Basque restaurant sounds nice. Maybe tomorrow, if we made reservations?"

"I can do that for you. One of them's real nice, family style, you know?"

"Great. Meanwhile, what about that steakhouse?"

***

The steakhouse was only a few blocks from their motel and the rain had subsided, so they opted to walk. When they arrived, Victoria pulled open the door to the redolent aroma of grilled food, beer, and the faint odor of tobacco smoke. The place was split down the middle with a bar in between. On one side was a casino with numerous slot machines and a roulette table towards the back. Cigarette smoke filled the air and spilled over onto the other side of the bar that consisted a western-style restaurant with booths and wooden tables. They selected a booth.

A waiter came to take their drink orders. When he returned with a bourbon and a beer, he gave Victoria a questioning look.

"You're sure not from around here, are you?"

"No, sir. I'm from Savannah, Georgia."

"So, what brings you to Winnemucca?"

"Funny you should ask," she smiled up at him. "You see, we're looking for our birth parents. We believe they may have come from around here. It would have been about thirty years ago now."

She leaned towards him conspiratorially. "This may sound strange, but we think maybe the CPS was involved. You ever hear anything about any children around here being removed from their homes by the CPS?"

"CPS?"

"Child protective services."

He crossed his arms and leaned in. "You know what? I did hear something about that. It happened before I was born, but folks still talk about it. I hear it was a very tense time in the town, 'specially over in the mining neighborhoods. Something about kids being taken into protective custody on account of child abuse."

"Really? So what happened?"

The man shrugged. "I don't really know. But folks were all up in arms. The sheriff, he tried to look into it."

"The sheriff?"

The waiter nodded. "Sheriff Nicholson."

"I see. And this Sheriff Nicholson. Is he still around? I suppose he's retired by now."

"Oh no. He's still the sheriff."

"Is that right? Well, we'll just have to pay him a visit, first thing in the morning."

CHAPTER 26

Winnemucca, Nevada

The sisters arrived at the sheriff's office promptly at nine the following morning. They had little hope that the sheriff could shed any more light on that long-ago case, but they had to at least try.

The office consisted of an open area with five desks. Three were occupied by sheriff's deputies, judging by their uniforms, and one was vacant. A woman of about sixty sat at a desk across from the door. The name on her desk said "Marsha Bascom". She glanced up from the pile of mail she was sorting when they entered.

"Good morning. May I help you?"

"I hope so," Victoria said, approaching her desk. "We would like to speak to Sheriff Nicholas. Is he in?"

"May I ask what this is about?"

Victoria glanced at Cate. "Well, it's about an old case. A very old case. We understand he might have some knowledge about it."

Marsha raised an eyebrow. "I see. Well, now, it might help if you were just a bit more specific."

"We...well, we would prefer to explain it to him. That is, if you don't mind."

The older woman leaned back in her chair and crossed her

arms over her ample midriff. She took in their appearance, her eyes roaming from their blond heads to their attire. Victoria had donned her business suit that morning, the same one she wore when she first visited Cate's family pub. Cate had pulled out her dressiest smart/casual outfit—a pair of khaki pants and a tailored button-up shirt.

"You'll have to give me something I can tell him."

"Tell him it's about a child trafficking bust back in 1993."

Marsha raised her eyebrows. Then she pushed her chair back and stood. "I'll let the sheriff know you're wantin' to see him. But I doubt he'll talk to you. Not if it's about that." She turned and walked to the door behind her that said "Sheriff." She tapped softly, then entered, closing the door behind her. Less than a minute later, she returned.

"It's just as I thought. The sheriff asked me say that he has nothing to tell you."

"I see," said Cate. "Nothing to tell us. Not that he doesn't *know* anything, just that he hasn't got anything he'd like to share with us. Is that about the size of it?"

"You're very perceptive, young lady. And I imagine you're right. But it won't help. Our sheriff is one of the most stubborn men I know." She shook her head, pensively. "In this particular case, hell might just freeze over before you'll get him to answer your questions."

Victoria surveyed the room, then turned back to Marsha. "Is there any way out of his office besides that door?" she asked.

A wry smile crossed Marsha's lips. "Nope."

"And I assume, if nothing else, he'll go out for lunch."

Marsha nodded. "Most likely."

"Okay, then. We'll just wait here." She gestured to a couple of visitors' chairs.

"Suit yourselves," Marsha said.

As they sat down, Victoria pulled two magazines out of her tote bag and handed one of them to Cate. It was fashion magazine. Cate shot her a questioning glance.

"You'd be surprised what you can learn from that," Victoria

whispered. Then she turned her attention to her own magazine. Cate perused the topics on the cover: skin care for a rosy complexion, the latest diet proven to lose fifteen pounds, new fashions on the horizon.

How on earth, she thought, could a woman as intelligent as Victoria read this tripe? As she flipped through it, she found herself glancing up at the clock, then at the other occupants in the room. One was a tall, good-looking man with short-cropped hair under a cowboy hat and hazel eyes. When his eyes met hers, she quickly bowed her head over the magazine.

Before long, she found her attention wandering around the room again. Next to the handsome cowboy was a squat, somewhat corpulent man with short curly brown hair. He was focused on his phone, making one brief call after another, and taking notes. Cate couldn't hear what he was saying. Then she caught sight of the third deputy eyeing her, a woman about the same age as Victoria and herself. She had long, shiny, dark hair pulled back into a neat ponytail. She was flipping through a bunch of documents on her desk, scratching her pen across the pages as she went.

"Stop fidgeting," Victoria mumbled under her breath.

"Yeah? Well maybe if I had something to read, it might help."

"That stuff is good for you. You should take it more seriously."

Cate sighed and moved to the next article in the magazine. When she next glanced at the clock, only forty-five minutes had passed. If they were really going to wait until the sheriff decided to go for lunch, they still had another two hours at least to go. This was more tedious than surveillance, she thought. At least then she could snack and converse with her partner.

When the phone rang, Marsha picked it up, spoke briefly, then transferred it to the cowboy deputy. He spoke for a moment, then stood to leave. "Got an accident out on 95," he told Marsha. As he approached the door, his gaze settled on Victoria for a moment and Cate could see a spark of interest in his eyes. Then, he ducked out the door.

She turned back to the last article in the magazine: "How to Keep Your Man Happy in Bed." Maybe she could learn something. If she had a man in her bed, which she didn't. With a sigh she settled in to read every blessed word.

* * *

While the two sisters waited patiently in the visitor's area of the sheriff's office, Hugh struggled to concentrate on the report in front of him. He found himself reading and rereading the same paragraph without comprehending a word, not since Marsha came in to tell him there were two women wanting to see him.

"Why?" he had asked her. "What did they want?"

Marsha had folded her arms across her chest. "Well, they weren't real forthcoming, but I believe they are interested in that old child trafficking case."

"That old case? Why ever for?"

"You'll have to ask them yourself, sir."

"Well what did they look like? Old? Young?"

"Blond, maybe late twenties, early thirties." Marsha paused. "Not bad to look at."

He thought for a moment. "I don't want to see them."

"Is that what you want me to tell them?"

"Just tell them I don't have any information to share."

Marsha raised her eyebrow in that imperious manner of hers. "Don't you think it's time to let this one go?"

The sheriff felt his face heat up. Sometimes, the woman could be most exasperating. "That's none of your business," he snapped.

"Right. I hear you." She turned, back straight as a rod, and left the room.

A few minutes later, she called him to let him know that the two women were waiting for him just outside his door. It looked like they had settled in for the morning.

He was trapped in his own damned office. He stood and paced. Then he sat down and tried to focus on the report due in at the state attorney's office. Then he stood once more and gazed out the window. Downtown Winnemucca wasn't the most picturesque town for sure. Just a hodgepodge of buildings of various vintages and a string of neon signs under a gray gloomy sky.

He'd rather be back at the home he and his wife had built, looking at the gently rolling hills spread out before him. Until he remembered the owl. It had waited for him every morning on the anniversary of the bust, just like the other day. Now these two women were sitting outside his door.

What did they want? Why were they asking about that old case? They couldn't possibly remember that case. They would have been babies. Unless they were some of *those* babies . . . Was it possible?

Hugh sat down slowly in his chair. Marsha was right about one thing. That case just wouldn't let him go. Thirty years is a long time to let something fester. Which is exactly what had happened. It had festered. Maybe it was time to let it go.

He stood and strode to the door and opened it abruptly. As he stepped out and approached them, the two women stood resolutely. The taller one clutched a magazine and eyed him with a determined expression on her artfully made-up face. She had a genteel look about her that seemed out of place in a dusty old mining town like Winnemucca. The shorter one had crossed her arms over her slender chest and gazed steadfastly at him. She was slim, clear-eyed, slightly tomboyish.

"Marsha, here, tells me you wanted to speak to me."

* * *

He was, Cate thought, the quintessential rural county sheriff: broad shouldered, with narrow hips and lanky legs. His face was leathery from years of high desert sun and wind. A permanent shadow of whiskers dusted his cheeks, upper lip and chin. Despite the fact that they were indoors, a cowboy hat rested low on this head. It was brown, worn soft from years of use, with a braided band around the brim. The brim bent low over his face and curled up on the sides. Light brown hair sprinkled liberally with gray was just visible around his ears.

Clad in a western-style, snap-front denim shirt, he stood with thumbs tucked into the pockets of faded jeans. The jeans hugged slender hips and rangy legs, crumpling around his calves and ankles, before resting atop round-toed cowboy boots. His belt sported a large silver western-style buckle embellished with turquoise.

He nodded at them and gestured to the two visitors' chairs in front of his desk. As they settled in, he took his seat in his old leather swivel chair that squeaked under his weight.

"Well, now. Tell me what I can do for you."

Cate took the floor. "We're here about an old case, a bust of a child trafficking ring."

Hugh nodded and waited for them to continue.

"You see . . . well, I know this may sound a little wild, but we think we were two of the children involved in that bust."

Hugh's eyebrows narrowed, but Cate got the impression he wasn't surprised by their declaration.

"Perhaps you can explain how you came to this conclusion."

"See, it started when my sister, here, had a DNA test on account of her mother dying of cancer. She was looking for genetic markers to see if she was at risk of getting the same cancer."

"That's right," Victoria interjected. "But what I found out was that my mother wasn't my mother at all. When I read the report, why shoot, I about liked to have died right there on the spot. I asked my father about it. All he would tell me was that I was adopted. Well, he could hardly deny it, not with that report right there in black and white. But then he refused to say anything more about it. Then I come to find out that I had a sister." She nodded towards Cate. "So, I tracked her down."

"Believe me," said Cate, "I was as surprised as she was. I have —or had—four older brothers, but no sisters. But I couldn't argue with that report. So, I talked to my parents. Unfortunately, my dad had a stroke so he couldn't tell me anything. My mom told me I came to them when I was three years old. It turns out that I was somehow rescued during a child trafficking bust with some joint task force in Nevada."

When Hugh nodded his head slowly, Cate said, "You know about this case, don't you?"

With a huge sigh, he pulled open a drawer and extracted an old, yellowed manila envelope. He passed it across the desk. Cate opened it. She stared at the first photo. A boy about five years old stood in nothing but a pair of underwear and a tag around his neck; his knees were knobby, and ribs stood out, but what caught her attention were the eyes; they stared into space with a vacant, hopeless look.

When she passed it to Victoria, her sister gasped. "Oh, my word." Cate then passed her a second photo of a young girl just verging on puberty wearing only underwear and a tag, eyes vacant. When Victoria saw it, tears sprang to her eyes.

As they shuffled through the photos, Hugh began talking. "We busted that ring and rounded up the children. Once they were safely under the protection of the CPS, I came home. I told the families we'd get their children home just as soon as possible. But when I contacted the CPS in Las Vegas, they claimed they had no record of any children being taken in on that date."

"No intake report," said Cate.

Hugh glanced sharply at her. "That's right. The whole business stunk. I already had my suspicions that the CPS up here in these parts were involved somehow. There was no reason to suspect those children were being abused or neglected. But then I started to thinking that the CPS was up to their eyeballs in the whole operation, not just here in Humboldt county, but clear across the state. I called the SAC on the case and asked him what in the hell was going on. He, too, was troubled by this information. He said he would make some inquiries."

"And then what happened?"

"I don't know if you know this, but Winnemucca is an old mining town," he began, apropos of nothing. "A lot of the country roads used to lead to mines here abouts. Now at some point, the county took them over, threw some pavement on them and called them county roads.

"The problem was, they weren't always the best designs. Like the road to my home. It had a sharp curve where it bent around the side of the mountain. It was always dangerous, that bend in the road. The county posted warning signs. But folks tended to misjudge it. We had a lot of accidents. That's where my wife had her accident. They reckon she was going pretty fast when she hit that bend. The vehicle flipped over as it tumbled down the slope. Broke her neck."

"I'm sorry," said Cate. Where is this going? she thought.

"The funny thing is, the highway patrol never found any skid marks. Like she hadn't even tried to use her breaks."

"Or . . . her breaks failed," Cate said.

Hugh nodded. "They towed the vehicle over to Karl's place. Back then, he owned the salvage company. Well, now Karl had a good look at it. He came to me about a week after the accident. Said the brake line had been cut."

Hugh paused, swallowed. Then he continued. "Now, that vehicle my wife was driving? It was mine. Hers was at the shop, so she borrowed mine to run some errands. The next day, I got an anonymous call. Said if I didn't back off, no one would be safe in this town."

By now, Cate had passed the last picture to Victoria. Carefully, Victoria placed them in a neat stack on the desk. They sat for a moment in silence. Then Victoria spoke up. "I'm real sorry to hear that. And I am truly sorry for your loss. But, well, you know that was a long time ago. I imagine by now it's safe to talk about. We really would like to find our birth parents."

"What makes you think they're from Humboldt County?"

"Why, isn't this Basque country?"

Hugh quirked a curious eyebrow at them. Victoria pulled out the DNA report and laid it in his desk. "Now see, right here is says that we have a high percentage of Iberian heritage."

Hugh took the report and stared at it for a moment. When he looked up, his eyes were glistening. He cleared his throat. "You really are sincere about finding your birth parents, aren't you?"

"Yes, sir," Victoria said.

He reached into his desk drawer and pulled out another envelope. "This might help." It was a report of all the families in the county who had been targeted by the CPS during the period from 1988-93.

CHAPTER 27

Winnemucca, Nevada 2013-2018

For the first five years since Art was elected governor, Janet had taken refuge in the governor's mansion in Reno. At Art's insistence, she continued to take the Xanax prescribed by their family doctor. Fears that her son Carl's real parents would ever be discovered disappeared into a pleasant euphoria that carried her through the day.

Her sons had grown up now and her job was done. She knew she was supposed to love each boy equally, and she did. But she had a very special fondness for Carl. The other two boys had grown up, gone to college, married well, and were now developing their careers. They were handsome and accomplished.

Janet had encouraged them every step of the way. Now, one owned a prestigious architectural firm in Seattle; the other was working his way up the ladder in an advertising company in Los Angeles. They were far from home and she rarely saw them, but it was all for the best, being away from Las Vegas and their past.

Carl, on the other hand, had chosen a completely different path. He went into nursing. His father had had a very difficult time with this decision. They had argued about it. Nursing was a women's profession, Art said. If Carl really wanted to go into the health profession, he should become a doctor, Art told him. After numerous heated arguments, Carl gave up trying to convince his father that nursing was the right profession for him.

Janet stayed out of the discussions between father and son. Carl was quite capable of making up his own mind and she knew there was no point trying to convince Art. The only time she ever interfered was when Art threatened to cut off his financial support for Carl's education. That's when Janet had a private word. She reminded Art of all his secret assets. All it would take was a leak here and there and he'd have the feds looking into them, and surely, he didn't want that.

To make sure that Art kept his word, she continued to keep up appearances, showing herself every now and then at an event to keep the gossip mongers from speculating too much. Over time however, that feeling of euphoria became harder and harder to tap into. At the slightest sign of nervousness, Art called the family doctor who agreed to increase the dose. Soon, she lost all interest anything but her flower garden.

It was Carl who pulled Janet out of the abyss. He had enrolled in a nurse practitioner master's degree program at Vanderbilt University in Tennessee. He hadn't been home in eighteen months. She had been so excited to see him, wanting to talk to him about his studies

But when he finally arrived, she had trouble formulating even the simplest sentences. Carl didn't like what he saw.

"Mom," he told her quite simply, "you need to get out of here."

He packed a few of her clothes, put her in her car, and drove her to the ranch. He stayed with her during his entire break helping to wean her off the drug. He called on a doctor who was a close personal friend to look after her when it came time to return to his studies. When the doctor saw the state that Janet was in, she was incensed and promised Carl that she would see to her recovery.

Janet worked hard to ween herself from the drugs. She went on hour-long walks on the ranch. She took on whatever chores she could to ease the burden on her aging parents. She started watching the news on a regular basis. She began photographing again. But this time, it was the vanishing ranching life that captivated her. As she photographed, she listened to the stories. Soon she had a large collection of photos and anecdotes to go with them. One day she hoped to publish her anthology.

By the time Carl returned from college with a master's degree in hand, she was back to the woman she once was. Her only regret was that she was still married to Art.

"Then divorce him," Carl told her.

"I would that I could."

"For God's sake, why not?"

She looked at her son who sat across from her at the old family kitchen table and place a hand on his cheek. Tears streamed down her face.

"Mom, whatever it is, you can tell me."

And so she did. She told him about the adoptions. About her suspicions about his true parentage. About how Art threatened to expose their little secret around the circumstances of their adoptions.

"Ah, Mom," he said reaching for her hand. "Do you think I care whether I was adopted? You're my mom. Always have been, always will."

"But what about your real parents?"

"You, Mom. You are my real parent. And quite frankly, I'm glad to know that I'm not related to the old man."

"Carl!"

"I never did like the son of a bitch."

A slow grin spread across Janet's countenance. "I'll do it. I'll divorce the son of a bitch."

CHAPTER 28

Winnemucca, Nevada

After profuse thanks Cate and Victoria left the sheriff's office with a copy of the report tucked safely into Cate's backpack. Just as they stepped out, the black clouds that had gathered while they were talking to the sheriff opened up in a torrential downpour. As they drove down Main street, Victoria spotted a café, its windows brightly lit from within, and suggested to Cate that they stop for lunch.

They got out and ran through the rain to the front door. The inside was cozy with a lunch counter. Wooden booths ran along the wall under the windows on the opposite side. It smelled of chicken soup and freshly brewed coffee and grilled hamburgers. The waitress greeted them warmly and told them to take any table they wanted.

When she came around with a coffee pot, they both accepted a cup. It wasn't Victoria's preferred lunchtime drink, but somehow it just went well with the dreary day in a small-town cafe. She opened the menu and struggled with the tempting selection of comfort food, from burgers and fries, to homemade soup and sandwiches, to a macaroni and cheese special. She finally settled on the macaroni and cheese special, calories be damned. Cate ordered a cheeseburger. They plowed into their food like they hadn't eaten in a week. Then they settled back with their coffee and opened the report.

It was two pages long. It listed the names of the families and the children who had been taken. The families were located all over the county. There were several families dated 1993. One, a family by the name of Eneko, parents Anders and Alana, had three children taken into CPS custody, ages eight, three, and three months.

Cate felt a tingle of excitement. "This has to be the family. It fits."

"Why, yes it does," Victoria looked up, a sparkle in her eyes. "Oh gosh. It just makes me shiver to think about it. What if this here family, this very one, is us?"

Cate sat back, pensive. "I don't know, Victoria. We've been so focused on finding them, I guess we never thought about what we would do if we did."

"I know, darn it. So what are we going to do? Are we just going to go up to the door and say, 'Hi, we understand your children were taken thirty years ago by the CPS?' "

"If we can even find them. Who knows if they still live here?"

They were so focused on their problem that they were unaware that the waitress was bussing the table behind them. Now she approached them and poured more coffee into cups that had barely been touched. "I don't mean to be a nosey parker, but I happened to overhear you ladies talking about children being taken by the CPS."

The sisters glanced up. "Why, yes, we were," Victoria said. She glanced at the woman's name tag. "Why do you ask, Lucy?"

"Might be I can help you some if you tell me why you want to know."

Victoria looked at Cate who nodded her head. Pressing her hand to her heart, she said, "You see, Cate and I," she nodded across the table, "we're sisters. But we didn't know each other until a couple of weeks ago. We only discovered each other through DNA testing."

Lucy set her coffee pot down on the table. "Well isn't that something."

"It is. I can't tell you how wonderful it was to finally meet her. I'm an only child, you see. And I always wanted a brother or a sister so when I learned about her, I just had to look her up. I was so lucky that she wanted to meet me. Anyway, besides finding my sister, why I've just had this hankering to find my birth parents, or at least learn who they were."

"So why here? You sure don't sound like you're from around here."

"No, ma'am. I'm from Savannah, Georgia. But my sister, here, she's from Arizona. She happens to know that she was adopted out of Nevada. It's kind of a long story, but the short of it is that we think our parents may have come from these parts. We think the CPS may have been involved."

The waitress scowled. "I tell you what, them people at the CPS, they ain't to be trusted. Claim to be all concerned for a child's welfare, but it ain't always the case. Why heck, a lot of folks these days, they keep a wary eye out. If they see the CPS coming, they close ranks. 'Cause once they got your kid, well, there's no such thing as parental rights with them."

"Such a shame," Victoria said.

"So, what's the CPS got to do with you two?"

"Well, we just had a talk with the sheriff about this case. It happened about thirty years ago."

"I remember. Folks still talk about it. There was one time when they took three kids away from their mother, claiming they were abused. I wonder if it was this family you're talking about. One of the kids was school age, the others were just babies. Anyway, the schoolteacher, Irene Fletcher her name was, she was real concerned about it. She was the boy's teacher, see, and she said she didn't see any signs of neglect or abuse.

"Now the way I hear it, that's when the sheriff started looking into matters. He even made a trip down to Vegas to check out some things. Then he just stopped. When folks asked him if he found out anything, he just wouldn't talk about it. That's why I'm surprised he talked to you."

"Well, not right away, he didn't", Victoria said. "We kind of had to force his hand. Wouldn't leave his office until he agreed to talk to us. Anyway, when he finally did see us, he gave us a copy of a report of the families targeted by the CPS back then."

"The thing is," Cate interjected, "we think we may have found the family."

"What family?"

"Where we came from," Victoria said. She pointed at the report. "This one. Anders and Alana Eneko."

"Why, them are the very ones I was telling you about."

"Do you know them?"

Lucy shook her head. "No, sorry, I don't."

"What about the schoolteacher, Irene? Would she be willing to talk to us?"

A look of sadness crossed over Lucy's features. "I imagine she would, if she could. She passed, oh, I'd say about a year ago."

"Oh, I see." Victoria's shoulders slumped in disappointment.

"But I tell you who you might try. Irene's daughter, Nel. I don't know that her mother ever told her anything, but you never know."

* * *

As Hugh watched the women scurry through the rain to their car, he began to feel uneasy about their encounter. Maybe he should have just kept his mouth shut. Would they be safer not knowing who their birth parents were? Was there any chance that word of their investigation would reach Las Vegas? Would it matter?

As the afternoon waned, his unease deepened. He picked up the phone and called his son. "Sam, you won't believe who just showed up at my office this morning. Two women looking for their birth mother."

There was a long pause on the line. He could feel his son's worry in the palpable silence. "Son? Are you there?"

"Yeah, Dad. I'm here. Tell me something. What are their names?"

"Caitlin Connelly and Victoria Saunders. Ring a bell?"

"It sure as hell does. You heard about Peterson, the SAC in charge of that child trafficking case back in 1993?"

Hugh felt his unease grow. "What about him?"

"He's been shot. They say it was a burglary gone wrong, but I think someone is covering something up. Those two women? They were at the scene when Peterson was shot."

"Holy Christ. Don't tell me that."

"I'm afraid it's true So what did you tell them? Did you give them any information?"

"I did. I turned over the file with those old CPS cases."

"Are you sure that was wise?"

"Of course not. But, well, you can't hold onto secrets forever. It was time to give it up. Besides, Winnemucca is a long way from Las Vegas. If they find what they're looking for, they'll likely go home. No harm. No foul."

"Let's hope you're right."

"And anyway, these women were downright determined to get to the bottom of things."

"Yeah, that's the impression I get. But listen, keep your ear to the ground. You never know what kind of skeletons they might dig up."

"You bet I will, son."

CHAPTER 29

Las Vegas, Nevada

Art hosted one of his famous barbeques at his home in Las Vegas. His guests consisted of the most influential men and women in the city: commissioners, club owners, politicians, and select members of law enforcement. As was his usual practice, their families were also invited.

Children splashed in the pool under the watchful eyes of the women while others sat at long picnic tables already spread with a bounty of food. Cold drinks nestled in wide, stainless-steel tubs of ice. On the lawn some of the older children played croquet or volleyball.

There was little that pleased Art more than a large crowded party of political cronies and their families. He nurtured the image of a family man that he had developed over the years, back when Janet stood by his side and his sons were young. Now Janet was no longer with him, but two of his sons had managed to make it to the party with their wives and children of their own.

He captained the enormous grill his oldest son had given him for his birthday. Over his polo-shirt and jeans he wore a bright red bib apron that invited everyone to kiss the cook.

As the grill smoked, he turned fat burgers, all-meat franks, and long skewers of vegetables brushed with his ex-wife's secret marinade. Detective Lawes stood next to him sipping a cold beer.

As Lawes relayed what happened at Peterson's home, Art smiled genially at the old cop for the sake of appearances.

"Do you mean to tell me that those two women went back to his house?" he asked in a gruff undertone.

"That's what my man told me."

"What were they doing in there? Did they find anything?"

"I don't know. When my men went into the house, the women were already there." Lawes told him what transpired.

"Unbelievable."

"Yes, sir."

As Art flipped burgers and turned hotdogs, he seethed. He had worked far too hard to get to where he was today to be thwarted by two interfering women.

Indeed he had always had big dreams. Born to lower middle-class parents in the then very small town of Henderson, he was constantly looking north to the glittering lights of neighboring Las Vegas. That's where the action was and he was determined to be part of it. After acquiring his engineering degree, he set his sights on becoming a Clark County Commissioner. It was but a stepping stone to bigger things.

Then came his marriage to Janet. She had been the perfect mate. Coming from a well-respected ranching family, she was beautiful and charming. It was a shame that she couldn't have children, for that was all part of the plan, his image as a family man. But he took care of that, didn't he? For that's what he did. He took care of things. From the many issues confronting the city commission and politicians as Las Vegas grew from a simple gambling town to "The Entertainment Capital of the World," to the resurrection of Las Vegas when it fell flat on its face during the pandemic. He saw it rise again from the ashes due in no small part due to his prodding and pushing both politically and behind the scenes.

His wife's perfidy—the divorce—annoyed him no end. He had done right by her. Provided her with all the wealth and influence she could possibly want. But she hadn't held up her end of the bargain, beginning with her inability to give him sons.

Then there was the increasing distance between them, ever since she confronted him about the adoptions. As she became more and more remote, other women gladly took her place. He didn't need her for sex.

But every now and then, he liked to bed her. He knew she hated it. And that gave him even greater pleasure. Nothing like having a woman against her will. Even if it was your wife. Especially if it was your wife.

But Janet's passing out at his debut event when he was running for governor then having a nervous breakdown was the last straw. He had made sure she got the best medical treatment, drugs to help her get through the election and beyond. Every now and then he would drag her out into the public eye. He selected her dress, arranged her hairdressing appointment, saw to it that she was sufficiently pacified with her mother's little helper.

His one vulnerability was the adoption of his sons. After all hell broke loose with the child trafficking bust, Art had gone about eliminating anyone who knew about, or even attempted to investigate, his role with the crime ring. At least until Peterson put a stop to it. He was the only person who held the goods on him. It may not have been enough to put Art in prison, but it was enough to destroy his reputation. So they had lived for a quarter of a century, he and Peterson, in an unspoken truce.

Now along come two women looking for their birth parents, of all things. They just wouldn't leave well enough alone. He no longer cared who they were, what families they came from.

"I want you to find them. I don't care what it takes. You find them."

"And then what should I do?"

"Make them disappear. For good."

CHAPTER 30

Las Vegas, Nevada

Sam ended the call from his father and paced. He had promised his good friend Michael that he would keep an eye on his sister. But then he lost track of them. He had put out feelers all over the city to let him know if anyone spotted them. So far, he had come up with nothing. And no wonder. The women had gone to Winnemucca. Did that mean they were safely out of harm's way?

If only he knew who was behind the assault on Peterson. Whoever it was must have been worried that Peterson had something on him. He had to have been covering his tracks. Someone who was still around after thirty years. Probably managed to evade detection when the whole thing blew up. So who? Who was around then that was still here today? And what did Peterson have on him?

Whatever it was, it must be pretty explosive. But against whom? It couldn't be the criminals that had been sent to jail. For them the game was up. No, it had to be someone involved in the Las Vegas machinery. A member of law enforcement? Someone in the gambling business? A commissioner? Sam homed in on that last thought. Could it be one of the Clark County Commissioners? Lord knows they were about as corrupt as they come. No one got anything done without the approval of the commission. It was all about bribes and favors and working the good-old-boy network.

The only problem with that idea is that commissioners didn't stay commissioners forever. The more ambitious ones moved on, many to higher political positions. On a hunch, he picked up the phone and called Jamie.

"Listen, Jamie, I was wondering if you could do a little digging for me. I'm looking for someone who served as a Clark County Commissioner about thirty years ago. Someone who is still involved in the political machinery of Las Vegas. I'm thinking politician, maybe here in Las Vegas or maybe at the state level."

Then he picked up the phone and called Michael.

CHAPTER 31

Winnemucca, Nevada

The house where the old schoolteacher's daughter lived was in an old neighborhood of Winnemucca. It was a tidy one-story house built perhaps in the sixties with white vinyl siding. By the time Victoria and Cate pulled up to it, the rain had slowed to a sprinkle and a late afternoon sun cast wan rays over the neighborhood landscape. Just as they reached the door and were about to knock, it flew open. A short, stout woman with a mop of curly red hair greeted them.

"Welcome, my dears, welcome." She pulled the door wider and bade them to come in. "Lucy told me a little bit about your mission," she said as she led them through a well-lived-in living room and into a cluttered dining room. She cleared a space at one end of the table that was otherwise buried in books and backpacks.

A tea kettle started whistling, turning into a high-pitched scream. "I thought we might enjoy a nice cup of tea while we visit. Just give me a moment. Have a seat." She glanced out the window. "It looks like it's stopped raining. Lord knows we needed it, so I can't complain but it does make for a dreary day." She prattled on, her voice fading as she entered the kitchen, which was visible through a pass-through window between the two rooms.

Cate and Victoria took seats opposite each other. From Cate's vantage point, she could see a fenced-in yard with a swing set and a slide, and a bright red pup tent. At least a half dozen kids were present. Three of them of varying heights had curly hair in shades ranging from auburn to strawberry blond. The others, Cate surmised, were kids from the neighborhood.

Soon, Nel placed a tray set with a tea pot nestled under a cozy, three cups, a sugar bowl, and a pitcher of cream on the pass-through between the kitchen and the dining room. Victoria stood and took it to the table.

"There now," said Nel, taking a seat at the end of the table between the two sisters. She looked them over for a moment. "You must be Victoria and you must be Cate."

"But how did you—" Cate began.

"Well, it couldn't be the other way around now could it?"

Cate gazed at her sister, trying on their names in reverse—Victoria, plain and a bit of a tomboy, and Cate, stunning and fashionable. She grinned. "No, no it couldn't."

"Right. So, tell me what this is all about?"

This time, Cate explained their quest. "So, you see, once we started down this road, well, it was kind of hard to turn back."

"Seems a bit dangerous, you ask me, digging into the past like that."

"You're probably right. If it weren't for some evidence someone entrusted us with, maybe we would leave it alone. But now, knowing what we do, it just seemed better to keep investigating."

Nel nodded. Her cheerful countenance was solemn as she sipped her tea. "My mother, she never believed that story concocted by the CPS. It really bothered her. They took those three kids away from their mother, claiming they were abused. One of the kids, Hektor, was school age, the others were just babies.

"Their parents about went out of their minds, trying to get their kids back. Them CPS people ran them around in circles, telling them they had to attend a hearing and get counseling.

Then they suspended their state benefits since they no longer had children living with them. They didn't have any money for a lawyer and the CPS provided one for them. But I don't think he was on their side.

"Anyway, my mother, she was real concerned about it. She was Hektor's teacher, see, and she said she didn't see any signs of neglect or abuse. And she should know, right? I mean she saw him every day. She knew his mama, too. She worked a lot of hours to support her family, but she always tried to attend his teacher's conferences and the like."

"And so then what did she do?" Cate prompted.

"She talked to her friend, Ellie. Now, Ellie's husband was the sheriff. So, of course, Ellie told him about it. He started poking around, asking questions, see? Next thing you know, he goes down to Las Vegas. I think he was working with the FBI or something on some child trafficking bust."

"And?" Cate prompted, sitting on the edge of her chair.

"Well they did bust up some operation. But then, things seemed to go pear-shaped. When he returned a few days later, he was mighty upset. That's according to Ellie, his wife. She's gone now, too."

"I see," Cate said and thought for a moment. "What about the mother? Is she still around?"

"Alana? Yes, she is. But she's never been right in the head since she lost her children. I don't know what all she went through, but it was real bad. She took to drinking and haunting all the local bars asking after her children. Then she tried to take her own life. Ended up in the hospital."

"What about the father, Enders?"

Nel shook her head, her expression sad. "Why, he took off. I guess he just couldn't take any more grief." She thought for a moment. "My mother did leave some old records in the house before she retired. I believe I know where they are. Let's have a look, shall we?"

The files were tucked away in boxes in the garage. Nel tried to reach for one box but could barely touch it with her fingertips.

"Here, let me," said Victoria, who was nearly a foot taller. Carefully she extracted the box and set it down on a small chest of drawers that stood along the back wall of the garage. She brushed the grime away. There was a label on the box: *Class of 1992-93*.

Inside were a variety of papers and pictures made by the kids. Some of them were drawings of their houses with stick figures of their families in front. Others were drawings of animals. Some were notes to the teacher. As the three women sifted through them, they began to despair that they would ever find anything pertaining to Hektor. Then under the papers, they found a manila envelope with Hektor's name on it.

Carefully, Cate slipped a finger under the flap and opened it. His report card sat on top. He was getting satisfactory grades for the first three quarters of the year. In the notes, the teacher had commented that he was very bright and well behaved. The fourth quarter was blank, like he just disappeared. Under the report card was a school photo of the boy. His blond hair was tousled, and he had a crooked grin on his face. His eyes were bright blue. Cate felt a prickle of recognition, then the memory was gone. She turned her attention back to Victoria and Nel.

"Doesn't exactly look like he was abused, does it?" Victoria said.

Nel gazed at the photo. "It sure doesn't. It just breaks my heart thinking about that poor Alana." She glanced out the window where her children were playing. "If they tried to take my children away, why I'd be fit to be tied. Is it any wonder she went around the bend?"

Victoria nodded and patted Nel's hand. "You say Alana is still around?"

"Yes, she is. They released her from the hospital after some time. She returned to her old house. 'Course, she wasn't fit to work. Now she does some cleaning for folks around town. And the neighbors take care of her. That's how folks around here are. We take care of our own."

"What do you think would happen if we paid her a visit?"

Victoria asked.

Cate was reluctant. "I don't know. I wouldn't want to cause her more grief."

"I think it would be all right," Nel mused. "If you are her daughters, she might finally find closure. And if you're not, then so be it."

* * *

The house was white clapboard at one time. Now it was gray and weathered. A spindly unpainted picket fence ran along the front. The shades were drawn in the windows. A gnarled stump of a large tree that had been chopped down long ago stood to one side. Next to it, was an ancient Ford. Its blue paint was rusted completely away on the hood and nearly so on the roof. The window on the driver's side listed half open; the tires were flat.

Victoria and Cate glanced at Nel as they approached the house. Nel nodded reassuringly. She grabbed the handle to the gate and pushed it open. Rusty hinges screeched in protest. Undaunted, she led the way to the front door and knocked firmly. "Alana, it's me, Nel. I've come for a visit."

They waited for several minutes. Then Nel knocked again. "Alana, are you there?"

They heard shuffling footsteps approaching. Then the door opened a few inches.

"Hello, Alana," Nel said. "I brought you some visitors."

Slowly the door opened wider. The woman stood in the dimly lit interior. She wore an old house dress and fuzzy slippers. Piercing blue eyes gazed out from a pale face laced with fine wrinkles. It was framed by fading blond hair hanging loosely to her shoulders.

"Nel?" Alana's voice was scratchy as though unaccustomed to use.

"Yes, Alana, it's me. Nel. Can you let us in? These nice young ladies would like to meet you."

Alana let go of the door handle and retreated into the interior of the house. Nel, Victoria, and Cate followed her in.

They stood awkwardly in a shadowy living room.

"Alana, I'd like you to meet Cate and her sister, Victoria."

Alana looked them over, then turned to Nel, a question in her eyes.

"Perhaps you should invite these two young ladies to take a seat," Nel said gazing around her. "My, but it's dark in here. Let me open a curtain to let some light in." When she drew back the faded drape, the sun cast its light through the grimy glass.

Alana uttered a little cry.

"Alana? What is it?" Nel asked.

Alana's gaze was fixed on Cate. She approached her slowly and reached out a hand to touch Cate's hair. "Katalin?"

This time it was Nel's turn to gasp. "Alana, what did you just say?"

"Katalin." Alana said. Tears streamed down her face. "I would know you anywhere."

At Cate's puzzled look, Nel hastened to explain. "Katalin is Alana's older daughter." She reached for Alana's hand and led her gently to a worn armchair.

"Have a seat, Alana. I know this is a bit of a shock."

Victoria and Cate sat next to each other in the couch opposite Alana. Victoria spoke gently. "Alana, are you saying that Cate is your daughter?"

Alana nodded her head emphatically, her tears left unchecked. "Yes. You are my Katalin." She stood and walked over to the mantel of an old fireplace and grabbed a framed photo. She stooped over to use the skirt of her housedress to remove a heavy layer of dust. Then she straightened, held it tenderly, gazed at the faces smiling up at her. She approached Cate and handed it to her.

As the older woman took a seat next to her, Cate examined the photo. Three children gazed into the camera: a boy who looked to be around eight years old, a girl of about three, and a baby held in the arms of a much younger Alana.

"That's you, Katalin," Alana said pointing to the three-year-old. "And that's your sister Maite and that's your brother

Hektor."

Hektor's arm was slung casually around Katalin's shoulders. As Cate gazed at her own image next to Hektor, a picture flashed into her mind: a boy with Hektor's face bending over her as he tucked her onto the back seat of a car. It was dark, lit only by a streetlamp.

"*Lie down, Kat. Stay there and don't say a word.*" *He grabbed a jacket that was slung onto the seat next to her and spread it over her.* "*I love you, Kat,*" *he said and bent down to kiss her on her forehead.* "*Remember what I said, now. You stay there as still as you can. Promise?*" *Cate remembered nodding her head. Then he was gone.*

"Cate?" Victoria's voice penetrated through the hazy memory. "Cate, are you okay?"

"I am. I . . . I remember something. From when I was very small. There was a boy who put me in the back seat of a car."

"What are you talking about?"

Cate hesitated, then said, "I've been carrying around this vague image ever since I can remember. Of a boy. He had big blue eyes. His . . . his face was very thin. He put me in a car and told me to lie very quietly. Then he kissed me goodbye. He wasn't one of my brothers. None of them has blue eyes. Only me. And this boy. It was Hektor, I'm sure. He put me in my father's car—Joe Connelly's car. He must have seen that it was a sheriff's car. He saved me. That's how I ended up being adopted by the Connelly's."

Victoria grabbed Cate's hand. "Well for heaven's sake, Cate." Her eyes filled with tears.

Cate looked at Victoria, eyes wide. "But Victoria, don't you see? That means you're the baby." She turned to Alana. "See, Victoria and I are sisters. We share the same parents. That means she is your other daughter."

Alana listened as Victoria explained about her mother's breast cancer which led to her discovery that she was adopted and that she had a sister. Then the two sisters went on to tell her about their quest to find their birth parents, leaving out many of the more harrowing details.

Alana smiled through her tears. "I am just so glad to know that both of you ended up okay."

***

Seeing it as a private moment, Nel slipped out into the kitchen. She rummaged around until she was able to find tea bags, an old tea pot and some cracked cups. By the time she returned to the living room, Cate had settled in to tell Alana about the family that took her in.

"They're Irish. A lot of Irish ended up in Arizona. They came to work the construction of railroad and to strike it rich mining for gold, of course. My father used to tell us all kinds of stories about his relatives. Anyway, he met my mother, also of Irish descent, and became a police officer while she settled down to make a few babies. I had four brothers," she paused a moment and swallowed. "But one of them died from the virus. The others are all in law enforcement."

Cate went on to explain what little she knew about landing in the family as a three-year-old, the only girl amid a rambunctious set of brothers.

Alana stroked her hand. "I am so glad to know that you found a good family." Then she turned to Victoria. "What about you?"

"I was lucky, too, I guess. I was adopted into a family in Savannah, Georgia. We were well off. Well respected. My father is a businessman and my mother was a Southern belle. She was always involved in community affairs and the like. Then my mother got breast cancer and died. I only found out I was adopted when I had that DNA test."

Victoria's eyes filled with tears. "I only wish I could have talked to my mother about it. But now she's gone." She wiped brusquely at the tears, then sat up straighter in her chair. "But tell us about you and your family. Are you Basque?"

Alana's eyes sparkled. "Oh, yes. My grandfather was one of the first to immigrate to Nevada. He and the others were cattlemen. They started in California, but when land got to be scarce over there, they came here. Spanish vaqueros are what they were. That's how the whole buckaroo tradition got started —the word vaquero eventually became buckaroo, see."

"But I thought the Basque were sheep ranchers," Cate said.

"Not at first." Alana told them. "At first they raised cattle. Then, you see, there was a hard winter back in 1889. Killed nearly all the cattle. That's when the son, my father, took to raising sheep. You know most folks think sheep farming skills were a Basque tradition brought from the old world. But it was the other way around. The Basque came here and learned sheep farming. They were tough, that's all. Most of them came from the mountainous country in Spain. Growing up on farms, they understood the land and the animals. Hard work was nothing new to the Basques. They were real stockmen. They were very dependable and could be counted upon to stay for long periods alone and not leave their flocks.

"Anyway, my father took to sheep farming. The land was just as good, if not better, for grazing sheep and sheep were tougher. He invited his relatives to immigrate from over to Spain and help out. That's how I met my Enders. He was fresh out of the old country. Didn't speak a word of English. Until I hooked up with him."

Alana's eyes glazed over as she stared into the past. "He was a good man, my Enders. We were poor, but we worked hard. We always made sure you children were fed and clothed. He was such a gentle father. That's why when they took our children away, why he just...well, I guess there's only so much a man can take."

Victoria reached over and patted Alana's knee. "I'm so sorry, Alana."

After a moment, Alana patted Victoria's hand and smiled through her tears. "Well, I'm glad, anyway that you two found good homes. You hear so many stories about children being sold for evil purposes. I just hope..."

"What, Alana?" Victoria asked.

"Hektor. I wonder what ever happened to him."

***

When Cate and Victoria got to the motel room, they were completely wired with excitement. Meeting their birth mother, hearing her story, sharing their own was beyond their wildest dreams.

They were deciding what to do about dinner when the motel phone rang. They looked at each other puzzled. Who would be calling from there and not on their cell phones? With a shrug, Cate picked up the phone.

"This is Mr. Lee at the front desk. I have a reservation for you at the Martin Hotel."

"Martin Hotel?"

"Yes, you wanted to dine at a traditional Basque restaurant. You have reservations for six o'clock."

***

The restaurant was situated in the older, somewhat seedier part of town by the railroad tracks and as they neared it, they began to have some doubts. Houses were old and rundown, much like Alana's home. But when they pulled up to the old historic hotel and took in the ambiance, they started to feel better about it.

It was pure vintage. An old-fashioned veranda ran the length of the front of the building and the original hitching posts lined the street. On entering, they found a bar running along one side of the room. It was filled with a lively group of customers. A woman approached them, noted their names, and led them to the dining room next door.

Here the heavy scent of home-cooked food mixed with a noisy crowd of diners. The walls were covered with an amazing variety photos. Long tables took up the entire floor area. Cate and Victoria were seated at the same table as a group of four men.

Ever the gracious one, Victoria smiled at their dinner companions and introduced herself. Cate watched their faces light up with interest. Never a dull moment with Victoria for company, Cate thought. The fourth member of the team was sitting next to Victoria, a man who looked to be in his early twenties. Blond hair fell over his brow and partially hid a smattering of acne scars. When introductions came around to him, he stuttered painfully.

"I'm B-B-Billy," he said. Victoria smiled at him warmly and commenced to put him at ease.

They learned that the men worked for the abandoned mines program. Their job, the team leader explained, was to locate abandoned mines and seal them off for safety.

"How interesting," Cate said. "Are there a lot of abandoned mines around here?"

"Hundreds. And they can be quite dangerous. So what we do is we drive to remote locations all over the state to inventory old mines. When we find them, we evaluate them for hazards, cultural value, and whether they support wildlife."

The waitress came to their table and explained that dinner would be served family style starting with traditional Basque soup and salad, then a main course of lamb, pork, or chicken served with Basque style side dishes and homemade bread.

But first, she served them a complimentary glass of house burgundy. As they enjoyed their drinks, Cate watched Victoria gently work to make the shy one comfortable. It wasn't long before he was laughing and talking with the rest.

They had just finished the second course when Victoria nudged Cate under the table with her foot. "Don't look now, but I get the feeling we're being watched," she whispered.

Cate lifted her head and started to look around.

"I said, don't look now!"

Cate snapped her head back. "But what makes you think that?"

"It's just that some of the staff and waiters have been, sort of, giving us the eye. And when I look their way, they quickly turn away."

"But why ever . . . ?"

The next thing they knew, the waitress served them each a small glass of strong punch. "Picon," she said. "From the owner. He wanted to be the first to welcome you home."

"What?"

"We've all heard about your meeting with Alana. We are just so pleased that you found her."

Victoria looked at her sister. "My, my but word travels fast," she muttered under her breath. Then she pasted a bright smile on her face and looked up. As the sisters raised their glasses, many people sitting at the tables raised theirs and smiled.

Throughout the remainder of their dinner, other diners came to their table to welcome them. Cate was completely choked up. Never in her wildest dreams had she envisioned such a reception.

CHAPTER 32

Winnemucca, Nevada

Finally, they returned to the room. Cate turned the TV on absentmindedly but had the volume on low. Victoria flopped on her bed in exhaustion and stared blankly at the screen. Suddenly she sat up. She grabbed the remote and turned it up. "Cate, look."

It was a special on Las Vegas, focusing on the early days and its rise to becoming the "Entertainment Capital of the World." Prominently featured was the Governor of Nevada as a primary mover and shaker in his days as mayor of Las Vegas. They flashed several photos of young Townsend working to promote the city. In one of them, standing right next to him was an attractive man with dark hair just turning silver at the temples.

She sprang from the bed and pointed at the TV. "That's my dad. Right there." They watched for a moment then the image was gone. In the next scene, Townsend was being interviewed.

They both stared at the TV for a moment as Townsend spoke. "That voice," Cate said. "Do you recognize it?"

Victoria grabbed the tape player and rewound it until she found the discussion about the sale of the child. "Holy mother of God. That voice is Townsend's." Then she grew thoughtful. "Isn't it interesting that my daddy and this Art Townsend are colleagues. I wonder if they knew each other thirty years ago."

Cate stood and paced. "That would explain a few things. I'm just thinking out loud, mind. But let's suppose your father and Townsend did know each other from way back. Let's say Townsend is involved in this whole child trafficking ring or knows what's going on and is turning a blind eye. After all, he seems to have done all right adopting three boys, wherever they came from.

"And your father is looking to adopt. So Townsend helps him out, either out of the goodness of his heart or because Forrest blackmailed him. In any case, Arthur helps him to adopt you. That would mean the Townsend babies and you and I were all part of the same child trafficking scheme."

"Seems quite likely, I would say," Victoria mused.

"And suppose your ex-fiancé told your father what you were up to, that you were going off to Vegas."

"Okay..."

"When your father learns what you're planning, he puts two and two together. He starts to worry that you are getting too close to the truth. So he contacts Art to warn him about your intentions."

"Go on."

"Now, Art has even more to lose than your father. He has another election coming up. If there is any kind of scandal around his children—"

"Whom he bought from child traffickers—"

"It could sink his political career. The one person who has the dirt on him is Peterson. I think those tapes were what kept him alive."

"I'll buy that."

Cate paced some more. "Somehow, he learns that we are going to meet Peterson. Maybe he's tapped his phone or bugged his home. So, he sends a couple of lackeys to force Peterson to give up the goods."

"And then we show up."

"Exactly. Then he learns that we have managed to get into Peterson's hospital room. So now he figures we have whatever evidence Peterson was holding onto."

"Well at least they don't know where we are. I mean we're in the middle of nowhere," Victoria said.

"Yes, but Victoria, the whole town has heard about us. I mean think about it. They have casinos here don't they? That means connections, snitches, a grapevine."

Cate stood and rummaged in her overnight case. She pulled out her gun and set it on the nightstand. Then she looked at the motel door. "We need to make sure no one can get in. That door would be too easy to bust down."

Victoria pointed to a small desk situated in the corner of the room. "How about that desk? We could move it in front of the door."

"Good idea. Help me move it."

With the desk barricading the door and the gun within reach, Cate fell into an uneasy sleep.

* * *

It wasn't until about four in the morning that Cate fell into a deeper sleep. When she opened her eyes, she could see the bright sun peeking around the motel's shades. She glanced at her sister. She was buried under her bedding, her long hair splayed across the pillow.

"Victoria, wake up."

"Hmm?" came a muffled moan.

"Victoria, we need to get up. Come on."

As soon as Victoria opened her eyes, she sprang to a sitting position. She gazed around the room, took in the neutral wallpaper, the closed curtains, and the desk barricading the door. "It's morning," she said dully.

"Yes," said Cate.

"And no one tried to break into our room."

"Apparently not."

"Do you think it's safe out there?"

Cate thought for a moment. "I don't know. Maybe we were being overly paranoid last night."

"Well, I say we skedaddle out of town."

"What about Alana?"

"I don't know. All I know is that we need to get out of here and fast. We'll figure out everything else later."

They wasted no time taking quick showers and packing up their bags. When they were ready, they pushed the desk away from the door.

And it crashed open. Before they could even react, a man grabbed Cate and thrust a needle into her neck. She caught a quick glimpse of her sister being held by another man before everything went black.

CHAPTER 33

Winnemucca, Nevada

Word of the reunion of mother and daughters after thirty years spread through the town like wildfire. The story that was nothing short of a miracle was passed from neighbor to neighbor, drinking buddy to drinking buddy, rancher to rancher.

But Janet hadn't heard the news. As she drove into town for her weekly grocery shopping, her thoughts were dark as she recalled last night's special. Art was made out to be the savior of Las Vegas. But Janet knew better. He was an evil, evil man, a man with absolutely no morals or scruples, a baby thief. But she couldn't prove it. Not any of it. No one would believe her, a disgruntled ex-wife who had even suffered a nervous breakdown.

She was standing in the check-out line when she heard the two women in front of her talking.

"You heard about Alana, didn't you?"

"I did. Isn't it just wonderful?"

"Yes, after so much heartache, to at last find her daughters, why I can't even imagine what a joy that must have been."

As they gathered their bags and headed out, Janet said to the clerk, "I'm sorry. I've been out of town. What is this about Alana?"

"You haven't heard?" The clerk's face lit up with the thrill of being the first to share the news with someone. "It was just the darnedest thing. Two women strolled into town the other day looking for their birth parents ..."

By the time Janet left the store, her head was buzzing. As she made her way to the car, she spotted two men sitting in a parked vehicle. She recognized one of them. He was a colleague of her husband's, a pal that went way back to those early days when Art was working as a commissioner. She felt a tingle of fear run up her spine. Quickly, hoping that they hadn't spotted her, she jumped into her SUV and pulled away from the curb.

She headed straight for the sheriff's office. She barged in, walked straight past Marsha, and pushed open the sheriff's door.

* * *

"Is it true?"

When Hugh saw the angry woman walk purposefully up to his desk, he stood. He had never met her before and he knew most all of the folks in his county. Even in her anger, or maybe because of it, she was stunning. Perhaps around sixty with short, spiky hair, sparkling blue eyes, and a tall, lithe build, she cut an imposing figure in his humble office.

"Ma'am?"

"Alana Eneko and two of her daughters. Surely you've heard."

"Ah yes, I've heard." Hugh said, eyeing her with a great deal of curiosity. Then he gestured to one of his visitor's chairs. "Perhaps you'd like to take a seat."

She stood stalk still, her gaze never leaving his face.

Hugh cleared his throat, gave her one of his engaging folksy smiles. It worked ninety percent of the time when dealing with angry people. Sort of took the edge off. But not with this woman. She didn't budge. Hugh's smile slowly faded. "Look, I'm happy to talk to you, but maybe you want to simmer down just a bit. Please, have a seat." This time it was more of a command.

Deliberately, she sank down, perching on the edge of the chair, her hands clasped at her knees.

"That's better. Now, why don't we introduce ourselves. My name is Hugh Nicholson, Sheriff Hugh Nicholson. And you are?"

"Janet Townsend."

"Nice to meet you, Mrs. Townsend."

"Janet, please."

"Right, Janet. Now why don't you tell me what's got you so riled up?"

"Those women, the daughters? They could be in grave danger."

Hugh gave her a dubious look. "Just what makes you think that?"

"My ex-husband is what."

Hugh studied the woman for a minute. There was something, some connection that he seemed to have missed. What was it? Then it clicked. Janet Townsend. His eyes narrowed. "Wait a minute. You're not talking about Art Townsend, as in our governor, are you?"

Janet nodded slowly, her eyes on Hugh's face.

"I'm not getting it," he said.

"Everybody thinks Arthur Townsend is God's gift to Nevada. Oh sure, he has helped the state get back on its feet after the pandemic wiped out the whole gambling and entertainment industry. Although, being a typical politician, he'll take the credit even if the recovery was inevitable. But he is no saint, trust me."

"Okay," Hugh said slowly, "I believe you. A wife knows a lot of things about her husband—"

"Ex-husband."

"Right. Ex-husband. But forgive me if I need a little more to go on."

"You heard about James Peterson?"

Now the pieces started to fall into place. James Peterson. Everything kept circling around to that old child trafficking case. Damnit to hell—that case. It hung like an albatross around his neck.

"Are you saying that you believe Art Townsend has

something to do with all of this?"

"Oh, I know he does."

Hugh stood and walked over to his door. "Marsha," he said, "please hold all calls and visitors." Then he closed the door and took his seat behind his desk. "Now why don't you tell me just what exactly is it that you know."

Janet laid it all out in sordid detail. There was no longer any reason to cover for her children. They all knew they were adopted, and Carl knew the sordid details. "So you see," she concluded, "Art isn't going to sit around and let this story get out. I have no doubt that those two women know things, things about what happened back then, maybe even implicating Art."

Hugh sat back in his chair, mulling over her story. Perhaps some of what she was telling him was true. It certainly fit with what he knew. But Arthur Townsend involved in the whole thing?

"Well, now, don't you think maybe you're overreacting? After all, that bust happened nearly thirty years ago."

"If that's true, then why did I just see some of Art's thugs hanging out right here in town?"

"Who?"

"I don't know their names, but I recognized one of them. They're sitting plain as day in a black van on Main Street." She stood and strode to the window that looked out over Main Street. Her shoulders slumped. "They're gone now."

Hugh joined her at the window for a moment. Then he walked to his door and opened it. "Marsha, did those women who came in yesterday sign the visitors' book?"

"Yes, of course. I make everyone sign it."

"Does it say where they are staying?"

Marsha grabbed the book and ran her finger down the page. "Yes, Sheriff. It says they're staying at the Value Inn."

Hugh turned to Janet. "Let's just go check on them, shall we?"

* * *

When Hugh arrived at the motel with Janet, he breathed a

sigh of relief. He recognized the old Jeep that the women were driving. It was parked in the motel parking area outside one of the rooms in a long the row of rooms.

"Right. Let's find out what room number they're in and have a talk with them," he said.

While Hugh went to the motel's reception, Janet got out and paced. The motel was located on the main street and morning traffic droned just beyond the parking lot. There were two other cars parked in front of a couple of rooms with their drapes drawn. The door to another room was open and a maid's linen cart stood next to it.

Soon Hugh emerged from the front office. "They're in room 103," he said and followed the walkway to the door. He knocked lightly. There was no response. He rapped again more sharply. Nothing.

"I don't like this," Janet said.

"Me neither." This time he banged on the door with his fists. Nothing.

"Let me get the manager to open the door," he said.

A few minutes later he stood with Janet and the owner in the empty room. Both beds had obviously been slept in, their linens in a tangle. In the bathroom, he found a couple of damp towels and a small puddle of water by the shower stall. A faint scent of perfume hung in the air.

He returned to the room and looked around. A desk stood right next to the door halfway under the window.

Janet turned to the owner. "Is that where the desk is normally located?"

"No," the owner said, "normally it sits in the corner. See where the chair is?"

At that moment, a maid came up to the door and hovered. She was breathless, her expression anxious.

"What is it, Linda?"

"I think I may have seen something. But I didn't know what I was seeing."

"Go on," Hugh said gently.

"Well, I was just getting ready to work, you know? I was in the changing room putting on my uniform when I heard a noise, like a yelp or a bang or something. When I glanced out the door, I saw a man carrying something into a van. Well, at the time, I thought it was our laundry service. But now, when I think about it, it wasn't the usual time for them to come. And it didn't look like a laundry van."

"What did it look like?"

"It was black. That's what struck me as funny. Those laundry vans are usually white."

CHAPTER 34

Somewhere in Humboldt County, Nevada

Cate came to slowly, opening her eyes and gazing around her. Wherever she was, it was nearly pitch dark. She had splitting headache. As she laid unmoving for a moment, she became aware of the rumble of an engine. The cold hard metal vibrating under her told her she was in a vehicle.

When she tried to lift her hand, it wouldn't budge; her arms were tied behind her back. When she tried to move her legs, they wouldn't budge: her feet were similarly bound. She swayed and rocked as the vehicle bounced over a dirt road causing her stomach to roil. She turned her head to her side and started to heave, but nothing came up. She hadn't had any breakfast that morning.

As she lay panting, waiting for her stomach to settle, she felt Victoria nudge her in the shoulder. "Cate, are you all right?"

"I will be. I think. What about you?"

"I feel like my head might explode. What happened?"

"I think we've been kidnapped."

"Holy mother of god. Where do you think they're taking us?"

"From the sound of it, out into the desert somewhere." Cate remembered the drive to Winnemucca, the inhospitable landscape with nothing but rolling hills and desert scrub.

They travelled over a few more bumps in silence. Then Victoria whispered, "Cate? I'm scared."

Hoping to give some comfort, Cate wiggled a bit until she came into contact with Victoria's hip. "We're going to get out of this."

"How?"

"We need to keep our wits about us. Sooner or later, the opportunity will come."

Just at that moment, they felt the vehicle slow and turn. Then the bumping got so bad that the two women were thrown from one side of the vehicle to the other. After what seemed an interminable length of time, the movement stopped. Cate could hear the doors to the cab open and shut.

"Remember," Cate whispered as footsteps approached the back of the van. "Stay calm. Wait for an opportunity."

When the back doors opened, she was blinded by the sudden brightness of the morning. Two men standing at the doorway cut black silhouettes against the intense blue of the sky. One man grabbed Cate's leg and dragged her to the opening while the other dragged Victoria.

"Where are we? What are you going to do to us?" Victoria's voice was shaky.

"Shut up." The man slapped her across the face and her head snapped back. Then he heaved her up on his shoulder like a sack of potatoes. The other man hauled Cate up. The men walked a short distance and stopped in front of a gaping hole in the earth and stood them on the ground next to it.

"Let's do this," said the man standing next to Cate.

"We're supposed to kill them first."

"Yeah? Well I don't do women."

"I ain't too keen on it either," said the other.

"So I say we dump them and let nature take care of them."

"Please," Victoria pleaded, "oh please don't do this." Her captor slapped her hard across the face once again. "Shut up."

Cate cringed when Victoria's head lolled to one side. She caught a glimpse of her assailant's face—a livid red birthmark just visible under a knitted cap. Then a look pass between the two men. In unison, they shoved her and a screaming Victoria into the yawning abyss.

* * *

Cate was falling to her death; the air whistled around her as she plunged downward. Suddenly, one foot landed on solid ground with a sickening thud. A searing pain shot through her ankle as it twisted beneath her. Then her body spiraled downward out of control. There was no way to break her fall; she tumbled, crashing on hard earth and stone, until she landed on level ground.

When she came to, she stared into blackness. Her body was a mass of bruises and scrapes. Her arms and legs were trussed up and she felt an agonizing pain in one of her ankles. She lay on her side. A rock pushed against her hip. Her cheek was pressed into gravel. Dust stirred up by her descent rose all around her, filling her mouth and nose.

She gazed around but could see nothing. She managed to raise her head just enough to make out a beam of light coming from the hole high overhead. Then she heard a sound, a soft movement. She froze. What was that?

"Cate?" came a soft whimper. It was Victoria! She was somewhere nearby and she was still alive. Cate's heart leaped with hope.

"Victoria?"

"I'm here."

"Oh, God, Victoria. Thank God you're alive. I am so sorry."

"Why, what in the Sam Hill for?"

"For getting you into this." She blinked back tears. "If I weren't such a stubborn, pigheaded . . . "

". . . obstinate . . . headstrong . . ." Victoria supplied.

"Victoria! Stop joking. This isn't funny."

"I know. I know. Truth be told I'm scared witless. Where are we?"

"I think we're in a mine shaft."

"Oh yes, now I remember. We were pushed, weren't we?"

"Yeah."

"So why aren't we dead?"

"I don't know," Cate said. "I think something broke our fall on the way down. If only we weren't trussed up like a couple of turkeys, we could maybe check out our situation."

"Well, hold on a minute."

Cate heard a scuffling movement as Victoria scooted over the rough surface towards her. Then she felt Victoria nudging her with her head. "Victoria, what are you doing?"

"I'm gonna try to get that rope off your wrists."

"How?"

"Well, I thought I'd start with my teeth. If I can't untie it, I'll gnaw it off."

Love poured through Cate for this woman, her sister. She grinned through the pain. "Is that what they teach you over in Georgia?"

"That and other things. Now hush. I got work to do."

Cate could feel the rope being pushed and pulled while Victoria grunted and panted. Every now and then she would stop and curse a blue streak the likes of which would have made Cate's brothers blush. Then the nudging would start again.

"Victoria?"

"Hmph," came a muffled reply.

"Victoria, I think I can feel the rope loosening. Let me try to pull one hand out."

"'Kay," Victoria said with a pant.

Slowly so as not to cause the knot to tighten again, Cate twisted and pulled at her hand. "Got it!" she said as her arm sprang free.

"Well hallelujah and thank the Lord," Victoria cried triumphantly.

Quickly, Cate pulled the rope off her other hand, then she started on the bindings at her ankles. Through a haze of pain in her ankle, she managed to get them off. Then she lay panting, waiting for the pain to recede. But it didn't. If anything, it intensified.

Steeling herself against it, she crawled over to Victoria and untied her sister's hands and then Victoria made short work of her ankle ropes.

Now untied, they set about exploring their surroundings, slowly, inch by inch, feeling the ground around them. Every now and then something crawled over Cate's hand. Like maybe a spider or a rat or some other critter. She bit back the urge to squeal.

"If only we had some light," Victoria said.

"Hang on," Cate said and felt her back pocket. She was in luck. They hadn't taken her cell phone. A moment later, a small light filled the cavernous space.

CHAPTER 35

Las Vegas, Nevada

Sam had had a rough night on an undercover operation. Smarming with some of the dregs of Las Vegas society, men bent on finding very young girls and boys to satisfy their perverted lust, was getting to him. When he finally got back to his apartment, he tried to shower away the filth. But it didn't sit on his skin or his clothes; it sat in his mind. He knew he would never be able to completely purge the memories of nights spent with such lowlife.

Emerging from the hot spray of the shower and rubbing his skin until it was raw and red, he poured himself three fingers of whiskey and downed it. Then he poured another and sat out on his deck, sipping it while he watched the lights twinkle over the city. When he finally tumbled into bed, he wanted nothing more than to sink into oblivion for a straight twelve hours.

But it wasn't to be. Barely two hours later, just as the sun was rising, his phone rang.

"Hello," he mumbled.

"Sam, it's Michael Connelly. I'm sorry to bother you so early in the morning but I wanted to give you a heads up. My brother Liam is heading your way. He's bound and determined to track Cate down. He should be arriving around nine."

"Right, okay."

"Look I am sorry, but Liam is pretty headstrong."

"It's okay, Michael. I'll do what I can for him."

Sam hung up the phone and sat on the edge of his bed for a very long moment. He wasn't at all sure if it was a good idea for Liam to come, but he had to admit to himself he couldn't blame the guy. If it were his sister, he would be worried. Hell, even though they weren't related, he couldn't get Cate out of his mind. She seemed so strong in spirit, but she was a woman and women just weren't as strong as men, physically. Call that chauvinistic but in his line of work, he had seen far too often how women could be abused.

Maybe she and Victoria were safely out of the way in Winnemucca, but then again, maybe not. Nevada may be large, but people knew each other. Either way, he would feel better if he saw them, spoke to them in person.

As he was pouring himself a second cup of coffee, the guard at reception phoned.

"Sir, there is a man here who claims to be a personal friend of yours. His name is Liam Connelly."

"Let him in," Sam said. "I'll meet him at the front desk."

* * *

Sam took the elevator down to the reception area with an overnight bag in hand. He found Liam pacing the spacious lobby. There was no mistaking him. He had the same build, the same hair, and, at the moment, the same intense expression on his face that Sam had seen when working a difficult case with his brother Michael.

"Liam," he said, offering his hand.

Liam shook it and looked him over. "Sam. Nice to meet you. My brother speaks very highly of you."

"I only hope I can live up to his opinion." He gestured to his bag. "I say we head on out to Winnemucca directly. It's a long drive."

They took Liam's vehicle, an SUV with four-wheel drive. They passed through Las Vegas and abruptly hit the wide-open road. It was always startling to Sam, who had grown up in Nevada, how suddenly they went from thriving metropolis to bare and lonely desert.

When they reached Indian Springs his cell phone rang. There was only one number that triggered that particular ring tone. His father.

Sam glanced over at Liam. Conversations on cell phones were often easy to overhear and this was one call he didn't want Liam to hear. He switched his phone to his other ear and covered it as he spoke. Fortunately, Liam's attention hadn't strayed from the road.

"Sam, we got a problem," his father began without preamble. "Those two women, Cate Connelly and Victoria Saunders?"

Sam's gut clenched. "Yeah? What about them? Did they find their birth parents?"

"Yes, yes they did."

"So what's the problem?"

"They've been kidnapped."

"Say that again."

"Kidnapped."

"But how? Why?"

"They were snatched right out of their motel room."

"Do you have any idea where they were taken?"

"The last time they were seen was in a van heading out into the desert."

"Christ. Any idea who's behind it?"

"Oh yes. I have a real good idea. But look, it's too complicated to explain over the phone."

"Right. I'm on my way. Should be there midafternoon."

When Liam glanced at Sam as he ended the call. "What is it? Is it about my sister?"

* * *

As Sam contacted the FBI's hostage rescue team, Liam put on the speed. By the time he finished his call, Liam was driving well over a hundred miles an hour.

"Look, Liam. I appreciate your worry, but you won't do Cate any good if you crash before we get there."

Liam let up slightly on the gas pedal. After some miles, he glanced at his travelling companion. "Michael tells me that you grew up in Winnemucca."

"That's right."

"And your father is the sheriff?"

"Yep."

"Quite a far cry from the apartment in Las Vegas."

"Yeah. That's all part of the image. For the job, you know."

"So, how did you wind up going from here to there?"

"It's a long story."

"We got a long drive ahead of us."

Sam settled into his seat and began his story. "It's ironic, really. It all seems to go back to that child trafficking bust. The same one that brought your sister to Nevada. My dad was involved in it because some of the kids came from our county. Now it seems that your sister and her sister were two of them."

"Yeah. Michael told me a bit about it. But I still can't quite get what happened. Why didn't they get rescued and returned to their parents?"

"Good question. The bust was a success. The perpetrators were apprehended. But then something happened to the children. From what I understand, they should have been taken to the CPS until they could be returned to their families. But then they just disappeared. My father tried to track them down. He was determined to get to the bottom of things. Until the accident."

Sam paused, gazed at the long highway in front of them that undulated across the rolling terrain. Then he went on.

"My mother. She died in a car crash. That ended any efforts by my father to search for the missing children. I was ten years old at the time. My father and I, why we did our best to rebuild our lives. We managed for the most part. Except when my father had one of his 'spells'. He'd like get all gloomy, drink excessively, wake up too hung over to show up for work. His deputies, they were loyal to a fault. They covered for him during those periods. Fortunately, he pulled himself out of it. In these past ten years, it only happens on the anniversary of the bust."

"Christ, that must have been tough."

Sam thought back to those years in his early teens. He had resented his father for his brooding. When he needed him to get through those awkward high school years, his father was mostly absent, at least in spirit.

Then one day they came to blows. High school graduation was approaching and, with it, all the plans for parties and celebrations. And of course, the prom. Sam had absolutely no interest in this event. But he had grown six inches in the past year and a boyish face was gradually turning handsome. The pressure was on for him to find a date because he was likely to be elected prom king. When came home from school to talk to his father about it, Hugh was in one of his gloomy funks.

Sam lost his temper. For once, just once, he wished his father was there for him. When he saw him slouched in an easy chair, eyes glazed, watching an old western, he walked up to him, grabbed his beer and smashed it onto the floor. His father stood to give him a good talking to and realized that Sam was looking at him eye to eye. Instead of lecturing him, Hugh stormed out of the house. Sam watched him walk away until he disappeared into the darkness.

The next morning, his father sat down with him at the kitchen table and apologized. And made a promise to his son to clean up his act. From then on, the only time Hugh fell into that hole was on the anniversary of the bust in Las Vegas. He began to treat Sam as an adult. He still tried to give fatherly advice when asked but showed a deep and abiding respect for the young man Sam was becoming.

"Yeah. I had to grow up fast," Sam said. "I spent a lot of time at the sheriff's office where the deputies took me under their wing. I got to know the kind of work they did. Crime doesn't happen too often in a rural county like Humboldt, but it does occur. By the time I finished high school, I determined that I, too, would become a cop. But not in a rural county.

"I submitted my application to Quantico and began training as an FBI agent. That's where I first met your brother. Eventually, I was assigned to Las Vegas and I'm now working undercover."

As Sam finished his story, he looked over at Liam, took in the bloodshot eyes, the worry etching deep furrows into his brow. "Tell me about your sister."

"Cate? What can I say? She's the most stubborn, feisty, fearless, awesome sister in the world. She would give her life for any one of us. She gave up her career in law enforcement to help our parents save their pub. See, they had poured their entire life savings into it. They nearly went belly up after the coronavirus shutdown. Then my brother died from COVID." Liam paused. His throat swelling up.

"It was just too much for Dad. He ended up having a stroke. So, Cate, well she stepped up to the plate, took over managing the pub and got us through it."

"Sounds like a hell of a women," Sam said.

Liam glanced at Sam, then quickly back to the road. "You'd like her."

"She never got married?"

Liam grinned. "No. She always blamed us for that. Said she had yet to meet a man who measured up to even one of her brothers."

"I can see that. I've only met two of you, but from what I can see, you're both pretty fine men."

Liam focused on the road and they drove on in silence for a while. Then he said, "I bet you could give us a run for the money."

"What are you talking about?"

"You and my sister. I can see it. I think you'd measure up, even in her eyes. If not, she'd be a damn fool." On seeing Sam's blush, Liam grinned. "You are attracted to her, aren't you?"

"Come on. I've never even met her. I've only ever seen her from across a bar."

"But you liked what you saw, didn't you?"

"Well..."

Liam's grin faded and worry wreathed his brow. "We have to find her, Sam."

"We will. If she's anything like you just described, she'll keep herself safe. Her and her sister."

CHAPTER 36

Austin, Nevada

State Troopers Davis and Garcia covered the sparsely populated Lander County, a vast and lonely territory located smack in the middle of the state. They had just finished their lunch in Austin and set out to patrol the highway south of town. While Davis drove, Garcia checked the messages on the computer installed on their console for any news or alerts.

"It says here to be on the lookout for two men involved in a kidnapping up in Winnemucca," he told his partner. "They're driving a black van. One man is in his late fifties, five-ten, two-hundred pounds, gray hair." Davis looked up at his partner and grinned. "That narrows things down to about half the men in Nevada." Then he read some more. "The other guy is easier to identify. Says he has a large port wine stain birthmark on his face. Both men are believed to be armed and extremely dangerous."

As they pulled onto the on-ramp of the highway, they caught sight of a black van travelling down the highway at well over the posted speed limit. Not that that was unusual; it was a long, lonely stretch of road. But the fact that it was a black van caught their attention. "Garcia, you don't suppose that's them, do you?"

Davis flipped on the siren and gave chase. "Let's find out."

The troopers followed the van, siren screaming, for quite a stretch before it finally pulled over. When it did finally stop and they drew in behind it, there was no sign of movement from it. They got out of their patrol car and approached cautiously. As they drew near, Garcia saw that the driver had rolled down his window. He could see him through the rearview side mirror. The man waited patiently. He was an older man, heavyset, with gray hair. His passenger huddled on the other side. Garcia couldn't see his face. He had pulled a knitted cap low over his brow and ears and was staring out the side window.

He said to the driver, "Sir, I clocked you at over a hundred-twenty miles an hour. Now, I'm afraid I'm going to have to see your driver's license and registration."

"Sure thing," the man said, reaching over the console. Something alerted Garcia, perhaps a look in the driver's eye. Instinctively, he snapped his head back, taking cover behind the metal frame of the vehicle. Suddenly, a flash and a horrendous blast tore through the window. Garcia dropped to the ground and flung his arms over his head. He felt a deafening pressure on his ears.

Just as suddenly, the driver hit the gas, tires spitting gravel, then squealing as they gained purchase on the tarmac. Davis had been hovering on the passenger side of the van. As it took off, he dropped to his knee and took aim at the back tires. On his third shot, one of them exploded. The van veered wildly before crashing into the ditch. It landed on its side, two wheels spinning in the air. Garcia and Davis approached with guns cocked.

As they drew near, the driver's door, which was now tilted towards the sky, popped open. The older man's head and shoulders emerged with his arms in the air. The patrolmen covered him with their pistols and watched as he crawled out of the van. The younger man followed. He had lost his hat and they could see a birthmark that covered half his face. They searched the van, but there was no sign of the two women.

CHAPTER 37

Winnemucca, Nevada,

The sheriff's office in Lander county contacted Hugh to let him know that they had apprehended the suspects, but there was no sign of the women. Hugh had just hung up the phone when Marsha tapped on the door.

"Sheriff, you have a visitor." Marsha nodded at a young man who was waiting for him in one of the visitors' chairs. "You're going to want to talk to him."

As Hugh approached him, the man stood and doffed his baseball cap. His blond hair was sweaty and mashed against his head. Much of his face was pockmarked with acne scars. "Sh-sh-sheriff," he stuttered. "M-my name is Billy. Billy Landa."

"Yes, Billy. What can I do for you?"

"Well, I heard about those l-l-ladies. You know. That got s-s-snatched."

"What do you know about this?"

"I d-d-don't kn-kn-know anything for s-s-sure. "

Seeing that Billy was clearly agitated, Hugh gestured him into his office. He motioned Billy to one of the only two visitor's seats. Hugh sat in the other one. He turned to Marsha. "Do me a favor and get this young man a glass of water." Then he turned back to Billy.

"Now, then, let's take this nice and slow. You may know

something about the two women we believe have been kidnapped."

Billy nodded his head and began more calmly. "S-see, me and my buddies, we work for the abandoned mines program for the State of Nevada. We locate old mines that aren't safe and b-block off the entrances."

"Go on," said Hugh.

"W-we were at this bar last night where we met a couple of guys. Th-they were asking us about the mines. I explained as how we first have to go out and identify them, take note of their location. Then we determine how dangerous they are. We block off the most dangerous first, see?"

"And these men were interested, were they?"

"Y-yes. R-real interested. They asked us if we had maps of the mines. I started to feel nervous. You know we get a lot of guys thinking maybe they'll strike it rich going into those old mines. The crazy fools, why they go into those mines to explore and are hurt or killed. There are all kinds of hazards in those old mines like collapsing wood structures, toxic gasses. Some of those mine shafts have severe drops, sometimes as deep as six hundred feet.

"So me and my buddies, we started to warn them. But I could tell they weren't listening. Well then, this morning when we got to our truck? Why someone had broken in. Only thing they took were our survey maps.

"I was sure it was them two fellows. I was pretty mad. That last thing we needed was to have to go out and rescue them. Well then, I heard people talking over to the restaurant where we were eating lunch. About those two ladies."

Billy smiled then. "We met them last night earlier in the evening over to the Martin Hotel. We were sitting right next to them. They were real nice. Anyway, I got to thinking. Maybe those guys weren't looking to explore those mines. Maybe they were . . ."

"Going to use one of them to hide those women in?" Sam asked.

"Well, m-m-maybe."

"Right," said Hugh. "And these maps, they're the only copies?"

"M-most of the locations are logged onto the computer, you know, latitude and longitude and all of that."

"How hard would it be to make new copies of the maps?"

CHAPTER 38

Humboldt County, Nevada

Victoria peered at Cate's cell phone. "Can you get a signal?"

"Nope. No reception. I guess we're too far underground."

"Well at least we have light."

With the cell phone's flashlight, Cate could see where they had landed. Just in front of them was a steeply sloping bank of earth, above which was a vertical shaft. At the very top of the shaft was a tiny enticing patch of blue sky. She wasn't sure how tall the shaft was, maybe the height of a one-story building. It must have been the slope just below it that had broken their fall.

"Think we can climb back up that way?" Victoria asked.

"We could maybe crawl up that slope, but I can't see any way past that up to the top, not without climbing gear."

"Yeah. You're right. Wishful thinking."

Cate lowered the flashlight and shined it about their more immediate surroundings. They sat on a fairly flat dirt floor in a hollowed-out space like a small cavern. On either side there appeared to be a tunnel. As she pointed her flashlight, she could just make out old mining cart tracks, rails mounted on wooden ties.

"Where do you think those lead to?"

Victoria shrugged and started to stand. "Only one way to

find out."

"Ah, Victoria?" Cate said. "There might be a slight problem. I think I sprained my ankle."

"Oh my goodness, Cate. How bad is it?"

Cate gently felt the swelling around her ankle. It was twice its normal size. "It's pretty bad, I'm afraid."

"Can you walk on it?"

"I can try."

Victoria helped Cate to her feet and propped her arm under her shoulders for support. As Cate put her weight on it, she winced. The pain was bad. She forced herself to take another step leaning heavily on Victoria.

"I think I can manage," she said through gritted teeth.

They turned their attention to the tunnels. "Do you think they're safe?" Cate asked.

"Like I said, there's only one way to find out."

"Yeah, I guess so. But I gotta say . . ."

"What?"

"Well, I mean these tunnels in these old mines, all that's holding them up are wooden support beams. What if one of them collapses? What if there's gas? Or wild animals?"

"Land's sake, Cate. Let's not be borrowing trouble. 'Sides, I reckon we don't have a lot of choice, long as you can walk."

Cate looked at Victoria's shoes—low heeled pumps. "Are you going to be all right walking in those?"

"Do I have a choice?"

"Yeah, you're right. So, which way do you want to go?"

"Your guess is as good as mine."

They chose to follow the tunnel to the right. As they approached it, they could feel the cold wrap around them. Victoria pulled her sweater closed and buttoned it up to her chin. Cate zipped up her sweatshirt.

"Ready?"

Cate nodded. With Victoria putting her arm under Cate's shoulder for support, they entered the tunnel.

Slowly, they followed the mining cart tracks into the deep

with only cell phone flashlight designed more for a roadside breakdown than an underground tunnel. The tunnel was barely high enough for them to stand. They could see the tracks disappearing into the dark. The ground was rough and the wooden railroad ties were in various states of decay. They had to step carefully over and around them. Every now and then they came across a wooden timber support.

Cate sent up a prayer that they were still solid. Then another thought came to her unbidden. "Victoria," she said, "how long does a cell phone battery last with the flashlight on?"

"Hell, I don't know. An hour? Two?"

"I think we better try to manage with the light as little as possible."

"You mean, like, walk in the dark?"

"We can see what's up ahead. If it's clear, we can turn off the light and navigate by the rails. We just use the light to check every now and then."

"Well, if you're sure."

When she turned off the flashlight, they were swallowed up in the dark. It lay all around them like a silent shroud. Cate could only imagine how deep under the earth they were. Her chest tightened and she felt her breath shorten as claustrophobia threatened to overwhelm her. Taking deep breaths, she forced air into her lungs. She focused on the putting one step in front of the other, fighting down the panic.

They had no idea how long they walked. Their hands and faces grew numb from the chill of the tunnel. Every so often, they turned on the light to assess what lay ahead, then they continued in the dark.

They were thirsty and hungry; the last meal they had had was at the restaurant the night before. They had only had time for a quick cup of motel coffee that morning. Cate's ankle throbbed dully. She set her mind to one thought only. The tunnel had to end somewhere, sometime. Unless, of course, they went the wrong way and were heading deeper into the earth. She pushed that thought away.

Finally, after what seemed like hours, Victoria stopped. "I have to rest, Cate. I am plum tuckered out." She eased Cate down and leaned her against the earthen wall of the tunnel. Then she plopped down next to her.

"Let's just rest for a bit."

* * *

Cate thought she would close her eyes for just a moment. And fell into an exhausted sleep. She woke up abruptly and opened her eyes. Black. That's all she could see—black. Her heart leaped to her throat. Had she gone blind? Then she became aware of the throbbing pain in her leg. Slowly, she remembered. They were in a tunnel deep under the ground and her ankle was sprained.

"Victoria?" she cried out.

"I'm here Cate. Right here." Cate felt the soft flesh of Victoria's hand and relief washed over her.

"How long do you think we were sleeping?"

"I have no idea. But I'm hungrier than a tic on a teddy bear."

Cate snorted. "Seriously? A tic on a teddy bear?" Then she started to giggle which started Victoria to giggling. Soon peals of hysterical laughter echoed up and down the tunnel.

Finally Cate got a grip. She stopped laughing. As the reality of the situation sank in, she felt the panic began to rise again. Her chest tightened and her breath shortened. She felt around for cell phone. She was sure she had put it in her pocket.

That was when she saw the very faintest of light. It wasn't coming from her phone; she still hadn't found it. It was shining into the tunnel. From the outside.

"Victoria, look." She pointed towards the light, then realized her sister couldn't see her. "There," she said, pulling on Victoria's arm.

"Oh my. Oh my," Victoria said. "Is that what I think it is?"

"It's coming from the outside." Cate's hand finally landed on the cell phone. She had stuffed it into other her pocket. Then she grabbed Victoria's hand. "Come on. Help me up."

The ground was still rough; there were still ties protruding from the ground. Cate's ankle reached a new level of pain and she leaned heavily on Victoria and took one slow step at a time. The light grew stronger. Soon, they could see the rails leading towards the light.

She could taste the freedom, smell the fresh outdoors.

Suddenly, they stopped. They were indeed at the entrance to the tunnel, but steel bars blocked it, preventing any hapless soul from entering. Or from exiting. Victoria help Cate up and they stumbled up to the bars. Staring outside, they realized that it was nighttime and what they were seeing was the full moon low on the horizon lighting the desert landscape in shades of grey.

Victoria grabbed a hold of one of the bars and pulled as hard as she could. But of course, it gave not a millimeter. She dropped to her knees and started scraping at the dirt with her bare hands.

Cate glanced around inside the tunnel. Her eyes having adjusted to the light cast by the moon, she could make out shadowy forms. She could see a fair amount of rubbish—food wrappers and plastic water bottles—littering the ground.

Somebody or some buddies had been there before them. Kids? Fortune hunters? She had no idea. Then she spotted the blade of a shovel. It had broken off at its handle. She crawled over to retrieve it, then returned to Victoria. Together, they dug away at the bottom of the gate.

Finally, they had a hole about two feet deep between the two metal posts that had been sunk into the ground.

"What do you think, Cate? Can we crawl under it now?"

"Let me try first. I'm smaller than you."

She laid on her back and scooted under the opening, first her head, then her torso, then she dragged her legs out.

And then she was free. She lay panting, gazing around her at the blessed earth and sky.

"Oh my Lord, Cate," Victoria said from inside the tunnel. "You did it."

Cate crawled back to the opening, dragging her leg behind her. "Here, hand me that shovel. I think I can make more space on this side for you to crawl under."

Ten minutes later, Victoria joined her. They lay on their backs and stared at the sky. It was just turning pink with daylight.

"Have you ever seen anything so beautiful in all your life?"

CHAPTER 39

Humboldt County, Nevada

Sam and Liam rolled into town in the late afternoon and met Hugh at his office, Sam could see the relief sweep over his father's face. Hugh looked like he had aged ten years since the last time Sam had seen him. Was it only six months ago? Sam could just imagine what was going on in his father's head. He had failed to rescue those children thirty years ago and now, two of those very children, all grown up, had been snatched right out of his town and taken God knew where.

"Thank God you're here," Hugh said.

Sam embraced his father awkwardly, then held his gaze. "We'll find them, Dad. It's going to be okay."

Hugh nodded, his expression grim. Then he turned to Liam and introduced himself. The two men shook hands, favorably sizing each other up. No words were necessary.

Then Hugh apprised them of the developments—the arrest of the suspects and the information provided by Billy. They proceeded to the local office of the Abandoned Mine Lands Program where they were met by the head of the program. He was focused on a large printer that was spewing out detailed survey maps.

They spread the maps out and created a search grid. By then the sun was starting to set. It was just too dangerous going out after dark in the kind of terrain they were talking about. They would have to wait until the morning to put their plan into action.

Sam and Liam decided to spend the night in the nearest motel to wait. They could have gone to Sam's father's house, but neither wanted to stray that far from the town. They had pizza and a six-pack of beer delivered to the room. Much as Sam would have liked something stronger, they had to keep their wits about them, be clearheaded in the morning. He watched Liam pacing inside the room and offered him a beer.

"We'll find them, Liam." He tried to reassure Cate's brother, to hide any doubts he might have. And there were plenty. He knew the countryside. He had grown up in the area. It was vast and empty, littered with abandoned mines. The women could be anywhere. But thinking negative thoughts wasn't going to help anyone, so he focused on the positive. They'd find them.

When they had finished the beers, he stretched out on the bed and settled into a uneasy sleep. Liam lay in the bed next to him, but Sam was sure he wasn't sleeping. In what seemed like an instant later, he woke to the sound of rustling in the dark. He looked at the clock. It was four in the morning. In the faint illumination of the clock, he could see that Liam was pulling on his pants.

They left their lodging before the sun rose, heading to the sheriff's office. As they pulled onto the main drag, they could barely believe what they were seeing. A crowd had gathered outside the office. Men and women with dogs, ATVs, and horses, all wanting to help with the search.

"Okay, folks," Hugh shouted. "We're going to do this in an orderly fashion. We'll need to form teams." Hugh wandered through the crowd to sort them out, pairing vehicles with dogs and those with experience in the back country. The deputies and Marsha had set up a table with a signup sheet and a pile of maps. Hugh directed teams to the table to sign up and get a map for their designated area. A couple of helicopters had arrived during the night; the FBI team would mount an aerial search.

* * *

As Liam and Sam looked over the map of their assigned area, Hugh approached them. A young man trailed behind him with a hound dog traipsing on his heels. A baseball cap shaded his face. Then he removed it and gazed at them with a determined look in his eye.

"Liam, Sam, I want you to meet Billy Landa. Billy, this is my son Sam, and Liam here is Cate's brother. This young man has been providing us with information about the mines around here. I want you to take him with you.

"Absolutely," Sam said.

Liam grasped Billy's hand in a firm handshake. "Nice to meet you, Billy. We need all the help we can get."

Liam sat in the front passenger side of the SUV while Sam drove. Billy sat in the back with his hound dog. Together, they scanned a terrain of rolling hills, rock-strewn ridges, and deep canyons. Occasionally, Liam held a pair of binoculars to his eyes, but the jouncing of the SUV across the unpaved roads made seeing through them almost impossible. How could they possibly hope to find Cate and Victoria in such a vast area?

Soon they reached a mining site and got out. While they searched for footprints, the dog sniffed around for scents, any sign that there might have been a human presence there in the past twenty-four hours. Finding none, they returned to their vehicle and consulted their map for the next abandoned mine.

The sun had risen and cast its rays over the high desert. Blue skies stretched from horizon to horizon. Yet it was chilly out. Liam worried about Cate and Victoria surviving the cold night. Where were they? Were they hungry, thirsty? Worse yet, injured? Trapped in some god-forsaken mining shaft?

* * *

Once the wonder of being alive and in the great outdoors subsided, Cate and Victoria debated what to do. They tried Cate's cell phone, but the battery had given out. Victoria wanted to follow the rough road that stretched out before them until they reached the main road. But Cate's ankle had grown increasingly worse. And leaving Cate behind wasn't an option.

"So what, Cate? What are we going to do?"

"A smoke signal. We build fire. There have to be people out there looking for us. The best way to signal them is with fire. You need to gather some tinder."

"But how are we going to light a fire?" Victoria asked.

"I think I have some matches somewhere." Cate rummaged through her pockets until she came up with a book of matches and held them up, grinning.

"How—" Victoria started to say.

"From the restaurant the other night. They were on the table next to the candle. I just wanted a keepsake of the place."

Victoria shook her head. "Land's sake, you are a wonder."

It wasn't difficult to find firewood; there was plenty of dried brush all around them. As Victoria returned with one armful after another, Cate instructed her to place them in three piles forming a triangle. Then she set a match to the dry twigs of the first pile. As they caught fire, she leaned over and blew on them until the flames grew larger.

"Aren't you just the boy scout," Victoria drawled.

Cate turned toward her sister and smiled. "Four brothers, remember?" When all the fires were lit, they sat near one of them and warmed their hands. It was cold there in the early morning high desert.

***

As the trio traversed over dirt trails that barely could be called roads, they listened to their high-powered radio. It remained silent as teams were instructed to call in only if they found something. Suddenly it crackled to life.

"Post one, post one, this is Little Bird 2. We're seeing smoke on the horizon." It was one of the helicopters.

Liam sat up straighter and grabbed the radio listening intently to the incoming chatter. As the helicopter drew closer, the team continued to radio in their findings. "We see three small bonfires northeast of our location. We're heading there now."

Liam let out a whoop of joy. "That's Cate. Three fires burning in a triangular fashion is an international signal for rescue. That's my girl."

As the helicopter drew nearer, Liam heard them report, "It looks like two people. They are waving their arms at us."

On hearing the latitude and longitude Billy exclaimed, "That's our sector. We're about ten miles away."

***

An hour into their wait, Victoria sat up straighter. "Do you hear that? It sounds like a helicopter."

She stood and searched the horizon. "There! It's over there," Victoria shouted. Cate gazed in the direction where Victoria was pointing. Sure enough, a helicopter was approaching. They raised their arms and started waving at it.

The helicopter stopped short of them as a cloud of dust mushroomed under it. They could see a man leaning out the door holding a bullhorn. "Cate and Victoria. Help is coming." Then it rose higher in the air and started circling overhead slowly.

"Well, why don't they come down and get us?" Victoria said.

"Yeah? And land where?" Cate gestured at the rough terrain. There wasn't even one small flat area on which to land. "They're sending a vehicle."

Twenty minutes later, a white SUV approached.

***

When Sam saw Cate limp towards their vehicle with Victoria's help, his heart lurched. She was covered from head to foot with grey dust. Her ankle was swollen up like a balloon. Her hair was in a tangled mess. Her face was scratched and smeared with ash. She was the most beautiful woman he had ever seen.

He got out of the vehicle and watched Liam run up to her and wrap his arms around her. "Oh my God, Cate. Oh my God. I was so scared."

"Not half as scared as I was, big brother."

He held her at arm's length and took in her disheveled appearance, her injured ankle. Then he lifted her in his arms and carried her to the back of the vehicle where he sat her down on the tailgate. "Help is coming soon. An ambulance is on its way. Can I get you anything?"

"I'm thirsty."

"Of course, of course." He reached inside and pulled out some water bottles. He handed one to his sister, then turned and handed one to Victoria who was standing next to Sam watching as brother and sister reunited.

Sam turned to her. "Victoria, I'm Sam. So very nice to meet you at last."

Liam also turned to Victoria. "Victoria, I don't know if you remember me. "I'm—"

"Liam, Cate's brother," she said. "I do remember you." She tipped her water bottle up, drained it, and handed it back to him.

Then Victoria spotted a young man lingering by the side of the vehicle. She walked over to him and smiled. "Hello, Billy."

A huge smile broke over Billy's face. "H-h-hello, Victoria. S-s-so glad to see you're all right."

CHAPTER 40

Winnemucca, Nevada

When they got to the emergency room the ER doctors and nurses went to work. They X-rayed Cate's ankle. Luckily, she suffered from a severe sprain, but no bone fractures. To bring down the swelling, they elevated her foot and applied ice. Once the swelling began to abate, they bound it tightly. For the first time, now that her foot was finally immobilized, the pain began to subside.

They eased the shoes off of Victoria's feet. They were in tatters; one heel had broken off. Her feet were scratched up, filthy, swollen, and blistered. Gently, they cleaned and bandaged them.

The nurses put Cate and Victoria on IVs to rehydrate and nourish them. Then they bathed both women gently, patched up their various scratches and injuries, all the while tut-tutting over them. Despite Cate's and Victoria's protests, the emergency doctor insisted on keeping both women overnight. Hugh insisted on posting a deputy at their door for protection. The deputies were told under no uncertain terms to let anyone in, including the countless town folk who were clamoring to see them.

Cate felt herself float away as the pain killer kicked in. She closed her eyes and drifted off to sleep. Even when a nurse came to check her vitals periodically during the night, she barely moved.

* * *

While Cate and Victoria slept, Hugh, Liam, and Sam met with Janet at the sheriff's office and talked until late in the evening. FBI Special Agent in Charge George Taylor, who had arrived the night before to head up the kidnapping/search-and-rescue operation, was also in attendance.

Janet told them her story, starting with the first time she met her husband, the adoptions, her investigation of those adoptions. Then she told them about her suspicions about Carl's parentage, her breakdown and addiction, her son's support when she filed for divorce. By the time she finished, she had run out of the tears that had been pouring down her cheeks. She ended her story with a wry smile.

"I divorced him. But not until he understood that I had more than enough evidence of his money laundering and graft that I could put him away for life."

"So why didn't you?" Agent Taylor asked.

"We still had this duplicitous pact, Art and me. I kept Art's secrets in exchange for him protecting my sons. And then along came two young women wanting to find their birth parents and the whole scheme was about to blow up in Art's face. He just couldn't allow that, now, could he? Not after all the years and time and effort he put into his career, into achieving his life-long ambitions."

"Do you think he is behind their kidnapping?"

"I have absolutely no doubt."

"But we can't prove it. Unless, of course, our two suspects talk."

* * *

Cate finally opened her eyes when the sun came shining into the hospital room. Her sister was in the bed next to her. She was snoring loudly.

"Victoria," she said, "do you think you can keep it down over there?"

Slowly Victoria opened her eyes and smiled at Cate. "We made it."

"Of course we did. I never had any doubts."

As they lay there, stretching luxuriously, a nurse came in with breakfast. She bustled around setting up their trays, fluffing up their pillows, and raising the beds to a sitting position. Both Cate and Victoria were ravenous and made short work of every scrap of egg and crumb of toast.

They were just settling back to drink their coffee when they heard voices outside their room. "I'm Cate's brother and this is FBI Agent Sam Nicholas. He's on official business. So let us pass."

When the door opened, two very tall, very masculine figures crowded into the room.

"Well, aren't you two a sight for sore eyes," Victoria drawled in her best southern accent.

Cate stared at the man standing next to her brother. She hadn't paid much notice of him when they were rescued at the entrance to the mine. But now, now she scrutinized his face.

"I know you. You're the man at the bar. At the casino. In Las Vegas."

Sam nodded and grinned ruefully. "Yes, ma'am. Guilty as charged."

Seeing Cate's confused look, Liam said, "Cate, this is Sam. He's a good friend of Michael. He works for the FBI. Undercover. When I decided to come to Las Vegas to find you, I looked him up."

Cate's gaze settled on Liam. "Maybe you should just start at the beginning."

Liam and Sam traded off telling the story, starting with Sam's surveillance of them following the burglary at Jim Peterson's house, and ending with Liam's decision to come to Las Vegas and the drive to Winnemucca. When they got to the part about Sam being from Winnemucca and his relationship to the sheriff, Cate interrupted.

"Hang on a sec. Are you saying that you are Sheriff Nicholas's son?"

Sam nodded.

Victoria, who had been silent during this tale, blurted out. "Well if that don't beat all."

Then the two men took up the story once again. Cate and Victoria were greatly relieved to learn that their captors were in custody.

"We know who put them up to it," Victoria declared. "It was Arthur Townsend."

Sam raised an eyebrow. "I don't suppose you can prove that."

"We have evidence on tapes. Tapes from Jim Peterson. Or at least we did. Lord only knows where they are now."

"Tapes?"

"They were surveillance tapes." Cate explained what they had heard

"Right," Sam said. "Well, I'd rather have the tapes, but I'll settle for your sworn statements."

"Fine," said Victoria, "but not until we get out of here."

"I'm with you on that," said Liam. "If the governor is involved in this, then I don't think you're safe here. We need to move you."

"My father's house," said Sam. "It's out of town a ways."

"But how secure is it?" Liam asked.

"There's only one road to the place. And my father has maintained a fairly sophisticated security system. We can get a couple of deputies to keep the place under watch."

"Well, what are we waiting for?"

"Ahem," Cate said. 'There is the little matter of the doctor signing us out,"

Then Victoria cleared her throat. "There's one other small matter. We can't be leaving here in these hospital gowns."

When the nurse stepped into the room to take their breakfast trays away, Victoria asked her what happened to their clothes.

"Oh, they're right under your beds. It's where we put a patient's personal belongings when they are checked into the

215

hospital.

The nurse extracted a large plastic bag from under Victoria's bed and handed it to her. When she opened it, she wrinkled her nose as she pulled out a filthy pair of jeans, a blouse that was equally as filthy with one sleeve practically torn off, and a once pale pink sweater that was now brown from the dirt ground into it,

Cate checked her bag. She found her shirt, sweatshirt, and shoes, but no pants. "Well, at least you have jeans," she said to Victoria. "They had to cut mine off in the emergency room. Remember?"

"What about your luggage?" Sam asked.

"Back at the motel room?" Cate said.

"No, my dad checked. Whoever took you cleared everything out."

"Well?" Victoria drawled. "We're going to need some clothes."

Sam looked at Liam. "I guess we need to do a little shopping."

* * *

As they headed out to their vehicle Liam said, "You're from around here. Any idea where we can get some clothes?"

"There's a shopping center near here. It's bound to have women's clothes, don't you think?"

"I'm not sure you could call it a shopping center if it didn't."

They found a Target where they were able to find sweatpants and t-shirts. What they knew about women's sizes would fit in a thimble. But a woman working there took pity on them and helped them out with sizes. He just hoped they would fit.

As they were returning to the hospital room, they passed by a waiting area meant for patients' relatives.

"Liam?" Sam said softly. "Do you see those guys over there?"

"Yeah. Why?"

"I think I recognize them. From Las Vegas."

Liam looked at him sharply. "Is that right?"

"Yeah. They work security for one of the casinos."

Liam felt the hair on his neck rise. "What say we get those

girls out of here, like right now."

They surveyed the hallway and made a quick plan. Then Liam tapped softy on the hospital door. "Are you two decent?"

"Barely," Victoria growled. "Just trying to get this brush through my hair. God what a tangled—" She stopped when she saw Liam's expression.

"No time for that Victoria. We need to hustle you two out of here. Right quick." He tossed the bag of clothes on the bed. "I hope something fits."

"But Liam, what's going on?" Cate asked.

"There are a couple of guys hanging out in the waiting area. Sam recognized them. They work for a casino in Vegas."

"Oh my God," Victoria said, her face turning white as a sheet. She grabbed a pair of sweats and a shirt from the bag and leapt from her bed, wincing when her feet, bound in bandages, hit the floor. She shuffled to the bathroom to change.

Liam grabbed the wheelchair that was sitting in the corner of the room and pushed it over to Cate. "Hop on," he told her. He stripped off his sweatshirt and wrapped it around Cate's shoulders. It enveloped her to her lap. Then he pulled off his baseball cap and shoved it onto her head. As a final touch, he grabbed a hospital blanket from the bed and tucked it around her knees.

Victoria emerged from the bathroom. The sweatpants were a little too short and the t-shirt swam on her.

"Now look, when I open this door," Liam said, "Victoria's going to push Cate's wheelchair. Go down the hallway to your right. There's a service elevator near the end of the hallway. Sam is waiting there for you. I will be right behind you. Got it?"

Victoria gritted her teeth as she pushed her sister's wheelchair, wincing with each step as she tried to walk normally down the hallway.

Liam felt relief when they caught sight of Sam. He had been holding the elevator doors open by keeping his thumb on the button. As Victoria pushed Cate's wheelchair inside, Liam slid in next to them. When the elevator reached ground level, Victoria pushed Cate through the lobby and out the front door and Sam and Liam followed closely behind, forming a human shield around them making sure they weren't followed.

* * *

They reached Hugh's place an hour later. Although Sam had billed it as a cabin, it was in fact a large rambling affair with four bedrooms, a family room, and large kitchen and dining area. Cate and Victoria made a beeline for the two bathrooms in the house.

As Cate stripped off her clothes, she looked longingly at the shower, but her bandage prohibited her from using it. Instead she settled for a bath, with her leg resting on the side of the tub. The warm water sluiced over her aching limbs and gently washed away the dirt that no amount of sponge bathing at the hospital could accomplish. She ran a washcloth over her face, neck, arms, legs, feet and everywhere else she could find. She ducked her head under the water, came up for a thorough shampoo, and ducked under once more.

Down the hall in the second bath, Victoria ignored the sting of her blistered feet as she stood under the flow of warm water. She let it run over her head, into her eyes and ears, under her arms, between her legs and toes, felt the hell of the past forty-eight hours start to dissolve along with the dust and dirt. She shampooed her hair, pulling her fingers through the length until it squeaked.

CHAPTER 41

Winnemucca, Nevada

They finished at about the same time and were putting back on the clothes that Liam and Sam had purchased for them just as Special Agent in Charge Taylor arrived. He had thoughtfully stopped at a pharmacy and picked up a set of crutches for Cate. They settled Cate on the couch with her foot elevated. Sam rummaged around in the kitchen and returned a moment later with a crudely made ice bag, which he gently placed on Cate's ankle.

Sitting comfortably in the living room, they spoke for over two hours, with Sam and George interrupting frequently to take down details. Liam listened from the porch where he stood watch. As Sam followed the story of the two women discovering they were sisters, tracking down Peterson in Las Vegas, saving his life, then sneaking into his hospital room, finding the tapes at Peterson's home while nearly getting caught by Detective Lawes's lackeys, travelling all the way to Winnemucca to search for their birth parents, he couldn't decide if Cate was the most careless woman in the world or the most courageous.

As the women described the daunting moments in the mine shaft, Cate with a badly sprained ankle struggling through the tunnel, and then digging their way out, his admiration for Cate and her sister grew.

As they spoke, the evidence against Arthur Townsend mounted. The agents told Cate and Victoria about Janet Townsend, her unwitting participation in the illegal adoptions.

Victoria frowned. "She never knew about the adoptions?"

"Not at first." Sam went on to explain how she eventually figured it out. "And when she did realize what had happened, she felt the need to protect her boys. She was their mother, after all."

"Well, bless her, the poor woman," Victoria said. "My heart breaks for her."

"What about Art Townsend?" Cate asked. "Can they put him away for life?"

"Well, it's not that simple," Agent Taylor explained. "We haven't gotten a statement yet from your kidnappers. And we only have circumstantial proof that he was involved in the child trafficking scheme."

"If only we had those tapes," Victoria said.

"What happened to them?"

"Those men who kidnapped us. They must have them. They were in our bags." Cate explained.

Just then, Sam's cell phone rang. When he finished the call he was frowning. The news was unsettling. When they had first arrived at the cabin, Sam had asked the sheriff's office to send around a couple of deputies to the hospital to keep an eye on the guys hanging out in the waiting room.

"Apparently, just as they arrived, all hell broke loose. The hospital staff discovered you two had disappeared. As soon as our thugs learned that you had somehow slipped by them, they left the hospital. The deputies followed. They watched them pacing outside in the parking lot. They had their cell phones glued to their ears, probably reporting back to the boss. When Dad heard what was going down, he hightailed it over there. He managed to arrive just as the thugs were finishing their calls. He approached them, questioned them about their business.

"Turns out that they were indeed from Las Vegas and worked security for one of the large casinos. When he asked them what their business was in Winnemucca, they were cagey. Since they couldn't give any plausible reason for their visit to the hospital, Dad advised them to head back to Vegas. Two deputies followed them out of town."

"I don't like it," Sam said. "The legal process could take some time and Art has a whole network of informants throughout Nevada."

"Which means the sisters still aren't safe."

"Agreed," said Sam. "I'm afraid you ladies are going to have to stay put until Art is brought into federal custody."

That night, Cate and Victoria slept securely while Hugh, Sam, and Liam took shifts watching over them.

CHAPTER 42

Winnemucca, Nevada

They woke up to the smell of frying bacon and fresh brewed coffee. Victoria helped Cate with her crutches, and they followed the smell to the kitchen where they found Sam hard at work. He turned when he heard them enter and smiled.

"Good morning ladies. I hope you slept well." He pulled out a chair at the table for Cate and pushed another one over next to her to prop up her foot. Retrieving a pillow from the living room, he settled her in solicitously. Then he grabbed a couple of coffee mugs and filled them with a rich dark brew.

Cate accepted the cup as she took in the homey scene: the country kitchen, the bacon sizzling on the stove, the man in jeans and a plaid shirt with his sleeves rolled up. She especially took note of the man. He was so very good-looking. Even more so in this domestic setting than when he was sitting at the bar in Vegas.

She remembered seeing him in Vegas all too well. Especially that second night, at the resort right after she had undergone a small makeover with an upgraded wardrobe and a stylish haircut. They had just ordered drinks and toasted each other when Cate glanced at the bar and spotted him.

He quickly looked away when she caught his eye, but if she

didn't know better, she would have sworn he was staring at her. Was it her new look? Even she could admit that the old Cate was washed out. It was amazing what a stylish haircut and some new clothes could do for a woman's ego.

But clearly, she had misjudged the situation. Now she knew that his interest was all business. And that annoyed her. She had been in law enforcement for a long time. She should have been able to recognize a surveillance job when she saw one. And she should have known her brothers had asked him to keep an eye on her.

But what really bothered her was that she'd let her ego get in the way of her judgement. She wanted this man to be interested in her as a woman. He was, after all, one of the most attractive men she'd seen in a very long while.

Now she sat at the table, sipping her coffee, feeling somewhat miffed. "Cate?" Victoria's voice brought her abruptly back to the present.

"Sorry. I was just thinking about something." She turned her attention to Sam and smiled brightly. "Anyway, everything smells delicious."

Victoria helped Sam set out plates and silverware. As they were setting up the table, Liam wandered in, his hair sticking up in all directions, his wrinkled shirt half buttoned, his face covered in day-old beard. He scratched his head and mumbled a sleepy greeting.

"Well, it looks like the gang's all here," Victoria said brightly and handed Liam a mug of coffee. "Except for Hugh," she said, looking around.

"He left early," Sam said. "He went to Austin to have a little chat with your kidnappers."

***

Special Agent Taylor and Hugh sat with the sheriff of Lander county in the small interview room facing Ted, the younger of the two kidnappers, across the table.

"You're in a lot of trouble," Taylor told him. "Near as I can tell, we have a number of felony crimes we can charge you with." He stared at the suspect. The man sat insolently with skinny shoulders slumped, head down. Hugh wanted to grab him by the collar and shake him. Or worse. But he would be damned if the little shit got off on any kind of technicality.

He waited for Taylor to continue. "Let's start with the shooting of retired FBI agent Peterson in Las Vegas. We have witnesses that you were there at the crime scene. Did you shoot him?"

Ted's head snapped up. "I never shot nobody."

"So, it was your accomplice, then. Funny, your partner claims you were the one pulled the trigger." Taylor lied. They had yet to apprehend the other man in the Las Vegas shooting.

"No, oh no. I didn't do it. He did."

"You willing to testify to that?"

"Damn right."

"Okay. Okay. But it'll be his word against yours. It will be left to a jury to decide who's lying."

Taylor let that sink in. Then he went on.

"Now maybe you could argue that it wasn't premeditated. And maybe you could argue that you weren't the shooter. Maybe. And then you might get a lighter sentence. Maybe even parole eventually. But I gotta tell you, you're facing other, even more serious charges: the kidnapping and attempted murder of two women in Winnemucca. Our victims, they got a peek at your face, you know. You can't hide a birthmark like yours. There's no question you're going to go down for this. Do you know what the penalties are for kidnapping and attempted murder?"

Ted gazed at his hands bound in handcuffs resting on the table.

"See, juries don't look too kindly on the kidnapping of two women." Hugh interjected. "And leaving them to die in a mine shaft? I'd say that was premeditated by anyone's book. We still have the death penalty for first degree murder in the state of Nevada. But you know that, right?" Hugh shook his head. "I sure wouldn't want to be in your shoes."

Ted continued to gaze sullenly at his hands.

"And other prisoners," Taylor said. "They don't take too kindly to crimes committed against women. Life could be pretty tough in the general population. There is one chance you got to save that hide of yours."

Ted glanced up sharply.

"See, we know that you committed these crimes on someone else's orders. If you tell the judge who was behind it, turned state evidence as it were, he might cut you a break."

Ted's gaze settled back on his hands. "I got no idea what you're talking about."

"Is that right? You don't know anything." Hugh scratched his head. "See, I'm trying to picture it. You just got it in your head to kidnap two women that you don't know and . . . what? Make them disappear? Who put you up to it?"

"If I tell you, I'm a dead man."

"I guess you've never heard of the protected witness program," Taylor said. "It also exists in prisons just for people like you. See, the government isn't nearly as interested in you. You're just a pawn. They are much more interested in getting the big guy. The one behind the scenes pulling the strings.

"So, to protect witnesses like you who are willing to testify, the federal government has created witness protection units within federal prisons. Protected witnesses live a more comfortable life than other prisoners, which includes having free and unlimited access to telephone and cable television and the ability to use their own money to buy food, appliances, jewelry, and other items. We can't keep you out of prison. Your crimes are too serious. But life could be made just a little easier for you."

Ted started to squirm. Sweat broke out on his brow. "It was Tony," he blurted out. "Tony told me he had a job for us. Yeah. That's right."

"Well, now, Tony's in another room. He's about to pin this entire rap on you."

"He wouldn't do that."

"You sure about that? Because he's about to cut a deal. He claims you came to him with this gig."

"Now that's a lie. You want to know why? Because he's the one with the connections. He's the one with the direct line to the boss."

"The boss?"

"That's right. Art Townsend. The governor."

* * *

They were just finishing up the large and very satisfying breakfast, when Sam's cell phone rang. When he finished, he was grinning from ear to ear. "Your bags are on their way, ladies."

They watched from the porch as a large SUV lumbered up the road towards the house. It was Billy and the rest of the crew from the Abandoned Mines Program. Billy got out first. He made his way to the back of the vehicle and, opening it, he pulled out a piece of luggage: a Louis Vuitton suitcase. It was filthy. Gray dirt was ground into its once tone-on-tone monogramed canvas and the beautiful silver-color hardware was all beat up.

"I'm s-s-sorry about its condition," he stuttered. "W-w-we found it in a mine shaft n-near . . ."

"Near where they found you," said one of Billy's colleagues, rescuing him from his tortured explanation. "When we heard that there was no sign of your luggage, our Billy, here, thought to look around. Isn't that right, Billy?"

"Y-y-yes."

"We didn't have to look too hard. The culprits had dumped it in a nearby mine shaft. Fortunately, it wasn't very deep. Once we got a light down there and found your suitcases, why Billy rappelled down to pull them out."

Victoria approached Billy with tears in her eyes. She hadn't wanted to complain about her loss. Shoes could be replaced. Clothes were just clothes. But there were things in that suitcase that were very dear to her. Irreplaceable. Like her mother's wedding ring and some college memorabilia and old family photos. She had taken everything she most treasured when she left Savannah because she never meant to return.

She walked right up to him and kissed him on the lips. "Thank you, Billy," she said simply. Billy's face grew bright red. As red as a beet. Redder even.

"Y-y-you're w-w-welcome."

Then he pulled out another smaller travel bag. It was old and worn and equally as filthy.

Cate smiled when she saw it. There wasn't a whole lot in it, mostly just clothes. But they were brand new, so it was nice to have them back. She stepped up to Billy and threw her arms around him in a huge bearhug. "You are a hero, Billy."

***

Returning to the house, Cate rummaged through her backpack. "I was afraid of that. They took the tapes."

"Well shoot," Victoria said, slumping in her chair. Then she sprang up, suddenly. "Hang on," she said and strode over to her suitcase. She unzipped it and swore when she saw that her carefully pack clothes and other items were in a mess. "Let's just hope it's here," she said and rummaged through the jumble until she found what she was looking for: the tape player.

"Well, look at that. Just as I thought. There is a tape left in the player."

Cate grinned slowly. "The last one we listened to?"

"Yup."

Victoria drawled. "I bet if you play it, you'll find your evidence, Sam."

***

As Cate watched Victoria make a valiant effort to restore some order to her suitcase, she stared absently at her stuff. Then a thought occurred to her. It had been pushed to the back of her mind as she and Victoria made their journey to Winnemucca and everything that happened since then.

"Sam, does the name Victor Belinsky mean anything to you?"

Sam's eyes narrowed. "As a matter of fact, it does. He was the head of that child trafficking scheme. Why do you ask?"

"Carol, the woman at the CPS mentioned him. Apparently, he got out of prison three years ago."

Sam nodded. "I'm aware of that."

"Well, according to Carol, he's been a regular visitor at the CPS office in Las Vegas in the past few months."

"At the CPS?" Sam asked.

Cate nodded. "When she gave us the intake reports from around the time of the child trafficking bust, she also gave us some other reports from the past few months. She was worried about things that have been happening recently at the office. Secret meetings and the like. So when we showed up, she saw an opportunity to report what was going on."

"What did she expect you to do about it?"

"She was hoping we would report it to the authorities. Liam, can you hand me my backpack?" When Liam got it for her, she pulled an envelope from it. "She asked us to give this to someone in law enforcement. At the time, I didn't know who to give it to, who to trust."

Just then Sam's cell phone rang. He strode out to the porch to answer it in private. When he returned to the kitchen table he was smiling. "Jim Peterson is out of ICU. He's just finished giving a statement to our colleagues in Las Vegas. They'll be putting together a task force to round up the governor and a number of members of the police department in Las Vegas and the sheriff's department in Clark County.

"Townsend will be brought into federal custody on multiple felony charges, including child trafficking for which there was no statute of limitation. He won't be allowed any visitors besides his attorney. With all those arrests, there should be plenty of plea bargaining going on and this time around we don't want Art to be able to seek any kind of retribution."

CHAPTER 43

J & R Ranch, Nevada

Janet sat in front of her laptop, opened her photo directory, and scrolled through the photos she had taken over the past few years: vaqueros at work on horseback, the sun rising over the Santa Rosa Range, old bunkhouses of various ages and states of repair, cattle grazing in vast rangeland where antelope roamed in the background. They meant so much to her, those photos.

She had a plan for them: a coffee table book. She could see it in her mind's eye. She thought creating it would be the perfect distraction while she waited for news about the investigation. But when she tried to put something together, she kept drawing a blank. In total frustration, she stood and paced the confines of her makeshift office in the old ranch house, glancing out of the window at the rugged vista before her. The sun was setting. Hugh promised he would get in touch the minute they had Art in custody.

That was yesterday. Only yesterday. It seemed like a year since she left Winnemucca and returned to the ranch to wait out events. How long did it take to gather enough evidence and arrest someone? For that matter, would they be able to get enough evidence? She had given them her records of his financial assets, but she wanted him to be put away for life.

She had reached for her phone so many times during the day, then stopped herself. She had to let them get on with their jobs. She wouldn't be helping by pestering them for progress reports.

As she stood watching the sun sink slowly below the horizon, she saw an SUV coming up the road, a huge plume of dust in its wake. In the gray light of dusk, she couldn't tell who it was. Hope and fear warred in her breast. Logic told her that it wouldn't be Art. He had no reason to come there. Her heart hoped it was Hugh. Not just because he might have news for her. But she also longed to see his rugged, but kindly face, hear his deep, reassuring voice.

And then the vehicle pulled into the driveway. The motion-sensored porch light came on and she could see the sheriff's emblem clearly stenciled on its side. She ran down the stairs to the front door just as her mother approached from another part of the house. Together, they stood on the porch and watched as the tall man unfolded himself from the vehicle and stood before them.

On seeing him nod, they both ran towards him, peppering him with questions. "Ladies, ladies. All in good time. It's a long drive out here and I'm parched."

* * *

They sat at the kitchen table, Janet and her mother and father, and listened as Hugh shared with them all of the events of the past thirty-six hours. By the time he finished it was close to midnight. At the family's insistence, Hugh spent the night. The next morning, Janet's mother cooked up good old-fashioned ranch breakfast with bacon, eggs, hash browns, toast, orange juice, and coffee.

Janet cleared the table and cleaned the kitchen. Then she joined Hugh enjoying his coffee on the porch swing in the front of the house. She took a seat in a rocking chair next to him. Two dogs romped in the front yard. One of Janet's brothers passed by in his pickup on the way to the north range. A hawked soared high above them in the deep blue sky.

She took a sip of his coffee. "I suppose I will have to call my sons, let them know what's happened."

"Have you worked out what you are going to say?"

"Not really. How do you tell your children that their father is a crook and child thief and an accessory to kidnapping and attempted murder?"

"You'll find a way, Janet. You are the strongest woman I have ever met."

Janet sniffed. "Right. I refused to see what was right in front of my face, Hugh. I had a nervous breakdown. I got hooked on tranquilizers."

Hugh stood and held her by the shoulders. "You think you're the only one who has stumbled and fallen? I left my son to be raised by my deputies while I wallowed in self-pity. But you, you raised three fine boys, protecting them the best you could. You have nothing to be ashamed of."

Janet looked up at Hugh's craggy face and broke down. He pulled her into his arms and held her while she wept and wept and wept.

CHAPTER 44

Winnemucca, Nevada

It took the rest of the day for Victoria and Cate to wrap up their affairs. Liam drove them to the motel to pick up Cate's jeep. Then they went together to see Alana. When she opened the door, Cate almost didn't recognize her.

She had cut her hair into a tidy chin-length bob. And she was dressed neatly in a pair of tan slacks and a flowery shirt. "Welcome, my daughters," she said with a broad smile. She wrapped her arms gently around Cate and her crutches and then embraced Victoria warmly. Then she turned to Liam.

"This is my brother," Cate hurried to explain. "He wanted to meet you."

"How wonderful to meet you," Alana said, offering her hand.

"And I, you." His gaze moved from Cate to Victoria to Alana. "I can see the resemblance."

Alana stood back, beckoned them to enter and Cate was again pleasantly surprised. What had once been a dark living space was now light and airy; the curtains were pulled back to let the sunshine come in; the room was tidy and the furniture glistened with fresh polish. On a table in the corner was a tea set and coffee cake.

"I hear you two girls have had quite an adventure," she said as she poured tea and offered them each a piece of cake. Then she sat with them and listened with great interest to their story. At times, her eyes glistened with tears, at other times, she shook her head in amazement. Still other times, when she learned of some of their scarier moments, she scowled darkly.

The tale was long in telling. They had finished their tea, polished off all of the coffee cake. Then Alana excused herself for a moment. She returned, awkwardly carrying a heavy stack of photo albums. Liam rose to help her set them on the coffee table.

"Now, then," she said. "These are yours to take with you."

"Oh, but we can't do that," Victoria said.

"But I insist. I had two copies made, one for each of you. Have a look." Her eyes twinkled.

Cate lifted an album from the top of the pile and sitting next to Victoria, she opened it. The first picture was of a handsome couple in their wedding attire taken in a church.

"Why, that's you and Enders, isn't it?" Cate said.

Alana nodded, her eyes filling with tears. "Yes, that's me and your father."

"Land's sake," Victoria said, "but you were such a handsome couple." Then they turned the page to a photo of a newborn.

"That's your brother, Hektor," Alana said, letting the tears fall. She brushed them away with a napkin. As they continued to turn the pages, the story of their earliest days was brought to life. It ended with the photo they had seen the first time they had visited.

The three women and Liam laughed and cried as they shared the photos. Then Liam addressed himself directly to Alana.

"You must come visit. Meet the rest of Cate's other family. We're only a day's drive from here. I know my mom and dad and my brothers will be eager to meet you."

Alana held her hand to her mouth as tears flooded her eyes and ran unchecked down the fine lines in her cheeks.

"Why, what a wonderful idea," said Cate. "Just say the word and we'll come and get you."

"Oh, my," was all Alana could manage to say around her tears.

***

By the next morning, Cate was anxious to return to Prescott. It seemed like she had been gone for months. Living out of a suitcase and eating road food got old real fast. And she was anxious to see everyone—her parents, her brothers, her staff at the pub, even their regular customers.

As they put their luggage into Cate's jeep, a vehicle pulled up. It was Nel with Alana in the passenger seat. Then the sheriff's car pulled up next to it. Hugh and Sam got out. A lot of tearful goodbyes and unrestrained hugs followed.

Finally, after more hugs and tears, they waved goodbye to their new friends and colleagues and set off. Victoria drove while Cate sat with her foot propped up under a couple of pillows. Liam following in his vehicle.

"I bet it'll be real nice to get back, to see your parents and your brothers." Victoria said, settling in for the eleven-hour drive.

"Yes, it will, after the dust settles."

"What do you mean by that?"

"I just have a feeling those brothers of mine are going to have some choice words for me."

"Pshaw. It only means they love you. And what about your parents? They are going to love learning about Alana."

Cate smiled. "Yes. I can hardly wait until they get to meet."

Victoria sighed. "I wish I could say the same for my father."

Cate glanced quickly at her sister. Victoria hadn't really said much about him, her feelings for him. "Have you thought about what you are going to do?"

"I don't know. Can a child divorce a parent?"

"It's called emancipation. But it's only meant for kids who are sixteen or older. Legally, if they are emancipated, they become adults. And since you already are an adult . . ."

"Well shoot. Can I disown him?"

Cate laughed. "In your heart, I suppose. But legally? Not really."

"Well, I don't ever want to see him again. The scallywag."

"What will you do then?"

Victoria sighed. "I just don't know." They drove on in silence for several miles. Then she said, "You're lucky, Cate. You have a life to go back to. Your mom and dad and brothers. I bet you're looking forward to getting into the swing of things at your pub."

"I am, of course. And yet . . ."

"What?"

"To be honest with you, I have been thinking about how much I would like to go back into law enforcement. I was thinking about child trafficking, maybe joining the FBI."

Victoria sat up straighter. "No kidding? I bet you'd be real good at it."

"I think so. But then there is the pub. I can't let my parents down. Dad still isn't well enough to go back to it. And my mom, well, she's taking care of my dad."

"Yeah, that is a problem, isn't it?"

They fell into a comfortable silence watching the miles fly by, each lost in her own thoughts.

Then Victoria said, "I wonder . . ."

"What?"

"No never mind. It was just wishful thinking."

"So? Tell me."

"Well, you may think this is a crazy idea."

"Try me."

"What if I took over running the pub? Why shoot, I have a degree in business administration and I know how to keep the books and I've had loads of experience waitressing and I make the best damn Bloody Mary ever." She looked at Cate, waiting to see her reaction.

Cate grinned.

"You think it's a dumb idea, don't you. Just forget I ever said anything. That pub belongs to your family and it was presumptuous of me to even think—"

"Victoria, I think it is an excellent idea."

"Do you? Do you really?"

"I really do. And it sure would solve a number of problems.

You'd have a place to settle. And you'd have a job you like. And I could join the FBI."

"Oh! Oh! Oh!" Victoria said. "I'm so excited."

CHAPTER 45

Las Vegas, Nevada

As Cate and Victoria wrapped up their affairs in Winnemucca, Sam returned to Vegas. He was anxious to follow up on the lead the women gave him. The first thing he did was to call Carol and arranged to meet at Javier's restaurant.

He opened the door to the familiar smell of spices and corn tortillas. It was Sam's favorite kind of Mexican restaurant. The place was about half full and noisy with boisterous talking and laughter. The crowd was a mix of Latino and gringo.

He sat conspicuously at the bar so that Carol could find him and ordered a margarita. The bartender returned with a frosty glass with a generous layer of salt on the rim, a bowl of salsa, and a basket of chips. Sam savored a crispy corn chip dripping with the spicy dip and took a gulp of ice-cold, tangy margarita.

When he was about halfway through his drink, a woman approached him. "Sam Nicholas?" She was perhaps in her late forties or early fifties with graying, light brown hair. She had a round, pleasant face; hazel eyes; medium build.

"I have a table in the back," she gestured with a nod of her head. Sam threw some money on the bar, grabbed his drink, and followed her.

"Thank you for agreeing to see me—"

"How do you know Cate?" Carol's question was abrupt.

"She's the sister of a man I have worked with for many years in the FBI," Sam told her. She seemed to like that answer. At least her shoulders began to relax. "I actually met her in Winnemucca," Sam continued. "That's where she found her birth mother. Thanks to you."

A huge smile spread across Carol's careworn face. "No kidding?"

"No kidding. She and Victoria finally met their mother. They are making all kinds of plans to share in each other's lives."

"Why that is just wonderful."

Sam's expression turned serious. "The thing is, when I met Cate and Victoria, they handed over some reports. Not the ones that helped them find their mother. These are very recent. And they gave me your name."

She gazed at his face intently. "You understand the significance of those reports?"

"I do. And I have been watching a man called Victor for the past few months. He and his associates are a tight-lipped lot. But they're up to something."

"Yes." Carol said then looked around. "Yes, I think something big is in the works. Those reports I gave you? There are at least two dozen more kids in the system."

Sam nodded and smiled as a waitress approached their table. He asked for the evening's special and Carol ordered a taco salad. Then he turned his attention back to Carol. "We're pretty sure that that same kind of trafficking is going on now. My partner and I have a good idea where it's going down, but we need to know when. Can you help us out with this?"

Carol thought for a moment. "I think so. You can't move that many children in one go without some logistics involved. I can let you know if I hear anything."

"That would be very helpful. There is one other matter."

"What's that?"

"The CPS. We can't bring those children back there."

***

Since his meeting with Carol, Sam focused a lot of time and energy into ensuring that any potential bust would take care of the children involved. Fortunately, things had changed since the tragic outcome of the child trafficking bust in 1993. Nine years later, in 2002, the FBI established the Victim Services Division (VSD) whose sole purpose was to inform, support, and assist victims in the aftermath of a crime. Within the division was the Child Victim Services program with teams focused on ensuring that any interactions with child victims or witnesses were tailored to the child's stage of development and minimized any additional trauma to the child.

Sam meant to make sure that this office was mobilized when the bust went down. He made sure that the division provided training and information to help to equip the FBI agents and other FBI personnel that would be involved in the bust to work effectively with victims.

Meanwhile, he and his partner continued to watch the club. All things appeared to be normal. They didn't see or hear of any suspicious activity. Sam's anxiety grew. Would Carol ever get back to them with anything solid?

A few days later, when Sam was just finishing up some paperwork, he got the call. It was Carol. He caught tension in her voice that he hadn't heard before.

"Sam Nicholas?" she said in a hushed voice.

"Speaking."

"I . . . I think, well, I've been seeing a lot of activity going on at the office today. Belinsky has been in several times. Then I heard one of our assistants on the phone arranging for a couple of vans to 'pick up some cargo.'"

"When? Did they say when?"

"This evening."

***

Just after the sun set, Sam and a team of FBI agents set out for Ramon's. They had discussed the best plan of attack. Their highest priority was to protect the children, but arresting the culprits was also very high on their list. To these agents, there was no worse crime than child trafficking. They welcomed any chance they got to put an end to this nefarious activity. Arresting them, incarcerating them would put at least one ring such out of business.

When they arrived within a few blocks of the club, they took up various positions with views in the neighboring streets of the service entrance. Among them were a half dozen female agents in plainclothes trained by the Victim Services Division. They stood by, ready to help with the children at the moment of the bust. Inside the club, two undercover FBI agents settled in to watch the pole dancing show. Meanwhile, several local police that Sam knew and trusted stood ready to set up roadblocks on the streets leading to and from the club. The sun had set an hour before. Sam could feel the nervous tension of the agents.

Finally, an hour into their surveillance, the first van arrived. As it pulled up to the service entrance, the door opened. A weak light from inside the building filtered out onto the tarmac. Then a half dozen men came out. They gathered at the door of the van.

One of them pulled open the door. Sam recognized him at once. He was one of the bouncers at the club that he had had the pleasure of meeting up close and personal.

He was large, at least six feet six inches in height. What may have been the physique of a star football player in his younger day had turned fleshy from over-indulgence in food, drink, and drugs. His skin had that pasty yellow complexion from never seeing the sun. His fine blond hair failed to conceal a large, fatty skull. Pale blue eyes that peered out from his sallow, corpulent face were stone cold.

The man reached in and roughly pulled a child out. Sam reckoned the kid was ten years old. The boy tripped and fell to the pavement as he was being shoved along. The man yanked him abruptly to his feet. As the boy started to whimper, the man backhanded him.

"Shut up, kid." Then he turned back to the van. "The rest of you, git on out here. We haven't got all night."

Slowly they stumbled out. Some of the smallest were being helped by the bigger ones. Soon they stood in a ragged group. Sam estimated their ages to be between four and twelve. They were wearing nothing but underwear. They stood so pathetically, nothing but skinny arms and legs and protruding rib cages. He could make out a tag reflecting in the dim light attached to a string around each of their necks.

"Easy," Sam whispered into his mike. He knew his fellow agents were chomping at the bit to get at these children. And their captors. But, according to Carol there was another van coming. "Wait for the rest of the kids."

The children were herded into the building and swallowed up inside. The agents waited edgily another fifteen minutes before the second van arrived. Like the first one, more than fifteen kids were shoved out onto the concrete driveway.

Sam watched tensely as the children were pushed and propelled into the club. When the doors closed, he gave the signal to the two men inside watching the show. One of them, pretending to be drunk, stumbled to the bathrooms at the back of the performance area. He lurched down the hallway but bypassed the restrooms. He passed a number of small private meeting rooms on one side, a large hall with its doors closed on the other, and headed for the back door.

"I'm in position," he said softly into a mike pinned to his collar.

Sam and Kyle approached the back of the club, pistols in hand. "Now," he ordered. The colleague on the inside opened the back door.

The team quickly entered. Inside the large hall, two heavily armed bouncers were swiftly surrounded and disarmed. Sam entered the hall and felt his stomach roil. The place was filled with men enjoying drinks and smoking cigars. At front and center was a large stage. More than thirty children were lined up before them. Their eyes were glazed over in a drug-induced stupor.

Victor presided over the gathering at the head of the main table. He was just lighting up a cigar when he looked up, stunned. Sam aimed his pistol at his head. Victor dropped the cigar and raised his hands in surrender. The FBI men quickly surrounded the tables; the FBI women mounted the stage and pulled the children into a protective ring.

CHAPTER 46

Winnemucca, Nevada

Janet paced from one end of the sheriff's office and to the other in anticipation of the meeting arranged by Hugh.

"Mom," Carl said, "it's going to be all right."

"Yes, Janet," Hugh said. "Listen to your very wise son."

"I know. I know. I think so. Yes, it will be all right."

"So stop wearing out the floor and take a seat," said Carl. "Can I get you some water?"

"Okay," Janet smiled up at her son. "Thank you."

As Carl stood to get the water, there was a tap on the door. Marsha stuck her head in. "They're here." She opened the door wider to let a man and a woman enter.

"Good morning, Mr. and Mrs. Jaso," said Hugh. "Come on in."

They entered and stood awkwardly in the office. Susie Jaso regarded Hugh intently. "What is this about, Sheriff?"

"Hugh. Please call me Hugh," he said.

Susie nodded her head, then waited.

Hugh gestured towards Janet, who was standing quietly to the side. "I believe you know Janet."

For the first time, Susie noticed the two other people in the room. "Yes, Janet. Janet Townsend," she said. Hugh could see the wheels turning in Susie's head. News of Art's arrest had been in the headlines for the past few weeks. Had she been paying any

243

attention?

"It's Janet Jones, now. I took back my maiden name."

"I see." Although, it wasn't clear what Susie saw.

Janet cleared her throat. "Let me introduce you to my son, Carl. Carl, this is Susie Jaso and her husband, Will. Susie and I grew up together."

"Nice to meet you," Carl offered his hand politely. An awkward silence followed.

"Please," Hugh said, "let's all take a seat." They settled into the four seats arranged in a semicircle in front of his desk while he returned to his chair behind it.

"The reason why I have arranged this meeting is because of something that happened a long time ago. Twenty-nine years ago, to be exact. Your children," he nodded towards the Jasos, "along with some others in this county, were taken by child protective services and never seen again. We know now what happened to at least a few of them.

"Although we don't know for absolute certain, we have reason to believe that this young man here, is your son, Chad. The resemblance is remarkable. And the timing fits. You see, Janet and Arthur adopted a baby boy on September 4th, 1992."

"Why that was . . . that was . . . Oh my God." Susie reached for her husband's hand. "Will?"

"That was the day after the CPS took Chad into custody, wasn't it?" Hugh asked them.

Will's expression turned dark. He scowled, first at Janet, then at Hugh, with disbelief and rage. "Now see here," he said. "I don't know what kind of game you think you're playing."

"I am not playing," Janet said forcefully. "I would never, ever, play that kind of game with any parent. This is my son. Art and I adopted him. I had no idea that my husband bought this child on the black market. You have to believe me."

As she spoke, tears sprang to her eyes. "By the time I started realizing that something wasn't right about the adoption, Carl was six years old. But it was many years later when I came to suspect that you were his birth parents. Do you remember the day I ran into you at the Farm and Fleet? The minute I saw you, Will, I knew. Carl was fifteen. And the spitting image of you. I don't have any real proof. There were never any adoption papers. That's what made me suspicious in the first place.

"I was so upset, when I saw the resemblance, realized what Art had done. I was afraid for Carl, what it would do to him if the truth came out. So, I ran away. I took Carl and my other sons back to Las Vegas. I counted on the fact that you would never see Carl, never recognize him. All I could think was to protect him and his brothers. It's what any mother would do, wouldn't they?"

Susie looked from Janet's ravaged face to Carl who looked so much like her husband it was hard to take in. Janet watched as Susie's expression slowly turned from pain and rage to acceptance and understanding. She reached over to take Janet's hand.

"Yes, yes, it is what any mother would do. What good would come of telling your secret to a fifteen-year-old boy? The damage had been done."

Carl leaned towards Susie and Will and said, "But then I grew up. And when Mom told me about you, my birth parents, we talked it over. We thought you deserved to know. And besides, ... I kind of wanted to meet you."

Susie looked into her son's eyes for the first time in twenty-nine years. "Your mother, Janet. She raised you into a fine young man."

* * *

The next day, Janet read an article in the Las Vegas Review Journal.

> Three current and one former employee of the Child Services Agency were arrested over the weekend. Among the former and current employees arrested were Phillis Cooper, the former director who had since moved on to a position with the Clark County Commissioners, Child Protective Unit supervisor, Kathleen Martin, and Agency Attorney, Edward

Long.

These three individuals were indicted with over three dozen felony and misdemeanor charges related to its alleged practice of separating children from their families without proper oversight.

The state district attorney stated that "this offense was done in secrecy and with malice; with deceit and intent to defraud; was infamous; and was done in violation of the common law, and against the peace and dignity of the state."

The indictment followed on the heels of the bust of the recent child-trafficking ring led by Victor Belinsky at the Ramon club in Las Vegas. Authorities are investigating alleged links between this case and the illegal intake of children by the CPS.

Forty-one charges will be prosecuted by the state's AG office. However, there could be more charges pressed down the road as investigations proceed.

CHAPTER 47

Prescott, Arizona

The morning finally came for Cate to catch a flight to Quantico. Although every member of the family wanted to be there for a big send off, Cate had put her foot down. Instead they had a farewell dinner at the folk's house the night before. She insisted on having Victoria and only Victoria drive her to the airport.

As Victoria watched the plane take off, she felt a pang of sadness. Cate wasn't just her sister but had become her very best friend. She would miss her terribly. But then she consoled herself that the training was only for twenty weeks. Of course, who knew where Cate would be stationed after that? But Victoria refused to think about that.

Now, she pulled her car into the reserved space at the back of the pub and grinned to herself. It was her spot now. She had been learning the ropes of managing the pub under Cate's careful tutelage and now it was her show.

She gathered her things from the car and headed to the back door of the pub. As she pulled it open, the familiar aroma of slow cooked corned beef, lamb stew bubbling on the stove, and brown bread baking in the oven wafted gently over her. As she reached for a pasty that was cooling on a baking tray, she glanced at Patrick. Cate would have gotten a smack on the hand for taking what was meant for the customers. But she and Patrick had a different kind of relationship.

"Go on, then, girl," he grinned as she took the pasty and poured herself a cup of coffee before going into her office. The office had gradually been transformed from the tidy but bare, no-nonsense place where Cate did her work to the softer, warmer ambiance that was Victoria. She had hung a beautiful Navaho tapestry on one wall. A tall basket filled with native grasses stood in a corner next to the shelf holding the pub's business ledgers. A hand-blown glass dish filled with hard candy sat at the corner of her desk for any visitors that happened into her office.

She sat at her desk and munched on the pasty while she gathered her thoughts for the day. She needed to review the order that Patrick had given her. Payroll was coming up. They needed to hire on another waiter or waitress. But first, she needed to catch up on some bookkeeping. She turned her computer on and buried herself in the numbers.

It wasn't until the din from the pub grew loud that she looked up from work. It was going on noon. She stood, turned off her computer, smoothed down her blouse, and went to work in the dining area.

* * *

The place was filling up fast, Victoria saw with great satisfaction. Since Cate began managing the pub and Victoria followed in her footsteps, the pub was running well into the black, finally, but every penny of revenue helped their bottom line. There were still plenty of little things that needed to be addressed: the exterior need a new coat of paint, there were still some appliances in the kitchen that were about to give up the ghost, the chairs needed recovering or replacing altogether, the tables could use facelifts. The worn look perhaps added to the charm of the place, but it wouldn't be long before it would begin to look downright seedy. And Victoria didn't intend for that to happen on her watch.

She grabbed a couple of menus and brought them to the most recent arrivals and greeted them with a smile. As she returned to the bar with their drink orders, she greeted many of the regulars along the way. She always strove to make herself visible and accessible to all of her patrons.

There was Pete and his brother Joe, who ran a construction company, but always took a break for lunch. Then there was George, the accountant whose office was right down the street. He usually came in for lunch unless it was tax time. Mandy, who owned the antique shop that was slowly pulling out of debt, liked to meet with her sister, the hair stylist, whenever business permitted it. Victoria knew each of them as well as many other regulars.

It was just as lunch hour was beginning to slow down and Victoria was clearing a table for a late arriving party that another pair of customers arrived. When she glanced at the door, she nearly dropped an armful of dirty plates.

The two men entering the place were none other than her father and her ex-fiancé. She focused on getting her load to a bus tray without breaking a single dish. Once safely deposited, she straightened and made a beeline to the back of the pub where Patrick was rolling out dough.

When he saw her face, white as a sheet, he laid down his rolling pin and wiped the flour off his hands with a towel.

"Victoria, darling, you look like you've seen a ghost."

"Worse. My father and my ex-fiancé."

"Where? Here in the pub?'

Victoria nodded.

"But I thought they were back east. Didn't you say they lived in Georgia?" Like all the old-timers who worked at the pub, Patrick knew about the circumstances of Victoria's adoption. And although they didn't know the details, they understood that her father's role in it was somehow underhanded.

Victoria nodded again.

"Well, what are they doing here, then?"

"I don't know, Patrick. I don't know."

"Do you want me to send them packing? I'd be more than happy to do it."

Victoria leaned against the old butcher-block table, unmindful of the flour powdering her backside, and thought for a moment.

"No, Patrick, no. If you did that they would just come back. No, I think I need to deal with this once and for all."

She squared her shoulders, dusted the flour off her bum, straightened her blouse, and returned to the dining area. She strode directly to the booth where Forrest and Noel where seated, looking over the menu.

"Hello, Father," she said.

He looked up and sat back, arms slung casually along the back of the booth. "Hello, Victoria. How very nice to see you."

She crossed her arms and scowled at him. "What are you doing here?" Her voice so low it was practically a hiss.

"Now, can't a father come see his daughter if he's a mind to?"

"You're not welcome here. Nor are you, Noel," she turned her glare on her ex.

"Come, come now," Forrest said. "We just wanted to see how you're doing."

By then, the few customers remaining in the dining room were watching the exchange, directing hostile looks at the two men. The bartender and the wait staff had abandoned their tasks to watch. They too regarded the two men with varying degrees of hostility. Patrick stood at the door by the kitchen. His arms were crossed and his look was belligerent.

The enmity of everyone surrounding them was not missed by Noel. "Ah, Forrest?" he said. "Maybe this wasn't the best idea."

Forrest opened his mouth to say something, glanced around, then seemed to think better of it. He held up his hands in surrender. As they stood to leave, Forrest growled, "You're going to regret this, girl."

Victoria stood nose to nose with him and spoke so softly that only he could hear. "I don't think so. In fact, if you ever come into this place again, I will contact my colleagues in the FBI. I have quite a few friends there these days. I am sure they would like to know about your many fraudulent business activities. I can provide them with more than enough evidence to put you away for a good long while."

Forrest's face turned a shade of purple as he glared at his daughter. "You wouldn't dare."

"Try me."

"Ah, Forrest?" said Noel, nudging the older man. "I think this is our cue to leave."

When the door closed behind the two men, the place was silent for a minute. Then, as though on cue, everyone returned to the tasks they had been about before the showdown.

Patrick strode over to Victoria and led her gently to the bar. Ben poured her a double shot of whiskey. Slowly, as she downed the strong spirit, the color returned to her face and the shaking of her hands subsided.

"I don't know what you said to him," Patrick said, "but it sure did the trick."

"Oh, don't worry, Patrick," Victoria told him. "He wouldn't dare show his face in this place again."

"Good for you, girl."

CHAPTER 48

Quantico, Virginia, November

Cate stood on the stage at the special graduating ceremony as the FBI Director swore her in and her many new colleagues as the new agents. In the audience before her, she could just make out the cluster that was her family. They had all flown in from Arizona to attend. She sat patiently as the class spokesperson, chosen by her mates, addressed the recruits and their families on the challenges they faced and the obstacles they overcame during the training. Then the Director called the new agents one by one to present them with their badges and credentials.

As Cate walked across the stage, the nerves she had been feeling earlier dropped away. Things were just beginning to sink in. She had made it. Just getting in the door to the Academy hadn't been easy. As she worked her way through one of the most rigorous and selective application processes in the nation, she found herself competing against hundreds of thousands of well-qualified men and women.

Then came twenty weeks of training. To prepare for potential deadly force encounters, they trained with a Bureau-issued pistol, carbine, and shotgun. Although Cate wasn't a stranger to the use of firearms, the FBI's basic law enforcement curriculum was rigorous. They learned the fundamentals of marksmanship, including instruction on firearms safety, weapons orientations, weapon handling skills. Through live fire training in marksmanship and practical shooting techniques, she honed her skills.

Then there was the physical fitness training leading up to a test: sit-ups, a timed three-hundred-meter sprint, push-ups, and a timed 1.5-mile run. She found this training to be punishing. But slowly, she found her rhythm as her body toned up.

She excelled in academics where they studied a broad range of subjects: law, ethics, behavioral science, basic and advanced investigative and intelligence techniques, interrogation, and forensic science. She learned how to manage counterterrorism, cyber and criminal investigations, and more.

Operational skills ran the gamut from defensive tactics including boxing and grappling, handcuffing and disarming techniques. She also received instruction on operations planning, handling of cooperating witnesses and informants, physical and electronic surveillance, undercover operations, and the development and dissemination of intelligence.

But by far her favorite part of the training program were the case exercises to test the trainees' mettle in real-life situations and mirror what they would experience in the field. As she played out a case scenario that started with a tip from an informant and culminated in the arrests of multiple subjects, she reflected on her experiences in Nevada. She had heard about Sam and his team bringing down the child trafficking ring with the help of a tip from one small, very brave CPS employee.

When the formal ceremony ended, a crowd had gathered in the reception area. Cate's colleagues pulled her from one group to another to introduce their families and friends and she did likewise.

They were all there. Her mother and father, her birth mother, her brothers, and Victoria. Many of her instructors made a point of greeting her brothers Ethan, who had worked closely with the FBI on many task forces, and fellow FBI Agent Michael.

That evening, to celebrate, they had made reservations for dinner and dance at a very popular restaurant frequented by marines and FBI agents alike.

* * *

And so, much as Cate might have liked to visit her family, that afternoon, at Victoria's insistence, the sisters left the rest of the family to their own devises and went to a spa. "The family can wait," she told her. "This cannot," she said taking in Cate's sadly neglected hair and rough hands.

Three hours later, they left with hair freshly cut and styled, nails manicured and polished, and facials. It was a first for Cate and she had to admit that after her grueling FBI training, the pampering felt wonderful. Most especially she reveled in the pedicure and foot massage that soothed and smoothed her hardworking, calloused feet.

When they returned to the motel room they would be sharing for the night, Cate was feeling loose and relaxed and thought to just melt into the bed. But Victoria reminded her that they were due at the restaurant in an hour and went straight to the closet. She pulled out the black dress, freshly pressed and sheathed in a drycleaner's plastic, that she and Victoria had purchased in Las Vegas.

"This poor old dress hasn't once seen the light of day. I bet it will look fabulous on that body of yours, all toned and sleek like it is. Why you look so good, I'm tempted to join the FBI myself just get in such good shape."

Cate laughed. "I promise you, that part of the program was the hardest. I thought I was in pretty good shape until I started the fitness program. For weeks, every muscle in my body hurt."

"Well, you know what they say. No pain, no gain. So come on," Victoria grinned, "put the dress on."

When Cate slipped it over her head, Victoria exclaimed. "Gorgeous. Just gorgeous. Here, have a look."

Cate turned toward the mirror. She had to admit, she looked fit to kill. She pulled the bolero jacket and admired how the metallic sequins sparkled in the light.

* * *

Liam knocked on the door fifteen minutes later. When Cate opened it, he did a double take.

"Cate? Is this really my sister Cate?"

"Doesn't she clean up nice?" Victoria said, with an impish grin.

Although it was November, the air was still fairly warm, and the skies had taken on that deep blue of the autumn. Alana was already in the car waiting for them. When they arrived at the restaurant, Liam dropped them at the door and went to park.

The restaurant was beautiful with white table clothes, low lighting, and tapered candles. The maître d' greeted them at the door. He was expecting them. He led them to a long table set for ten.

As soon as they sat, a man approached from the bar. He was tall and wore a dark suit. As his face was backlit, Cate didn't at first recognize him. Then he stepped closer.

"Hello, Cate," he said. When she saw his face, her breath caught.

"Sam," she said. "Sam Nicholas. What are you doing here?"

"I'm here to teach a course. When Michael heard I was here, he invited me to join the party. I hope that's okay with you."

"I, well, of course."

"Great," he said and took the seat next to her.

Soon the rest of Connelly's and Alana arrived. Amid all the clamor, Cate was able to hide her sudden angst at having Sam sitting so close. She still hadn't forgotten those days in Nevada. Nor had she forgotten the man. Damn him. And now he turns up looking gorgeous in formal attire.

She turned her attention to the rest of the people at the table. Her family. They were all smiles and happiness. Proud to attend the celebration of Cate's success. Soon, the waiter brought champagne. Ethan stood and raised his glass.

"To my sister."

They all raised their glasses and then the party was underway with much talking and teasing. Michael, Ethan, and Sam told old war stories from their days in the field, Victoria joined in with her soft southern drawl, Alana managed to get a word in every now and then. Even Joe managed to say a few words through his wife.

The dinner was fabulous. Cate ordered a large prime rib with all the trimmings, which she had no trouble tucking away while her brothers teased her about it. As the plates were cleared away, a small band set up in the back corner of the restaurant with an area cleared for dancing. The music was a delightful mix of country, old rock-n-roll, and blues.

As the dance floor began to fill up, Sam asked Cate to dance. By then she had had a few drinks and a heady feeling enveloped her. As she and Sam stepped onto the dance floor, she felt the energy of the dancing pairs. Before she knew it, she was rocking and rolling with the best of them. Then the DJ slowed it down with an Elvis Presley number. As Elvis crooned "But I can't help falling in love with you," Sam pulled Cate close.

They swayed to the shmaltzy melody and Sam whispered into her ear. "You are so beautiful."

Cate, who had been snuggling ever so closely against him, suddenly stiffened. Her moves became robot-like as they stepped through the song. When it was finished, she excused herself and made a beeline for the ladies' room.

* * *

That's where Victoria found her, standing in front of the mirror dabbing at the tears that threatened to spill over.

"Cate?"

Cate started when she saw her. "Oh, Victoria, I feel like such a fool."

"Thus speaks the woman who just crushed her FBI training at Quantico. You are no fool, sister. Now tell me, what's got you all in a dither? Is it Sam?"

"Why do you say that?"

"Why one minute you're dancing and the next minute, you're in here crying. Did he say something to you?"

Cate nodded.

"Well now, what did he say?"

"He said I was beautiful."

"Well, my goodness gracious, why on earth would that make you cry?"

"It's just . . . it's just that I have been so attracted to him for the longest time. And the only interest he ever shows is professional. It's so humiliating."

"Why sometimes I just don't understand you. Not one itty bitty bit. Of course he's got his eye on you. I could see that the first time he looked at you at that old resort in Vegas."

"But that was just business, him keeping an eye on us."

"Honey, trust me. I know when a man is interested in a woman."

"Really?"

"Really."

"But then why hasn't he ever tried to contact me? Not since Nevada?"

"I think maybe that's something you should ask him, don't you?"

Cate bowed her head. "I suppose."

Victoria put her hands on Cate's shoulders. "Now, why don't you just pat those tears away and go out and find out for yourself."

As they exited the bathroom, they saw Sam standing uncertainly at the bar. Victoria held tightly onto Cate's arm and steered her over to him. "Sam," she said, "this here sister of mine has something she wants to ask you." Then she left them alone and returned to dinner the table.

Cate looked around, feeling quite embarrassed. But then she realized that no one was looking their way. They were all drinking and laughing and dancing. As she gazed up into Sam's face, everything else, everyone else, seemed to fade away until it was only herself and Sam.

"Did you mean that, what you said on the dance floor?"

"That you are the most beautiful woman I have ever known?"

Cate blushed. "Don't make fun of me, Sam."

Sam gazed directly into her eyes. "Cate, I meant what I said. Hell, I've been around the block a time or two. And I can tell you there isn't a woman in this world that can hold a candle to you. You're strong and courageous and," he looked her over from head to foot, "and sexy as hell."

Cate felt her face burn even redder. "Then why haven't I heard a word from you since Nevada?"

"Well, let's see. First, I had to bring down a pedophile ring. Then I heard that you had signed up for training at Quantico. I sure didn't want to distract you at that time. I've been biding my time."

"You have?"

"Yes, I have. Your brother has been keeping me up to date."

"I see."

Sam reached out to brush a hand on her neck and Cate felt a shiver run from her head to her toes. He pulled her in closer and brushed his lips over hers. "Hm," he said, "why don't we dance before I lose my head?"

EPILOGUE

Winnemucca, Nevada

Many months had passed since Cate and Victoria had taken Winnemucca by storm in search of their birth parents. Sam had kept Hugh apprised of the most significant events since then: Alana's visit to Prescott and meeting the Connelly's, Cate's training at the FBI. But most important to Hugh was the bust up of another child trafficking ring.

He learned from Sam that the children had been taken in by Catholic Charities where the slow process of counselling and returning the children to their families had been taking place. Most of the children were reunited within a month or two. There remained but a brother and sister, ages four and six, at the charity. Their paperwork, the intake reports, seemed to have been temporarily lost in the shuffle. Today, Sam called him to let him know that the parents had finally been tracked down.

Hugh ended the call and settled on his porch with a beer. He propped his feet up on the railing to watch the sun set. An owl glided overhead, then descended to the land on the old pinion pine to the side of the house, settling on a gnarled branch. Hugh knew him well. They say that owls can live up to twenty years, more in captivity where they are protected from predators, disease, or accidents and have an abundant food source. But

Hugh knew without a shred of doubt that something else had kept this old owl around for nearly thirty years.

The owl hooted softly, cocked his head to the side. Then he turned back and stared directly at Hugh.

"Hoo . . . Hoo." He called again, his throat expanding with each hoot.

Hugh lifted his beer to him in a toast.

The owl turned his head all the way around before spreading his wings and taking off, soaring silently up into the dusky sky. Hugh nodded farewell and felt peace descend over him.

AFTERWORD

A few years ago, I met a woman who was interested in the fact that I wrote novels. She told me she had a great idea for a novel based on a true story. Back in the late 1990's, she stumbled on a group of town folk in West Virginia who had been the victims of the Child Protective Services. According to these people, the CPS was stealing their children without cause. Parents were then stripped of their child welfare benefits and faced a system totally lacking in legal recourse. They never saw their children again. Upon further investigation, it was discovered that the children were being sold to child traffickers.

Although I was not able to identify this particular case, there is plenty of evidence reported from reliable sources online of the lack of oversight of child protective services and the link between our child welfare system and child trafficking.

I struggled to envision writing a book about such a heinous crime. Imagine being poor, on welfare, and having your child taken from your home on the grounds of neglect or abuse and then having little to no recourse with the CPS. As an author and a mother, I chose to put some distance between myself and the crime by setting the incident in the past. The story begins when two adult sisters discover each other thirty years later through DNA testing.

ACKNOWLEDGEMENT

I have to start by thanking my awesome husband, William Brands. From reading early drafts to being a sounding board to encouraging me when I got frustrated or filled with self-doubt, he was as important to this book getting done as I was. Thank you so much, my best friend.

I would also like to thank my dear friends, Lynn Hampton and Dennis Auld, both of whom read my final draft, noting typos and inconsistencies which made it an all-around better book. Most importantly, thank you for giving it your solid approval. Cheers to both of you!

ABOUT THE AUTHOR

Eliza Mccullen

For nearly a quarter of a century, Eliza lived and travelled throughout many parts of Africa, the Caribbean, Latin America and Asia. She has survived a coup in Honduras, an attempted Al Qaida attack in Uganda, an army/paramilitary shootout in Malawi, earthquakes, dengue fever and malaria. This has provided fodder for some of her books. Others are inspired by current events or trends.

Her career path was as varied as her geographical wanderings, ranging from social scientist to business manager to editor of the U.S. Embassy newsletter. Two interests have sustained her throughout her many travels: textile arts and writing fiction. She began by writing middle grade mysteries then moved on to adult novels. Her one requirement when a writing book is that it has a happily-ever-after ending.

Eliza is enjoying life as an empty-nester in Sedona Arizona where she and her husband of thirty plus years have retired amid the majestic red rocks. She has two adult children who share their father's passion for globetrotting. As of this writing, they are launching international careers in finance and public health.

BOOKS BY THIS AUTHOR

Hidden Archives: A Cozy Mystery

Eliza Hamilton, professor of literature, drops in on her father at his beloved bookshop early one morning . . . the very morning that he has fallen victim to thugs, a fatal blow to the head, in a random break-in. Or was it random?

The bookshop, nestled in a row of colonial buildings in historic Old Town Alexandria, has stood immutable to Alexandria's changing fortunes since Eliza's forefathers built it before the Civil War. Within its venerable old brick walls, it houses an eclectic selection of new and used books, historic documents and archives.

Patrons come from all walks of life, old and young and every age in between, local residents who have been visiting the shop since they were tykes and the many tourists that crowd the streets of the colonial town. Is one of them the murderer?

Eliza is determined to find her father's killers even as she grapples with the fate of the shop that has been in her family for so many years. A rash of break-ins and attempted arson together with missives from her family ghosts and the spirits of long dead slaves convince her that buried in the old historic documents from Virginia's plantation days are secrets that someone doesn't want uncovered . . .

The Infinity Tattoo: A Gripping Suspense Thriller (Northern Triangle Trilogy Book 1)

An exciting international suspense thriller with plenty of romance and adventure

"A great read: it's got action, romance, and danger." Beth Boyd

Meg Goodwin's best friend Alex disappeared when they were reporting the violent unrest in Honduras. But Meg thinks her dangerous life is behind her when she settles back in Sedona, Arizona. Then a mysterious bleeding man turns up in her barn, and her life will never be the same again.

In this gripping thriller, Meg must face not only drug cartels and corrupt politicians, but also an international conspiracy And if she survives, and solves the mystery of her lost friend, can she also find love?

"I couldn't put this romantic suspense novel down. Fans of Lisa Gardner or Sandra Brown will enjoy 'The Infinity Tattoo'." Sarah Yorke

A romantic suspense thriller you won't want to put down.

Undocumented: A Suspense/Thriller (Northern Triangle Trilogy Book 2)

Fourteen-year-old Ricky Hernandez witnesses a murder. Authorities want his testimony. The mafia want him silenced. Ricky makes a perilous journey across Mexico to escape gangs back home in Honduras. Finally arriving safely in South Tucson, he witnesses a homicide—and recognizes one of the murderers. His name is Chava, a ruthless narco-trafficker.

Ricky must navigate through the harsh world of drug smugglers, immigration authorities, and law enforcement. His only chance of survival lies with Detective Rosalie Diaz and veteran DEA Agent Scott Smith. But even they have traitors in their ranks.

And trusting the wrong people could cost him his life . . .

De Leon's Ring: A Gripping Novel Of International Suspense (Northern Triangle Trilogy Book 3)

Unearthing long buried secrets of terror and politics in Central America leads to dangerous consequences...

Maya archeologist, Ana Chan, seeks to excavate mysteries of her ancestors in the rugged mountainous highlands of Guatemala. Instead she uncovers a mass grave. Danny Martinez, a ladino who rejects his elite upbringing, works in the highlands with the rural poor to boost food production. Ana and Danny are drawn inexorably to each other despite the huge social gulf that separates them.

Then Ana discovers a ring in the grave and someone seeks to make her disappear...permanently. She is forced into exile, crossing over the border into Mexico. Danny fears the worst until he chances upon her in the United States three years later.

Was it fate that led him to her? For it is only by working together that they can uncover a deadly secret buried since the war and keep them both safe.

The Rise Of Eagles: A Gripping Novel Of Mystery And Suspense

White supremacist are launching a cyberwar to destroy the government...

Financial fraud, hacking, and murder... a hate group will do anything to build their all-white homeland in this gripping conspiracy thriller.

Tony, the owner of a tourist lodge, is gut-shot and left to die. His estranged sister, Jackie Robertson, returns to her hometown in Montana to sort out his affairs. A computer geek extraordinaire, she begins digging into the inner workings of the resort. There she uncovers a money laundering operation controlled by an internet spy.

Former Chicago homicide detective, Walt Hanson, has escaped the murder capital of the nation. He decides to take a job in the small town of Kalispell, gateway to the soaring peaks of Glacier National Park. His peaceful life is shattered when he is tasked with investigating Tony's murder.

Tension rises as he tries to protect Jackie, who dives headfirst into high-tech espionage to catch a thief, all the while living among her brother's most loyal employees.

But cyber theft is merely a means to an end. A far more insidious and sweeping threat looms, one that may shake the very foundations of America. Before she can uncover this plot, Jackie is kidnapped, bringing the entire sheriff's department, an FBI agent, a search and rescue team, and a three of former Delta Force operatives down on the white supremacists.

Made in the USA
Monee, IL
17 July 2022